Overstars Mail: Imperial Challenge

Overstars Mail: Imperial Challenge

Roberta Gellis

Five Star • Waterville, Maine

First Edition
First Printing: August 2004

Published in 2004 in conjunction with Tekno Books and Ed Gorman.

Set in 11 pt. Plantin by Liana M. Walker.

Printed in the United States on permanent paper.

Library of Congress Cataloging-in-Publication Data

Gellis, Roberta.
    Overstars mail : imperial challenge / by Roberta Gellis.—1st ed.
      p. cm.
    "Five Star first edition titles"—T.p. verso.
    ISBN 1-59414-228-9 (hc : alk. paper)
    1. Life on other planets—Fiction. 2. Letter carriers—
Fiction. 3. Space flight—Fiction. 4. Imperialism—Fiction.
I. Title.
PS3557.E42O94 2004
  813′.54—dc22   2004047086

Overstars Mail:
Imperial Challenge

CHAPTER 1

The job, Cyn thought when he first applied for it, had everything. If you didn't call yourself a mail-carrier, the work sounded romantic. Star-hopping always sounded romantic to the planet-bound. Cyn knew differently about that, of course; he had been born in space on a Free Trader. It was no news to him that space flight was actually made up of endless sdays of total boredom, when there was nothing to do, punctuated by moments of acute terror, when you had to do everything—most of it usually impossible—all at once.

Nonetheless, saying you were a star-hopper was a sure key to the bedroom door of nine out of ten dirtside fems—and a key with no strings attached. Few fems wanted a husband who would show up about once in a decade. Surprisingly just as few wanted to go along. The adventurous ones mostly spaced on their own terms; the others had a strong core of practicality, even the most romantically-minded. And even those few who toyed briefly with the idea of life-mating with Cyn and traveling with him gave up when they saw the interior of the Piss Pot.

Austere was not exactly the right word; austere, in relation to the Piss Pot, was a miracle of understatement. Naturally Piss Pot was not the official designation of the ship. She had an Empire IdentNo—OMS 16.8.19/19—but Cyn's first glimpse of her ungainly shape had named her irrevocably.

That first sight—which simultaneously tickled Cyn's warped sense of humor and twisted his gut with pity (for to him ships were never simply dead mechanisms, and the Pot's ugliness woke a need to protect her)—forged another bond to his job. Ugly was not all the Pot was, however. As he came to know her, a deep respect overshadowed all Cyn's other feelings about his ship. Ships came in myriad shapes and sizes, from the tiny, graceful needles of felanthrop pleasure yachts, which could sprout wings for atmospheric travel, to the nearly planet-sized, grape-clusterlike cargo vessels of the redis, which never left deep space. The Pot was an all-around compromise. If it was a speck compared with a redis cargo carrier, it was a giant compared to a totally automated, one-man needle-ship. It could, in a real emergency, land on and take off from a planet. Usually, however, the Pot remained in orbit and Cyn made his pickups and deliveries in a shuttle that was docked in the "handle" of the inverted chamber pot the ship so closely resembled.

Inside the Pot, at the top of the flattened dome, was the control room and Cyn's personal quarters—the luxury spot on the ship. There was a fresher, a bunk for sleeping, a thumb-lock closet for clothing, two chairs, one of which had padding, and a table. The seven passenger "staterooms" that surrounded the dining/recreation area on the next deck down were nattily furnished with the inevitable fresher, double-decker bunks, a closet, and one hard chair—no table. The recreation provided by the recreation area was space enough to walk around and around the large table into which the autochef—a spartan variety of limited resources—was built.

The third deck down was for living cargo and hydroponics—not the veritable gardens of the ordinary spaceship, which provided fresh fruit and vegetables and even flowers, but a basic algae-tank air-and-waste recycling system. Below this level lay the cargo space, floored by the safety walls that contained the massive fuel tanks, and, in the largest area, which looked like the flared flange of the pot—what would be the seat of a chamber pot—the engines.

The engines aroused an awed admiration in Cyn, whose experience was with generations-old power plants nursed tenderly in the hope they would last more generations. The engines of the Pot, unlike its furnishings, were not "utility" models. They were the very latest, the up-to-datest, the super finest—and powerful enough to move a dreadnought cruiser at racing-ship speeds. In fact, the ship's ungainly shape had been dictated by the thrust of those engines. The Pot was built as a shell to house the engines. Everything was subordinated to speed and reliability. The Piss Pot could, without question, outrun anything in the known universe.

That should have been no surprise, since the purpose of the ships of the Overstars Mail was simply to get from one place to another as quickly as possible. And since their ships had no official armament, it was just as well that they had long legs because sometimes the Pot and her sister ships carried startlingly valuable cargo, sentient and otherwise. If a box of priceless jewels, the deed for a planet, a precious serum, a being involved in a fabulous Deal, or a scientist carrying the plans for weapons that could explode suns or machines that could build them had to be transmitted from one world to another in a hurry—then they went aboard an OMS.

Fortunately it was rare for Cyn's cargo to be particularly valuable. Most of it was simply perishable, time-dated, or a delivery to one who was impatient for some reason. More was plain old-fashioned written or printed letters and electronic recordings. There were many reasons to transmit written or electronic material. On a personal level, some needed the touch and feel of a message in a loved-one's hand to make it real, or the ability to replay a message many times.

On other levels, there was the matter of speed and security. Although carrolling was faster than sending a message by a ship, depending on the Overstars Mail schedules, it might not be much faster. Carroll waves leapt from spiral to spiral of condensed space in little time, but they could come no nearer the carrollpause of a sun than could a ship. At some point, the gravitic and magnetic influence of any star canceled the effect of the carrolling system. Carrolled messages had to be recorded at that perimeter and sent on by laser at no more than the speed of light; unfortunately there was no way to prevent anyone from tapping those messages. In addition, there was some chance that a message might be garbled in transmission. So, anything really important was still committed to written words or electronic media and transmitted physically.

That was the kind of cargo Cyn liked best because Cyn's second reason for becoming a mail-carrier was that the job was safe. Born to a couple on the Free Trader Lystris, Cyn had had his fill of anthropophagous natives, poisonous atmospheres, indigestible edibles, and carnivorous plants by the time he was thirty. He was tired of taking his life in his hands every time he planeted. On the other hand, he had vacuum bubbles in his blood and bones. He knew he could never settle dirtside. The vibration of a ship around him, the star-studded blackness or distorted colors of space, were as necessary to him as eating. He could do without both for a little while, but not for long.

After a particularly bad delivery, Cyn had gone so far as to have a fleeting thought of signing aboard an IntraGalCorp liner or trader, but it was only a fleeting thought. For one thing, the Free Traders hated the huge IntraGalCorp organizations so much that it would have meant breaking contact with his family, and Cyn, scared witless or not, could not contemplate that. For another, Cyn knew that shipping out on an Empire liner or cargo vessel would not satisfy him. He might be tired of convincing primitives of wildly varying species that he was not a part of the dinner menu; he might have a yen for bright lights, soft music, and decorative fems; but escaping the former and enjoying the latter could not pay for a life of sameness. Cyn had a strong taste for new things; he just preferred them not to be inimical.

Cyn discovered the answer to his problem about five syrs earlier, quite by accident, when Lystris made a rare stopover on an Empire planet. He had been sent to pick up a payment for a delivered cargo at an Overstars Mail office. Just at the door he passed a large poster, showing a being even Cyn didn't want to recognize, a repellently handsome galactic-hero type homo male, and an exquisite felanthrop fem. The poster was blazoned across with Universum type reading, **"THE EMPIRE'S NOBLEST SERVICE/Promote Understanding/Be a Mail-Carrier."**

Although Cyn wasn't overly impressed with either nobility or understanding, he did know that the nearly galaxy-wide Empire comprised only water-based-life-type, civilized planets. The forms of the creatures on them might be weird and wonderful, and the political and social systems might make a species homo Free Trader blanch, but whether the inhabitants flew, squirmed, rolled, leapt, or walked, whether they were slave or free, related in masochistic or sadistic or neutral lifestyles, they all breathed air roughly twenty percent oxygen, ate d-sugar/l-amino acid food, and had complex technological societies.

Nonetheless, Cyn had had no immediate revelation. He had walked toward the clerk's cage occupied by an urso fem and while he waited for those ahead to be served, his eye had been caught by a flickering light. It was only the poster again,

11

with "Be a Mail-Carrier" in flashing colors.

The revelation had come when, as his turn came, Cyn had looked from the poster to the cage in which the clerk worked. He had raised his head quickly and stared at the poster again until he was roused by a sharp voice asking impatiently—not for the first time, he suspected—how she could serve him.

"Oh," Cyn had said, somewhat absently, still bemused by the idea that had come to him. "Mail for the Lystris."

The urso had checked, acknowledged mail was waiting, and touched a control that opened a cavity on Cyn's side of the counter into which he could deposit his identification and authorization. When the cavity had snapped shut, she pointed to a spot on the clear plastel of the cage front, said "Look here," and pushed the button that photographed him and took a retinal pattern. Meanwhile his genetic code had been recorded (particularly easy in species homo, where it could be obtained from a few cells of the eternally flaking epidermis) while the clerk slid the cards Cyn had passed into the reader. Finally the mail appeared, with Cyn's cards in the counter hollow.

Cyn looked up at the poster again. The Overstars Mail might not be any more concerned with the well-being of its employees than any other business, but it was very conscious, indeed, of the safety of its trade goods—and willy-nilly the employee was also protected.

"Next," the urso said, even more sharply.

"Where do I get information on joining up?" Cyn asked.

"They don't take ones that sleep on the job," the urso snapped caustically, but before Cyn could respond added, "Out to the corridor, turn left. Hiring office is four doors down. Next!"

Cyn really had only one question to ask the hiring officer. He wanted to know whether mail ships ran the same route all the time. He got a long lecture on time and motion studies that implied . . . fuel efficiency studies that proved . . . crime statistics that showed . . . What it all added up to was that a mail ship seldom touched down on the same planet twice in ten syr.

"You convinced me," Cyn said. "I want to enlist."

"Apply. Apply." The hiring officer replied testily. "This isn't the Patrol. And we're more particular than you are. We have more than one question to ask you."

Only as soon as Cyn identified himself as a Free Trader born and bred, most of the questions became irrelevant. The hiring officer lost his testiness, turning almost effusive, until he came to the final blank on the application. When he asked, "What is your purpose in joining the Overstars Mail Service?" he clearly expected Cyn to give one of the many possible reasons for his ship to be grounded.

Instead, Cyn grinned and replied, "I'm nervous. It seems like a peaceful job."

"I don't have time for facetiousness, homo male. Please state your real reason for applying to the service."

"That's it," Cyn said a little more soberly. "I'm tired of carrying the goods I have to deliver in one hand with a stun rod in the other. I want to walk into an office and not worry about whether the clerk I see is going to serve me or try to serve me up for dinner."

"I don't have room for all that," the officer said slowly, but his stylus moved to the next line up and darkened the mark beside the "security check necessary?" box. Free Traders were a notoriously in-group type. It was very rare for one born to the Trade to leave it, except in a shroud out in space or if the ship were lost, through mechanical or financial failure.

Cyn had shrugged at the reply. "Okay," he said without

any further tinge of humor. "In a word, I want security."

It was possible, the officer thought as he filled in the last blank. Any being could lose its nerve, but Cyn didn't look as if he had; he laughed too easily and his stance wasn't that of a broken one. Still, it wasn't the hiring officer's job to worry about security. There was a whole department concerned with keeping the mail-carriers honest. He handed over a sheaf of plas sheets and punched the keys of a device that spat out a new temporary IdentCard.

"Top sheet tells you where and when to report for training and indoctrination," the urso said, "but you'd better read all of them or you'll get some nasty surprises. Close the door as you leave."

Thus, Cyn had never lifted off with Lystris. There were no tears at parting. With the increased efficiency of communications, there was no danger of losing touch with his family. And, although in one sense space was immeasurably huge, to those who inhabited it as a way of life the distances were easily traversed. Lystris carrolled its new destination from each port of call, and as soon as Cyn was assigned, he carrolled his route in Trader code to Lystris, picking up messages directly from the system transmission satellites at each destination.

In the five syrs of his service, Cyn had no regrets about the choice he had made. Sometimes he was lonely and missed his human companions on Lystris, but mostly he reveled in his privacy and freedom. He was accustomed to filling the empty time of travel in space, and the periodic two- and three-sdays layovers while new routes were computed and mail and cargo assembled were eminently satisfactory, for he was totally free all of that time. Though many of the planets he visited were not inhabited by species homo, he didn't mind. Cyn liked friendly aliens, and on nonhomo planets there were always new things to see, smell, and touch. And if he wanted to play—well, every spaceport had a section devoted to diversions suited to each of the major space-traveling species.

For the whole of his present transit, Cyn had been particularly pleased with his decision to strike out on his own. At the last stopover of the previous run, he had jerked out of his usual relaxed slouch when he examined his route sheet and saw his final delivery was to be made on Healtha. Cyn liked willing and decorative women, and there were none more willing or more decorative—or more expensive—than the nymphs of Healtha.

Before he let himself get too enthusiastic, Cyn checked his credits to the last minum, added what he could safely borrow against the future, and then, satisfied with the total, carrolled his request for an appointment, giving as his address the Overstars Mail office on Healtha. Rumor implied a certain amount of danger. Cyn had heard tales of both males and fems who had been so enslaved by what the nymphs offered that, after their own fortunes were despoiled, they would do anything at all to purchase a few more standard time units—stus of joy—in the Garden. But that only added to the spice.

On and off over the swiks of that last transit, Cyn wondered whether he had been a fool—not out of fear of enslavement but because of recurrent doubts that the widely spread tales were true. On and off he reconsidered the reputation of the nymphs, who were famous or infamous according to one's attitude regarding sex as an article of commerce. The only solid facts were that they inhabited a closed area on Healtha called the Garden and that they serviced only species homo.

All the rest was rumor: First and foremost that the nymphs by some mysterious means had discovered entirely new twists in the labyrinthine art of love and that they were able to match perfectly the mind and spirit of each client. Because species homo was not telepathic, the latter hinted that they were not homo fems, although Healtha had no native intelligent life and had been colonized by homo direct from Old Terra. As far as Cyn had heard, no one had ever asked the nymphs—or they would not answer. Another persistent rumor was that they were clones, despite the fact that no successful cloning of species homo had ever been reported.

There was some factual support for the clone theory. Patrons gave different names to the nymphs they had visited, but descriptions were identical. Still, if they were cloned, Cyn wondered, why were there said to be so few true nymphs? Surely cloning could produce any number of copies of the absolutely flawless beauty of one particular type for which they were known. Or could it? If the process were delicate—could it miscarry in minor ways? Was that the reason for the existence of near-nymphs who had failed to obtain residence in the Garden by some gossamer-fine lack in face, form, or disposition?

For a lesser price a man could enjoy these simulacra; some even bought them for life companions. Cyn's strongest doubts, when he remembered that he would not be able to afford so much as a new pair of boots for some time, arose from wondering if there was any real difference—whether the "true nymphs" had engendered the myths about themselves to raise their price.

By the time the Pot settled herself comfortably into orbit around Healtha, Cyn was resigned to the loss of his credits. It was far better to need to watch every minum for a syr than to spend the rest of his life wondering what he had missed by not paying full price for the genuine article. Nonetheless, he was uneasy enough about the cost to thank the Powers that Be

16

that he had no passengers. If he had had to direct debarkation or program the robos to take only particular parcels with his mind mostly elsewhere, as it now was, disaster would have overtaken his efficiency record. At the final stop, he merely had to order the robos to sweep everything off the shelves in the cargo hold into the shuttle. His delivery record had been made up sdays before.

His final trial was keeping his mind on his landing long enough not to disgrace himself or kill himself, but that really wasn't much of a trial. Self-preservation being an even higher priority than the fear of having allowed himself to be gulled out of his credits, his landing was impeccable. But Cyn nearly ran into the scheduling room to hand his delivery record to the clerk. The robos had already unloaded mail and cargo and stored themselves in the OM storeroom; the shuttle was sealed to him. Cyn barely restrained himself from pawing the ground as he waited for the clerk to stamp the records, hand his copy back, and tell him how many free sdays he could take.

The clerk glanced down at the routing sheet, raised his brows, and whistled softly. Cyn's heart sank, but only because he thought he was to be sent out immediately. He braced himself to argue, to demand a layover, but before he could start to complain, the clerk thrust his stamped copy of the delivery record at him and said, "Three sdays."

At that moment, Cyn should have known he was in for trouble, but he was in no condition to understand anything beyond anticipation. He realized vaguely that a three-sday stopover meant a complex route was being calculated, but he didn't care a pin—which was just as well because that was all he was likely to have left after paying for three sdays of a nymph's time.

"Can I get transport to the Garden?" he asked the clerk.

The male's brows shot up again and his eyes goggled in

mixed surprise and suspicion. "It's waiting," he said. "The golden flitter in the parking lot. I wondered who—"

But Cyn was gone before the clerk could finish. He stared at the door as it swung shut, then slowly drew a set of forms toward him and began to fill one out. Mail-carriers who could afford a nymph were few and far between. What was worse, any homo who developed a taste for nymphs could be easily bought.

Cyn had no trouble spotting the flitter. It was a luxurious robo, hinting that entry was a prelude to satisfaction of the senses. He hesitated before he gave his name and the door slid open, feeling a vague sense of disappointment. Were the nymphs just like any other expensive seller of pleasure? Cyn had ridden in the flitters of enough of those, and there was always something about them that made clear the profession of their owners. Without being garish or obvious, the type of music, the type of scent . . . something . . . heightened sexual anticipation.

If this was no different, Cyn thought, he had wasted a lot of hard-earned credit. But then he shook his head. A guess based on the outside of a flitter was stupid. Uneasy but determined, Cyn stepped inside. He sat stiffly on the cushions and looked around. There were no controls—but he had expected that. The facing panel showed only a screen with the name "Myrrha." Slowly his suspicion began to dissolve and he relaxed, stretching his long legs and allowing the lids to droop over his startlingly pale eyes. This flitter was different. Its interior was harmonious, soothing to the eye; it smelled nice, and soft music beguiled the ear. Somehow, however, it was not at all like the conveyances with which he was familiar. Actually, it was remarkably free of sensual enticement. It was simply . . . pleasant.

"Let's go," Cyn said.

The door slid shut and the flitter lifted. Cyn wondered how many words it was programmed to accept. "Go" must be one; "Garden" was almost certainly another. He was almost tempted to command a stop just to see how intelligent the little ship was, and then laughed because he had already been beguiled. He was not particularly in a hurry any more. He watched with idle pleasure as the city and then open, rather rugged countryside, passed below until the flitter landed.

An ornate gate in what must be a symbolic stone wall—it was low enough to step up on and down the other side—was invitingly open. Cyn walked through and looked around: lovely; not exquisite, not startling, just peaceful and lovely. Cyn stood for a little while breathing in peace, watching the sun dapple the gently moving leaves of graceful trees and the smooth grass below. From where he stood, he could see no sign of a building—not that it mattered; he was quite willing to walk as long as necessary in this landscape. But if it rained . . . Why should he think of rain?

Suddenly Cyn grinned, then puckered his lips for a whistle of awe, although he did not allow the sound to emerge and disturb the natural murmurs of insect and leaf. He had thought of rain because outside the place where the flitter landed the swollen clouds of a dark grey sky had promised a deluge. Here the sky was blue and the sun shone. Cyn knew why the wall was so low, the Garden so seemingly open to invasion. The whole area must be protected by a force field.

Now Cyn chuckled softly. He also knew why the fees the nymphs charged were so high. Maintaining a field of such dimensions could not come cheap. Then he frowned. One practical thought had engendered another. Cyn began to wonder how he would find Myrrha.

As soon as the thought entered his mind, a silver bell chimed. Cyn looked expectantly around for another conveyance. A whole cascade of chimes followed. Chimes? The sound had nothing metallic in it. Only the purity of the tone was truly bell-like.

Longer, slower, the sounds were repeated. That was no bell. Quite clearly the chimes said, "I'm here, Cyn, by the feather tree."

His eyes followed the sound to a slender fem, one hand stretched toward him. "Are you truly a wood nymph to spring out of a tree?" Cyn asked, moving toward her.

The cascade of bell tones rang again as she laughed. "Sometimes our companions are nervous or fretful. The Garden brings peace, and they wish to wander a while. I was waiting until you wanted me."

Now that he was listening, Cyn found the words in the silver chimes easy enough to understand. Lovely, his mind repeated. She was like the Garden in which she dwelt, lovely and peaceful. But the nearer he came to Myrrha, the more aware he became that in her the placid welcoming warmth of the Garden was enlivened by an active aura of friendliness, by human warmth, and by a hint of playfulness. Her long cornsilk hair was loose and moved gently in the soft breeze; her eyes, a peculiar misty grey-blue, twinkled; her small rosy lips smiled—wickedly.

CHAPTER 2

Laughing, Cyn tightened his encircling arm to give Myrrha's waist an affectionate squeeze. He kissed her welcoming lips one last time and then withdrew, without the slightest sense of loss, to pass though the gate and enter the waiting flitter. Just inside, Myrrha raised a hand in farewell, her expression a delightful compound of happiness, satisfaction, and curiosity—which could only be for her next companion, Cyn thought, settling himself with a tired sigh; there was nothing about him she didn't already know.

He leaned back and closed his eyes, completely, totally content. The nymph had been worth every minum. He had had an experience he would carry to his grave—a warm core of peace; joy mingled with a kind of sexual excess of which he had not suspected he was capable. Cyn sighed. That fem had muscles in highly unlikely places and could do even more unlikely things with them. Every fantasy Cyn had ever dreamed had been fulfilled, and each would remain a bright memory—and never require repetition. Cyn's brows drew together, remembering what he had heard about those who became addicted. He shook his head, unable to understand wanting to return. It could never be the same, never hold the same freshness and wonder. To come again could only soil or dim what had been perfect.

His eyes opened again and he looked out over a scruffy

21

field dotted with garbage on the outskirts of Healtha's spaceport. Ugly compared with the perfection of the Garden, where every leaf on every tree seemed to have been placed deliberately to produce the greatest beauty. But who wanted to live in heaven? Peace and joy were all very well, but they'd cloy soon enough. They were only wonderful as islands in the normal sea of trouble that was life. To enjoy peace and joy properly, you had to be bored, scared, hurt, and grief-stricken from time to time also.

Cyn smiled. He knew he would never reach sexual climaxes to match those Myrrha had produced, but he also knew he would be quite content with his ordinary responses. He felt the warmest friendliness toward Myrrha. She was lovely and she was fun, and he didn't doubt that she truly reciprocated the friendliness. But Myrrha would never, probably could never, feel more than friendliness for anyone. Myrrha didn't need him, didn't need anyone. Unlike most of species homo, she seemed able to walk alone without fear of falling or needing the certain knowledge that a hand would be extended to lift her to her feet again.

Three sdays of complete freedom from all demands had been a revelation. The Garden was worth any price for a single visit. It was like the cornerstone of a building; knowing it was there was a kind of solid block on which to rest ordinary life, but Cyn had no desire at all to be buried under total security. In spite of his fatigue he sat up alertly as the flitter settled into the parking area of the OM office; he was looking forward to his new routing—new places, new faces, new customs.

When he looked at the sheets the clerk handed him, however, he didn't know whether to laugh or scream. Served him right for being a wide-eyed optimist, he thought, and groaned aloud. Six passengers! Passengers were the all-time nuisance.

No matter what warnings and explanations were given to them, they could not or would not accept the spartan conditions aboard the Pot and they would act as if the mail-carrier were responsible for the discomfort. Complaints and appeals would bombard Cyn from the moment they arrived to the moment they departed, as if there were something he could do to change the situation.

Cyn's eyes had been traveling down the sheet as he thought about the passengers, and they fixed suddenly. Oh, help! A large living organism to be delivered to Ingong. Cyn looked at the size of the cage and gaped. Then he shoved the sheet under the clerk's nose and shook it before he pointed to the item.

"Is it dangerous?"

"It's caged," the clerk responded without sympathy. Then he shrugged and consulted a file. "No comment on the original more than what it says there—don't unwrap the beastie until it's fixed aboard the ship. There's usually a warning if the creature is likely to attack without provocation, so they may be afraid it will get scared and hurt itself—but I wouldn't let it out if I were you."

"I'm not an idiot," Cyn remarked dryly, "but I suppose I have to feed it and give it water. Food? There's nothing listed here."

"Maybe an automatic feeder attached to the cage, or the food is in an attached compartment. The cage is sure big enough for that."

Cyn had been barely listening. "Ingong—" he muttered, shuffling plas sheets to consult the printout of the routing imbedded in the data button the clerk had handed him first. "Wow!" he exclaimed, "that's a long side jump and it's after the Mantra stop. Oh, hell, that means cage cleaning too."

The clerk smirked. Damn superior mail-carriers, fathead

'overstars heroes,' stamping in in their space coveralls with their tanned faces and everyone oohing and aahing over them. It was nice when one got a dirty job once in a while.

Oh, well, Cyn thought, it couldn't all be roses. He was unaware of the satisfaction his dismay had given the clerk and how close their thoughts had been. "Right," he said resignedly. "I'll take the mail and freight first. There won't be room in the cargo hatch for the cage and the boxes, and I'll have to set up life-support in the shuttle hold and the live-cargo hold. I'll be back at 4:00 standard for the beastie and the passengers. Takeoff at 5:00. Anyone not here gets left."

He ambled out to the shuttle, unsealed it, and settled into the pilot's seat to enter codes. The port-puter responded promptly with its "working" symbol, and the robos' ready lights came on immediately. Cyn began to punch each code on the manifest sheet. After a few smin, the robos came trundling out with their loads. Having dropped the ramp for the robos to enter, he went to the cargo hold and checked each item with a reader as the robo deposited it. Lots of mailcarriers didn't bother, and Cyn had never found a disagreement with the manifest; nonetheless, Trader habits are drilled deep into the bone.

When the robos had secured themselves into their niches, Cyn went back to his seat. The port-puter was displaying three acceptable times in five, fifteen, and thirty smin for liftoff, and an approval of liftoff at 5:20 standard in the morning. Cyn coded acceptance of the five smin slot, and engaged his engines. Half a stu later he was locked into the Pot's handle. Patiently he checked all systems: the seal between the two vessels, the levels of life-support in the ship, the state of the ship-puter, and on down the list. When he was satisfied, he transferred control from the shuttle to the ship. He had done it all hundreds of times before and not once had there been a glitch, but the first glitch in space is all too often the last if it goes unnoticed.

Through the shuttle's upper live-being lock, Cyn entered the corridor to the rec room. He walked round and stuck his head in each cabin door, but his examination was cursory. He had looked carefully after he put off his last passenger on the previous run. Had anything important been left behind, there would have been a carrolled message at the OM office; the robos had cleaned up, and he didn't care much anyway if they had missed something. Passengers were a nuisance. They'd complain anyway.

Opposite the entry passage from the shuttle was the companionway that led up to the control room. At the door, Cyn paused and his eyes swept the area in a swift, automatic survey. The puter console was locked in front of the pilot's recliner, now adjusted to a sitting position. The second recliner, to which the console could be slid along a track, was extended to a sleeping position. That feature had at first seemed to Cyn a miracle of forethought—in an emergency in which the pilot was injured but not mentally incapacitated, anyone could run the ship with the pilot alongside to give instructions.

Later, when he considered the two desks in the center of the floor with their sliding and locking seats set so that the occupants would face each other, Cyn realized that the moveable console was not a result of practical consideration but an archaic design. No doubt at one time two beings were needed to run even so simple a ship as the Pot. Imperial designers, notoriously conservative, simply never bothered to change anything until a pressing need for change was hammered into their brains.

In the pilot's seat, Cyn pressed his left thumb on a little box nestling under the console—not that it mattered which

25

finger he used; the puter would accept any finger or any toe, since accidents could happen. Print recognized, the screen lit. Cyn had heard that some new puters were voice-operated. He wondered how many voices in how many accents they accepted and then shuddered slightly, imagining the results of a voice-print-activated puter's reaction to what he might sound like after a night of howling at a drinking house or being hit in the throat in a brawl. In this case the old system seemed better.

Cyn set the controls for life-support in the live-hold compartment and, after a moment's thought, in the cargo hold also. Often he didn't bother, preferring to keep the extra air as a reserve against catastrophe. He was so accustomed to working in a life-support suit that he found it no real trouble to shift cargo and sort mail suited-up, but with six passengers aboard he had no idea what to expect. Probably several of them would discover that some article s/he couldn't live without had been sent with the baggage to the cargo hold and must be fetched out. Or one would decide some particularly delicate item had fallen or been placed where it would be damaged and insist on examining it. Cyn was within his rights to refuse to admit anyone to the cargo hold and to refuse to retrieve forgotten items, but then the passengers would complain even more all through the journey and complain about his treatment of them too. It was simpler to do what they wanted.

Chores complete, Cyn turned to the printout of messages from his carroll receiver. At the beginning of each route, Cyn carrolled his schedule in Trader code to Lystris. Sometimes his mother, who was cargo officer, would carroll ahead to one of his stops and ask him to buy certain items to be shipped to a future port Lystris or an allied ship would make. Cyn made a commission; Lystris made a profit and also was getting a reputation for being able to supply Empire goods—which few Free Traders could easily obtain. All in all, Cyn's move to Overstars had been an advantage all around. Even when he did no trading, Lystris was usually willing to spend the credits to send him family news and any other bits of gossip or information that might be useful and interesting.

At the time he had left the Pot, the message bin had been empty; now there were two sheets of plas in it. Cyn reached for them with a frown. If Lystris had an emergency that required two messages . . . But the topmost sheet, to Cyn's surprise, was headed by the comet-tailed OM of Official Communications. He scanned rapidly and his brows shot up in surprise.

"Pirates?"

He said the word aloud, grinning. By the Powers that Be, did the Imperial Postmaster think they were back in the sdays of ships that sailed the waters? Had whatever being was Postmaster taken leave of its senses?

Carroll's equations coiled space up quite safely, but no one could tell at what point a ship would emerge on the sphere that made up the carrollpause of the target solar system. It would take an armada to patrol such a sphere of space, even if someone had a copy of a mail ship's routing—which was why Cyn knew it was safe to send his to Lystris. And even an armada could not patrol closely enough to catch the Pot or any sister ship running at speed. Only if a ship were within tractor range when the Pot came out of the Void could she be trapped.

Cyn frowned, wondering if emerging into real space within tractor range would be possible. He knew a ship could not impinge on a planet; even the minor gravity of a planet ejected a ship from the Void a safe distance away. But ships emerging from the Void had been struck and damaged by small asteroids—not seriously damaged, but contact had occurred. A ship would have even less gravitic pull than a small asteroid but might have a very high magnetic field. Since both gravitic and magnetic fields were involved in the inactivation of the Carroll system . . . Cyn shook his head; it was beyond him to figure the possibilities. Then he shrugged, realizing it didn't matter. If his ship came out within tractor distance of another, all his proximity detectors would be screaming their speakers right out of the walls. Before any tractor could fix on him, he could snap back into Carroll's void, come out somewhere else, and run.

The Postmaster must be out of its weird head. Piracy was financially impractical in space—except possibly for a lightsday or so around a planet. Even then the number of ships needed to make a capture would be high. Of course, a ship in orbit, a shuttle, or a private yacht might be attacked in near-planet space . . . Cyn reread the com more carefully to make sure he had not misunderstood. The frown regathered between his brows. The piracy apparently wasn't a freak born of the Postmaster's mind. Two mail ships had disappeared in this quadrant after entering the Void quite normally.

In the words of the Bard (still the one and only Bard after almost 10^2 centuries) "something was rotten in the state of Denmark" (wherever that was). If two mail ships had disappeared in this area, wouldn't it be more sensible to send out a request to check engines against sabotage than silly injunctions to watch out for pirates? Unless the pirates were aboard the ship? Cyn began to gnaw gently on his lower lip. Six passengers? Six? The whiff of rottenness suddenly attached itself to his scheduling sheet. Cyn spun his chair back to the console, tapped in the code attached to the Postmaster's warning, and asked for the routing and passenger list for each of the missing ships.

While he waited for an answer, Cyn picked up Lystris's

message, which he expected to be family gossip. It consisted of two words that sent his eyebrows skyward again: "Data button." That meant Lystris's message was in High Code. It wasn't the mythical state of Denmark where something was rotten, but right here in the Empire!

Cyn withdrew the data button from a second, smaller bin in the com unit. With that in hand, he opened one of the many panels that faced the interior of the ship-puter and began to disconnect a chip box, which looked just like every other chip box. He was very careful to unhook the delicate wires in a particular sequence. A single mistake would not only destroy the box and its true contents but probably remove both his hands, although the self-destruct would not be violent enough to damage any critical part of the ship-puter. High code was a private language, top secret to each Trade ship. It was rare for a code box to leave the Free Trader on which it originated, and Cyn had no intention of failing Lystris's faith in him. When the box was free, he inserted the button and plugged a short cord into a hidden socket in the com. The printer hissed into action.

The message was absorbing enough to make Cyn ignore the renewed hissing of the com printer that indicated the answer to his query was coming through. When he finished, Cyn's wide, good-natured mouth had thinned to a hard, ugly line. Lystris wanted him to quit Overstars and come home. In view of the profits accruing from his employment, which Lystris would give up only with the greatest reluctance, the remainder of the message took on an urgency that did not appear in the words themselves.

There was, the high-code message stated tersely, trouble brewing in the Empire. The old Emperor had been assassinated—Cyn had known that already, of course, but Lystris reported that on unfederated planets the rumor was that the new, young Emperor was dissatisfied with his largely ceremonial position. He wanted greater control over the Patrol and the Navy so he could add new planets (willing or not? Cyn wondered) to the federation and enforce the "civilized standards" implied by Imperial rule. The Empress—a strong supporter of the independent rights of each system and thus of the Planetary Council's control of Imperial armed forces—opposed him.

This, too, was not new to Cyn, but Lystris implied that the rift between the new Emperor and his mother, which had long been sealed over with patch after patch by the diplomacy of the old Emperor, was coming unsealed. Again implied was that the trouble this time was likely to be bad enough to shatter the huge, loose federation and, to some planets, make the approach of any Empire agent, even so innocent an agent as a mail-carrier ship, a threat to be vaporized on recognition.

If Lystris said the trouble would be bad, the word was probably a miracle of understatement as others would understand it. Cyn had still been with Lystris when she had arrived with a load of nuclear arms, which was supposed to enforce the peace, to discover that war had already broken out. A contract being a contract in Lystris's opinion (the captain had already taken payment; arms were carried only if paid for in advance), Cyn's father had taken the shuttle down and his mother had shepherded the paid-for missiles to their destination right through a full-scale battle. Lystris was not given to needless panics.

Cyn wrinkled his nose as he read the com one last time; he didn't like trouble. That was why he had left Lystris and joined Overstars in the first place. Mechanically, he popped the button, wiped it, fed the plas sheets into the regenerator, and replaced the code box. By then, he had decided to put off his decision until he completed this run. Although he didn't doubt that trouble was coming and that it might be bad, he didn't think the situation as critical as those aboard Lystris. A Trader was accustomed to reaction times at planetary speeds—sdays, sometimes stus. The Empire moved more slowly. Also, the Empire capital, Mantra, was the third stop on his route. Cyn wanted to sniff for news and rumor himself near the source.

Without any comment, aside from "Button received," Cyn carrolled the list of planet names at which he would be calling in ordinary Trader code to the Lystris. He might have to take the advice to quit Overstars in the long run, but for now he would wait and see. He felt differently about the Empire than most Free Traders, who usually were either totally indifferent to the federation or felt that its collapse would be an advantage. Because the big Combines controlled trade within the Empire, Free Traders dealt mainly with those planets that were too primitive, too poor, or too dangerous to be included in the federation. They assumed that if the Empire removed its protection, the Combines would fall apart and the Free Traders would capture many more trade routes.

Cyn did not agree with that simplistic view. He did agree that the first result of a conflict between the Emperor and Empress would be paralysis, or worse, of the Patrol and the Navy. That probably would spark an open war among the Combines, but it would also free them to eliminate any Free Trader that dared infringe without fear of reprisal. Beyond that, although he had laughed at the poster that urged beings to "Promote Understanding, Be a Mail-Carrier," he had come to believe in his service. If the Empire fell apart, the long-range result for every solar system would be near-isolation, and isolation could only lead to stagnation and, eventually, to degeneration.

Whistling softly between his teeth, Cyn considered the

two warnings he had received. Lystris warned of trouble in the Empire, but the Postmaster's com had indicated that the two lost ships had both disappeared in this sector. And he would be carrying six passengers. Six! He had never carried more than three in the past. If the other ships—the thought reminded him that the answer to his queries about them had come in while he was reading the message from Lystris. Cyn pulled the sheets from the com.

Interesting. Very interesting. Both ships had carried four passengers. In Cyn's opinion the odds that passengers and disappearances were connected had just gone up by an order of magnitude. From none to three passengers was a normal load for a mail ship, with none far more frequent than three and one the most common. In his five syrs of service, most of his jumps had been made alone; only once had he carried three.

A tight, mirthless smile broke the grim line of Cyn's lips. Forewarned, there was little chance that whoever was playing these games would get away with it on his ship. Cyn went to his quarters, where a palm-lock cabinet held a set of strictly unofficial tools. A mail-carrier was neither required nor expected to know anything about the complex inner operations of his ship. There was training in certain testing procedures and simple gross repairs, but for any more serious malfunction, the ships were provided with elaborate distress signals that would bring a repair ship and crew—or a Patrol ship—within a few sdays.

Basically Cyn had no quarrel with the system. Carroll's void spit a ship out into real space the moment its drive failed or the moment it came within the carrollpause of a sun. Therefore any malfunction put you well within reach of quick rescue. Nonetheless, Cyn's Free Trade background made him unwilling to leave his safety in the hands of others. Free Traders were not assured of instant reply to a distress call because they often traveled far from heavily trafficked areas, and outside of the Empire the incidence of space-going repair crews was zero. Habit, which made Cyn check each item on a manifest, also made him obtain and study the engineering manuals on the Pot until he could take apart and put together anything that did not require a shipyard or a micromanipulator.

Carefully, so that no tool marks would show, Cyn removed the panels that covered the navigation equipment. He was grinning when he finished making his adjustments. Anyone who tried to send the Pot to an unofficial destination was going to get a rude surprise. No one was going to kidnap his Pot.

The grin faded quickly as Cyn considered the other, more unpleasant, alternative. If obtaining the use of the mail ships was not the objective, he was still in trouble. For the life of him, he could not see how destruction of a mail ship could benefit anyone or harm the Empire. Nonetheless, it was a possibility he had to consider. He tried to think of methods of destroying a spaceship from the inside and was relieved to discover how few there were. Then he shrugged. There was nothing he could do about a kamikaze passenger anyway, except watch and listen. On that note, Cyn descended to the passenger level and inactivated all the OFF switches on the av equipment.

Having done everything he could think of to protect himself and the Pot, Cyn checked the time and grimaced. He had hoped to snatch a nap. Sleeping had seemed a waste of expensive time while in Myrrha's company. Now he wished he had been less eager to experience her infinite variety. He made do with a brief session in the fresher and clean clothes before he shifted control to the shuttle and left to pick up his load of trouble.

CHAPTER 3

The passengers, Cyn thought, were a particularly motley group. Then he chided himself inwardly for lack of charity. From a lifetime of rotating periods of duty, all stus of the sday and night were about the same to him. For these people however, it was barely dawn and they could scarcely be at their best.

He greeted them politely, gave his standard little speech apologizing for the lack of amenities aboard his ship, mentioned his inability to do anything to mitigate the spartan conditions, and asked them if they would like to cancel their travel plans and ship out on a passenger vessel. As usual, everyone assured him they were prepared. Cyn nodded and turned away, ostensibly to watch the approach of the large cargo robo carrying the caged "whatever." Actually he wanted the freedom to let his face express his mingled disgust and disbelief.

When his expression was under control, he directed the passengers into the shuttle, told them to take seats, and instructed them how to strap in for the shuttle trip—all without really seeing them. Doubtless, he thought sourly, he'd have all too many chances to look at them over the next swiks. Then he went out again, directed the small robo to bring in the baggage, and finally brought in the large robo.

Cyn watched as the cage was gently settled into the cargo

area and secured. He checked the chain bolts twice himself, a little disturbed by the utter silence behind the curtains. Now he was sorry he hadn't taken the time to investigate the cage the previous night, but the instructions had specifically said not to disturb or excite the animal by removing the curtains. He could only hope that the creature was well protected and lift off gently.

His care won him a twittering compliment from the only passenger who seemed wide awake. Frefem Rocam was a small, thin, elderly fem dressed in an ultraconservative dark suit with a bit of white lace at the throat. The only notable thing about her, aside from her bright-eyed alertness, was her hat. Tied square on top of her head with a swathe of veiling, it was a flat, black pancake topped with the body, head, and wings of a glossy black bird. The creature could have been alive, except for its immobility and the fact that it did not appear to have any legs.

"Such consideration," Frefem Rocam chirped to the much younger fem strapped in beside her. "It's my first trip and, although I'm not frightened—indeed, I've been looking forward to it—somehow all the talk about how fast the mail ships travel made me think it would be a rather bumpy ride."

Cyn could see the younger fem's head turn in the mirror above his console. The mirror, specially surfaced so that it looked like a dull metal strip from any position except his own, permitted the pilot to watch the cargo and passenger section without turning his head. It was set up so the mail-carrier could forestall any silly moves, like unstrapping in freefall, or render aid to anyone seriously affected by weightlessness.

He must have missed that one when he called the group motley, Cyn thought. Her travel wear was really something— a jumpsuit of dully glistening gold that concealed and yet clung revealingly from throat to ankle and still managed to give a definite impression of toughness and utility. No loose ends to float in freefall, tangle in straps, or catch on things in close quarters. As she shifted, Cyn caught a glimpse of a wide brown belt studded with dark gems. He was willing to bet credits against minums that those gems were chips, and that what they controlled was housed in the elegant pouch secured by straps to the fem's shoulder and hip.

She turned, smiled, and said, "*I'm* Fr. Aimie. He is lifting off a little slower than usual, probably because he doesn't want to frighten the animal in the cage and set it squalling, but it wouldn't be a bumpy liftoff in any case. These mail-carriers are like lift operators. They go up and down so often, a smooth ride is almost a habit."

"You sound as if you've traveled on these ships very often."

"Almost as often as the mail-carriers, I think," Fr. Aimie replied with a chuckle. "I work for Vie Parer, and fashions are only fashions when they're hot. If you get there the firstest, you make the mostest."

That accounted for the lacquered perfection. Cyn regarded her with some interest. Right now he wasn't hungry, but she would be aboard to Mantra. Very often the professional fems that traveled the spaceways were not averse to a little light dalliance to while away the dull sdays. An interesting contrast to Myrrha, Cyn thought. The nymph was all genuine friendly responsiveness; Fr. Aimie was probably hard as the gems on her belt—as polished, and possibly just as fake: Glossy chestnut hair, its brown fired with red where the light touched it, was dressed and frozen into the elaborate swirls of the highest fashion. Her skin was pale: cosmetically shielded from all radiation, no doubt. Her lips were full and dyed very red. Cyn couldn't determine the color of her eyes because of the way the mirror reflected, but he was sure, whatever the color, they would be bright and unrevealing.

"From Vie Parer, eh?" a bulky man across the aisle remarked. "We might have a lot in common."

"Don't tell me I have a rival aboard," Fr. Aimie groaned with mock dismay. "I thought I was way ahead on this jump."

The man laughed. "Fremale Demoson, and this is my assistant Fr. Wakkin. No, I'm no rival for Vie Parer, but I am interested in your business—financially interested. Fact is, I'm headed for Mantra for the meeting of the GMA."

Something flickered across the fem's face very swiftly. Had Cyn not been studying her features intently—with only the most dishonorable motives—he would not have seen the fleeting change of expression before a look of horror was deliberately fixed on her face.

"Oh, help!" she exclaimed. "Pilot, I want to unstrap. I have to triple lock my sample cases. There's a thief aboard! Do you know what members of the GMA do? They come to fashion shows, steal our ideas, and turn out two-credit versions of two-hundred-credit items."

Cyn had swiveled his seat slowly, well aware that the fem was merely indulging in a little barbed humor. The look that had so briefly crossed her face had, however, nothing to do with either humor or the real sense of grievance the joke covered—unless Cyn was mistaken in what he thought he saw. Once out of the atmosphere, Cyn only faced his console to allow passengers who were ignorant to feel comfortable because the pilot was "flying" the ship. Actually, aside from landing and docking, the shuttle was almost completely automated and Cyn had little to do but cancel a maneuver he didn't like or let the shuttle alone. Now he turned because he was more interested in watching his passengers' faces directly than reassuring them.

"I cannot allow that, Frefem," he responded, smiling, "but I will allow you to leave the shuttle first so you may be sure of being present when the robos bring in the baggage."

"Now, now," Demoson interjected, "that's not fair. We don't steal the stuff, and you know it. We pay through the nose for the right to reproduce." He shrugged. "I guess the people in sales get the raw end of that deal, but I assure you your front office loves us dearly. We profit, they profit—and you know that a lot of them wouldn't be in business at all without us—and Everybeing can afford to wear the latest rage."

"Yes, but I don't think that's a good idea at all," the little old lady in the funny hat put in before Aimie could answer. "Not everyone profiting, of course—that's a fine idea—but everybeing wearing the latest fashion. High fashion is nearly always extreme and most of it is most unsuitable to anyone who isn't young and beautiful."

"I'm afraid my motives aren't as pure as yours," Aimie said, "but I agree with you completely. I don't think high fashion is for Everybeing."

"Oh, no," Fr. Rocam twittered, "my motives aren't really pure—not if you mean that my modesty is offended by high fashion. It's my taste. Just think of me in that very lovely suit you're wearing."

A guffaw burst briefly from the short, rotund, pink-faced fellow in the rear seat. The tall, saturnine-looking man opposite glared at him.

"I beg your pardon, Frefem," the little man muttered, abashed.

"There's no need to beg my pardon," the little old lady said with a decidedly impish grin. "You've made my point. For me to wear a suit that is completely becoming on Fr. Aimie would be dreadful. Really, beings should be protected against making such fools of themselves."

Demoson laughed aloud and grinned. "But that would be far worse than looking silly. To deny freedom of choice, even wrong choice, as long as it does no harm to anyone else is the worst choice of all." His expression was surprisingly boyish and lent considerable charm to his heavy face. "Now, you see, that's just what GMA does. It provides freedom of choice and actively prevents harm—"

"Don't all choices bring some harm with them?" the saturnine-faced man interrupted, his mouth twisted.

Demoson laughed again. "There's harm and harm. After all Fr. Rocam can look away if her taste is offended, but if a fem or male drove its spouse to suicide or to breaking a mating contract because it couldn't get one of the real Vie Parer outfits, that would surely be worse harm. If you want to restrain someone, Fr. Aimie, and put us out of business, it's the right to send carrollpics you should complain about. If no one saw the styles, no one would want them."

"Do you think there was no high fashion before star travel?" Aimie asked.

"Oh, dear," Fr. Rocam sighed, "I didn't mean to start an argument. I was joking!"

As everyone turned to assure her that they had understood, that they were not arguing, merely having a friendly discussion on a subject of particular interest, Cyn swung his chair back to face his console. A number of the remarks had— in light of what he suspected—given him food for thought. While he made mental notes of Rocam's casual statement about protecting beings against themselves, Demoson's cynicism, and the sardonic man's remark—Hachisman, Cyn recalled from his list—his eyes were automatically scanning his instruments. All systems were green, speed and approach to the Pot were right on, no signs of—But there were! The rs screen showed two widely-spaced blips.

Pursuit? But it was the mail ships themselves that had disappeared. The Postmaster said nothing about attacks on the shuttles. Cyn watched, thinking about what he could do. The shuttle was completely without defenses and no faster than any standard model. Of course, ground control was watching, but that wouldn't do him any good if all they did was report . . . If they reported he had been pursued or seized at all. They hadn't warned him he was being followed!

Cyn moved the speed control forward cautiously, not wanting to alarm the passengers. The blips began to fade, but before Cyn could breathe out his relief they began to grow again. Pursuit then; if not, they wouldn't have increased speed too. Cyn checked the distance to the Pot and swallowed an oath. If he accelerated any more, the gravity compensators in the shuttle wouldn't be able to deal with the deceleration necessary to match the Pot's orbital speed. And it wouldn't help anyway. Even if he had extra speed, he was too close to the Pot to outrun his pursuers before he reached her.

The moment he thought it, Cy had to set his teeth to keep from cursing himself aloud. He had forgotten one essential thing because of his "clever" conviction that the passengers were involved in the mail-ship disappearances. He had forgotten that the Pot was most vulnerable when the shuttle approached it. The hangar opened automatically when it picked up the shuttle's signal. Any other ship, or even a man in a suit, could slip inside and open the emergency hatch into the ship itself.

But not whoever was behind him, Cyn realized. The blips had kept pace, but neither had deviated from the original path to intercept. Cyn blushed under his deep tan and hoped none of the passengers could see his ears burning. The Postmaster had used an ancient word that evoked drama and mystery—pirates—and he, fool that he was, had generated a melodrama in his head. If he had the brains of a segmented worm he would have realized that two blips like that had to be guards assigned to make sure the shuttle was not intercepted.

Not a total gain. The fact that the following ships were guards only increased the possibility that one or more of the passengers intended to capture the Pot. Cyn quietly activated the small force field designed to protect the pilot and console from accident. It was a serious drain of energy, but would protect him until the passengers were actually aboard. Once inside the metal shell of his ship, Cyn felt the advantages were all with him. He had already taken certain precautions, and he knew the Pot—every nook and cranny, every nut and bolt, almost every electron and positron. He couldn't believe that anyone could beat him at any game played inside the Pot. He kept one eye on the blips, which maintained their distance, but gave his primary attention to a smooth deceleration and docking that would eat up the least power.

Cyn was almost disappointed when all the passengers sat quietly while the hangar closed on the shuttle. He finished his checks, and flipped the relay that transmitted the psuedogravity from the ship to the shuttle. While the passengers' seats rotated to the new upright position and the debarkation ladder slid down the aisle, Cyn unsealed the airlock between the vessels and closed the switch that slid the doors aside. Since pressure and temperature were already equal, both opened immediately onto the corridor that led directly to the passenger level. Just as Cyn started to swing around to tell the passengers to unstrap, a violent blow struck the ship.

He was flung sideways against the console and then held there as the Pot was dragged forcefully out of orbit and drawn along. However no shock could break the training that in generations of space travel had become almost a phylogenetic instinct. Even before his brain had caught up with what had happened, Cyn's eyes flew to the telltales. No damage. All glowed a steady green. Ignoring the shrill shriek startled out of Fr. Rocam and the oaths from the men, Cyn forced himself into his seat over the pull of the acceleration. He closed the doors of the airlock and shoved his thumb against the plate under the console that would connect the shuttle to the shipputer, which he instructed to transfer rs and other visuals to the shuttle's screens.

Only then did Cyn have time to realize they had been caught by a tractor beam. He hadn't considered that possibility because neither of the pursuing ships had been close enough nor indicated mass enough for traction—not of the force that had been applied. And then Cyn spat an oath and flung his hands up to protect his eyes. A tiny sun had blossomed out on the real-space visual he had scarcely glanced at in his concentration on the rs blips. Almost simultaneously, two further shocks hit the ship—the first when the tractor beam was released and the second when the Pot's engines fired briefly but violently to counter the applied pull and reachieve orbit.

Cyn snapped the relays that reopened the airlock doors. "Right," he snapped. "Demoson, unstrap and out into the ship. Quick as you can move."

The heavyset man reached for the straps, but before he could pull the release, Hachisman began to rise. He had one leg out in the aisle on the ladder, but he never actually freed himself from the curve of the seat. As he turned, Cyn had cancelled the force field and a stunner had appeared in his hand as if by magic. Hachisman sank back with staring eyes.

"When I give an order on my ship, it's obeyed," Cyn snarled. "Demoson, out! Wakkin, out!" As Wakkin's heels cleared the rung of the ladder level with Hachisman's head, Cyn gestured with the stunner. "Now, Hachisman, out. Sorry about the gun, but I know what I'm doing." His eyes shifted to the little, round fellow. "Mortchose, out."

As soon as the smaller man cleared his position, Cyn dropped down past the two women. "Fr. Aimie, do you need help?" he asked. "Go then, now!" he said as she shook her head wordlessly.

When she was out, the gun disappeared into his tunic as fast as it had emerged and he bent and released Fr. Rocam's straps and helped her to her feet. After the single shriek she had uttered, the old lady had been silent, one hand pressed to her lips and the other, comically or pathetically, holding down her funny hat. She was probably light as the bird that perched on it, Cyn thought, and prepared to lift her.

"Thank you, pilot, but I'm quite capable of walking," she said calmly.

Rocam's tone was a shock. Cyn really looked at her and would have reached for his stunner again, except that it was far too late. If the old lady had intended to take him, she would have done so already. He was a fool for mixing up age and apparent fragility with helplessness, and would have deserved his fate if she had attacked him. Clearly she was capable of walking or of sliding a knife between his ribs, had she wished to do it. A nice pink color showed in her cheeks, and her eyes were bright. Cyn bit his lips to hold back a grin. He had suddenly realized why he thought her helpless. It was her determined clutch on her hat. As she climbed the ladder, Cyn did grin behind her back. People surely grew attached to the oddest oddities.

As soon as he had herded Fr. Rocam through the ship's lock, Cyn raised the manual lever to slam it shut. He had suddenly remembered his other responsibility—the beastie in the cage. Had they been in any danger, he would have had to ignore the creature, but Cyn had figured out what had happened and knew they would be safe for a while. Nor was the Pot in any danger from the passengers. Because some were curious as fflathores and some seemed to think they had bought the ship with the price of the passage, Cyn always locked the companionways to both cargo level and control level when he had passengers. That effectively imprisoned them on the passenger deck, and allowed him to take care of his duties without fearing that one of the idiots would try to adjust the heat in his cabin by pushing the Carroll's void switch or decide to get his own baggage out of a hold with no life support.

Cyn turned toward the cargo area, then hesitated. What he could do for anything that large if it had been hurt, he didn't know. Then he went down toward the end of the shuttle. If the beastie was hurt, he would insist someone come up from the planet to help it or take it dirtside again, where it could be treated. He and his ship would be safer in the void, but he couldn't let a living creature, no matter what it was, suffer.

At that moment from behind the curtains came tiny, half-stifled snuffles and whimpers. Cyn flung himself down the rest of the ladder. Oh, damn! It had been hurt. Cyn's heart contracted painfully; that anything so large should make such little muffled whimpers hinted at great timidity or serious injury. Singing a soft litany of curses, Cyn unfastened the curtains and flung them back.

A sensation of surprise so strong as to result in total paralysis gripped him. Finally his brain and body caught up with what his eyes were transmitting, and Cyn gasped.

CHAPTER 4

"Myrrha," Cyn breathed, his eyes starting, his heart sinking right into his metal-inset space boots. Sexual gymnastics were all very well and he had had a wonderful time, but a lifetime of Myrrha outside the Garden was not what Cyn had bargained for.

The head lifted from the disconsolate heap lying on the padded floor of the cage; the cornsilk hair was flung back from the flowerlike face. Cyn took a deep breath. Not Myrrha. In spite of the striking similarity of features and coloring, the difference was clear. For one thing this girl was many syrs younger than Myrrha, barely more than a child. Her eyes were different, a pellucidly clear pale blue instead of the older nymph's misty grey-blue.

"Child," Cyn said softly, soothingly, "are you hurt?"

"Just bruised a little. I was frightened." The clear eyes clouded with tears.

No nymph at all, Cyn realized. Her voice was pure, high, and clear, but it certainly did not chime like a bell. A failed nymph then? But caged? To be delivered to Ingong? Cyn frowned. If his memory served him right, Ingong was a member of the Imperial federation but its inhabitants were not even vaguely humanoid. What the hell was this? What would an Ingongian want with a failed nymph?

"What are you doing in a cage, child?" Cyn asked.

"I am not a child," she protested. "I am ripe for marriage and my name is Niais."

Her tears had already dried and she smiled sweetly at Cyn as she sat upright. Her denial of childhood was a trifle marred by the convulsive way she clutched a soft package to her small breasts. However, no matter how sweet the smile, it had not answered Cyn's question.

"What are you doing in a cage?" he repeated.

"I am going to Ingong."

Cyn swallowed. The voice was sweet, the eyes, wide with innocence, met his brightly, but she still had not answered his question. "But why in a cage?" he insisted. "People do not travel in cages."

The rose petal lips parted, closed, parted again. Her expression clouded; the lips pouted. "That is not a nice thing to say, fremale. I am a person, and I am traveling in a cage."

Now it was Cyn's turn to open and close his mouth. "I was not implying you weren't a person," he got out, his voice sounding a bit constricted. "I was trying to find out why a person like you was traveling in a cage."

Joy returned to the exquisite face. "To go to Ingong," she replied with a blinding smile.

This time Cyn's mouth did not close after it opened, not until he had fought and won a battle with his inclination to bellow at the top of his lungs. Either the girl was truly an idiot, in which case bellowing at her would be cruel and accomplish nothing, or she was a good deal cleverer than he, in which case bellowing would be equally useless. While he got his mouth closed and swallowed hard, Cyn examined the lovely, childish, slightly vacuous face. She must be an idiot. Or, perhaps she didn't know the answer to his question and was ashamed to admit it. In any case, this was neither the time nor the place to continue the argument with her.

"Well," he said firmly—without raising his voice—"people do not travel in cages aboard my ship." He reached up, slipped the key that hung beside the lock off its hook, and unlocked the door. "Come out at once."

Niais stood up obediently, but fear leapt like a flame into her eyes. "I must be delivered to Ingong in the cage," she faltered. "I must."

Tears hung, crystal jewels, in her lower lids. Her beauty was incredible. "All right, all right," Cyn assured her, "you can get back in when we get to Ingong, but that will be more than a swik. Surely you'll be more comfortable in a regular passenger cabin."

As he spoke, Cyn wondered whether what he said was true. Now he realized why the cage was so large. It had a couch-chair, a tiny but perfectly adequate fresher, a small table with what looked like a miniature autochef attached, all beautifully made and most luxurious. No cruelty had been intended in the method of transport. Still, the child—Cyn smiled; no, she insisted she was a fem—would be horribly lonely in the cargo hold. She realized it too, he guessed, as he saw the trouble disappear from her face. She shifted the package she had been clutching with both hands to her left arm, snatched a small travelbag from under her couch, and stepped out, making Cyn a little curtsey.

"Thank you, fremale. I am happy to obey you."

She was that much a nymph, Cyn thought; she was happy to obey him, happy to do anything that gave pleasure. And she was surely beautiful enough. Then why . . . Cyn recalled his wandering mind. It was not his problem, he told himself. He had troubles enough without wondering why Niais had not been accepted into the sisterhood.

He half turned toward the ladder leading to the passenger level, then hesitated. The moment he showed his face, he would be set upon by the passengers to explain why they had been jolted about and why he had drawn a stunner on them. It would be better to get the shuttle unloaded, go directly into the control section—he would have to take Niais with him, but he could keep an eye on her—and get the ship started toward the carrollpause.

While he directed one of the robos to take the passenger's baggage, Cyn ran through his mind what he was almost certain had happened. The Postmaster was not as far out of its mind as Cyn had first thought, it seemed, but the piracy had not taken place in Carroll's void or when the target emerged from the void. Someone had been very clever and very skillful and had caught the ship at the logical place to board—the takeoff point.

The "pirate" had matched orbits with the Pot in space, spiraling closer and closer but always directly behind her with respect to the distant rs screens in the planet's port, so that only one blip would show. Once the two ships were close enough, only one blip would show, no matter what position the raider took with respect to the Pot. The real-space screen in the shuttle might have showed the double image when he closed on the Pot, but the raider had avoided that by a repetition of the maneuver, by keeping opposite the ship from the shuttle as Cyn approached. When the shuttle hangar closed, the tractor had gone into action. From the planet, only one blip would show and that blip, just as usual, would move away into space.

Clever, but not clever enough. Overstars might be a little slow on the uptake, but they were not idiots. The scheme had worked twice in this sector, possibly as many times in other sectors, but the raiders should have realized that it could not work forever. The blips that had followed Cyn from the planet were indeed guard ships. Because they were angled well to each side of his approach to the Pot, the raider that was invisible to Cyn was a clear mark to them on real-space screens.

At that point Cyn frowned. Had the raider not seen the guard ships coming? Not guessed what they were? Why had it not simply moved away without trying to take the Pot with it? The Patrol certainly would not have fired at them, and even if the ships were those of the Planetary Police, they would have given a warn-off before shooting. He shook his head sharply. It was ridiculous to second-guess that situation. The miniature sun that had momentarily blinded him was clear evidence that the guardian ships had fired and that that particular raider would not trouble anyone again. Nor would any other pirate trouble the Pot. Cyn was sure his guardian angels were still there, watching. They might be willing to accompany him right to the carrollpause, but Cyn had an idea of his own that he preferred.

The loaded robo scuttled toward the cargo lock and beeped plaintively. Cyn went to open it, and glancing back at the cage, decided that could remain where it was until needed, since Niais was not going to travel in it. The fem was right beside him, and Cyn smiled at her. Another very pleasant nymph characteristic was hers: she neither chattered nor fidgeted. With the robo gone, the shuttle was suddenly so quiet that Cyn heard a futile clicking at the passenger level shuttle lock. He looked at it in surprise and "tchked," tongue against teeth. He had dogged it shut without thinking in response to his general anxiety.

Likely enough the attempt to re-enter was totally innocent. Any one of the passengers could have left some small item behind; he hadn't bothered to search the seats yet. Cyn ran up the ladder to open the door, but he put a hand on his stunner before pulling out the dog and pushing up the lever.

The corridor was empty. Then the attempt to get in was not so innocent. But if someone wanted to leave the ship, there would certainly be enough excuse to do so without suspicion after the knocking around they had taken. Steal the shuttle? Insane. He would merely have to report the defection and the shuttle would be picked up. It was a common type, no special engines like the Pot's, and not worth stealing. He stared down the corridor for a moment then slowly closed the door, but he did not dare dog it shut again. Once he left and would not be there to open the lock, the passengers had to be able to get into the shuttle on their own in an emergency.

He dropped down the ladder and gestured for Niais to follow the cargo robo, which trundled out of the lock he opened into a square chamber that housed the small lift. She waited while Cyn closed the cargo lock and reset the palm seal. By then the robo had unloaded the luggage into the lift; it was a tight squeeze but Cyn maneuvered Niais into a corner and squeezed in after her. At the control level, he gestured her out, and got out himself. When the lift door closed, he locked it so no one could get into the control level that way.

"Come with me," he said to Niais, and took her through the door into his private room. "Get into the bunk."

She had been looking around with bright-eyed curiosity, but had not moved without his permission at any time. Now she lay down without protest, although her eyes had widened. Cyn patted her cheek and said she was a good fem, then went out, closing the door behind him. She had hardly made a sound since their conversation ended. As he slid into his seat and started flipping switches, Cyn thought that the instant responsiveness of the nymphs was more precious than their agility in bed. By the time the thought had passed through his mind, Cyn had cut off system interpenetration from the shuttle. He hesitated a moment and then cut off life support from all cargo holds. The warning lights would go on over the companionways and in the lift. He flipped a last switch.

"Frefems and Fremales, your luggage is now in the lift opposite Cabin Six. You may collect it at your convenience. There is no need to do so now. We are about to accelerate. There will be an increase in gravity, as this ship has more power and less corrective capacity than most passenger liners. Please be careful. If you have any doubt about your ability to adjust to gravitic change, please lie down in your bunk. The automedic available is of a very rudimentary character; however, you need have no fear of ultimate recovery as it has good freeze-preserve ability. I also wish to warn you that there is no life support in any area except the passenger and control decks. If you must visit any other area of the ship, please call me and I will either provide a suit or arrange for life support in the area."

But Cyn didn't get away with trying to act as if nothing had happened. Three faces blurred together on Cyn's av screen and three voices made an incomprehensible cacophony.

"Please," he protested, "the av doesn't have split channels. I can assure you that whatever caused the unexpected movements of the ship, it was not a malfunction. If any passenger wishes to leave, I will inform the OM office and the port-puter to arrange a pickup, but this will mean suit transfer since this ship has no extra shuttle ports. Let me remind you that a mail ship is as fast or faster than any other known vessel so it is unlikely that anything can catch us before we reach the carrollpause. Once in the void, nothing can touch us. I do not believe there is any further danger."

Cyn felt a little guilty about that flat statement, but there was a chance it was true. An attack from outside did raise the possibility that the passengers were not involved with the ship disappearances. In that case, Cyn was reasonably sure they would arrive without incident at their destination. Unfortunately, Cyn still felt the probability of all six passengers being innocent was as near zero as made no difference.

Far more likely one or more was supposed to take control of the ship to prevent any alarm and to open the ship to those in the tractor-bearing vessel—only Cyn, forewarned, armed, and ready, had reacted faster. Since Cyn had no idea whether the agent of the pirate ship still intended to seize the Pot or would be the first to desire landing, he was no longer as eager to be rid of any of the passengers as he had been. Certainly he was too practiced in the art of self-preservation to wish to be alone on the ship with a clever and determined enemy. All those innocent bystanders milling around in the cramped passenger quarters would certainly curtail any agent's freedom of action, and short of mass murder, s/he wouldn't dare harm anyone for fear of self-betrayal.

There had been no immediate response to Cyn's offer, but the faces on the av shifted and blended as, presumably, the passengers moved or tried to consult one another. Cyn was sorry it was impossible to pick features or expressions out of the mess on the screen. Then another babble directed at him broke out.

"One at a time," Cyn remonstrated. "Please go to the central area, talk it over, and use the av there. Will each of you please identify himself or herself and give me a decision? Then I will have a record that will eliminate future disagreements."

The delay was no longer than it took to walk from the cabins to the central av. "Demoson here," the stocky man reported. "I want to go ahead."

"Wakkin. I want to continue."

"Aimie. I'll go."

"Mortchose. I'll go too. I wouldn't be on a tub like this if time wasn't important."

"This is Fr. Rocam. I will continue on, I think. Well, I must or I will miss my great niece's wedding. Anyway, it's—it's thrilling."

Cyn bit back a spontaneous protest. If she wasn't one of the villains and anything happened to her, he would never forgive himself. The face of the saturnine man replaced Fr. Rocam's delicate features.

"Hachisman." He grinned wryly. "Well, that did it for me. I was going to ask to go back, but if Fr. Rocam has enough nerve to go ahead—I'll go."

"Thank you all," Cyn said. "Please return to your cabins and prepare for acceleration."

He made the adjustments that shifted the Pot from orbital mode to acceleration, fed in a t-d angular correction of 5.27 degrees, and slipped the journey button that the clerk in the office had given him into the navigation slot. As he closed the switch, he had a brief qualm of doubt. Could the journey buttons be involved in the disappearance of the mail ships? No, that wasn't logical. Journey buttons would be the first things security would check.

On the rs screen the two blips still appeared at widely divergent points. Cyn touched intership com. "OMS 16.8.19/19. Request identification of ship at coords—" he reeled them off from the screen.

Without delay, the com screen lit to show the tight control room of a PP vessel. The ship was slightly larger than the Pot, but its interior was much reduced by the thickened hull and the space absorbed by the offensive and defensive armament with which it was crammed.

"PP ship 273. Sorry about the bumps," the officer said. "I thought I would get them before they grabbed you. What are you carrying?"

"Not a thing of value, as far as I know," Cyn replied. "Maybe someone is collecting OM ships to start a rival service."

The screen fuzzed with interference, then cleared to show a different face in a similar interior. This officer was older, with hard-bitten features and a suspicious expression. There were more stripes on this man's shoulders too.

"PPS 104. Maybe you're carrying something you don't know anything about, but we do. You'd better match with us so that we can come aboard and look you over."

Cyn hoped that his sender had not carried the brief expression of the shock he felt. The Planetary Police, even on a rim planet, knew better than that, and Healtha was one of the first members of the Empire. Once anything was aboard an Overstars ship, it was sacred against any interference, except by the Patrol, which was the armed force of the Empress. It might be that the suggestion was innocently intended. The officer had not actually ordered him to match, but Cyn's suspicions were reinforced.

His hands flew over the console, ejecting the navigation button, switching to manual, bringing the Carroll system engines to life. "I don't think that's necessary," he remarked slowly, as if he was thinking about the suggestion. "I do have one thing of value—just never thought of it until now—I've got a failed nymph. I've heard that some people would sell their souls for one, not to mention trying a raid."

The officer's eyes flicked down and the sensitive com picked up the rustle of plas sheets. His eyes sought Cyn's in the screen again. "Only Fr. Rocam and Fr. Aimie—no nymph. What are you trying to pull, mail-carrier?"

Hoping the expression would not look like a rictus, Cyn grinned. "You're looking in the wrong place." He stole a glance at the Carroll telltales. "It's the craziest thing. She was the beastie in the cage."

"What?"

Cyn's mouth felt dry. Not ready yet. "Look," he said, "I was just as surprised as you. Instructions were to keep the cage covered until it was settled in the cargo deck, but after those bumps when the tractor grabbed and let go, I went to see if the 'animal' was hurt. What I found was a fem that looks like a clone of the nymphs."

An expression of triumph flitted across the officer's face. "You should have reported that right away," he said severely. "The traffic in nymphs is forbidden. We'll have to remove her. Now you'll have to let us match."

"Wait a smin," Cyn protested. "That's a planetary rule. It's your business to catch them before they get into Overstars hands. You know I have to get approval from the Imperial Postmaster to let anyone remove anything from an OM ship. Only the Patrol—say, there must be a Patrol ship around. Healtha's an important planet. You put in a complaint; Patrol takes her off. That solves both problems."

"Don't be a fool," the officer snapped. "Do you want to be held up for stus? You won't be blamed for obeying PP orders. I have a record—"

The telltales were half-green, and Cyn had heard all he needed to confirm his suspicions. When PP wouldn't pass a responsibility to Patrol, some kind of dirty politics was involved. He hit the stud that engaged the Carroll system. The face disappeared from the screen. The Pot's metal screamed as the ship tried to enter the void and was flung out again by the gravitic and magnetic forces of the sun and planet. Cyn was driven right and left with bruising force by a convulsion that might have torn a needle ship apart. The Pot's rotund form was far less delicate and designed to endure strain, and all structural telltales were still green when the shock had passed.

Cyn's mouth twisted. That must be two surprised PP ships. They wouldn't have expected a mail-carrier to use a Free Trader trick. Not that the Free Traders used planet-hopping except in cases of real emergency. The violent collision of Carroll's void and a sun's field did neither ship nor cargo any good, but it flung the object at the point of the collision about 50 million kim. The distance was more than enough, considering the Pot's speed, to take her completely out of pursuit range.

Naturally, enough noise burst from the intraship av in moments. Hachisman's face, eyes starting with alarm and rage, filled the screen. "What the hell was that?" he bellowed. "You said we wouldn't be—"

"I'm very sorry," Cyn replied, hitting the all-channel switch so that his face and voice would be carried to all av outlets, "but that bump saved us half a sday's travel. We will be at Healtha's carrollpause by tomorrow evening. In view of what happened earlier, I just decided we would be better off if no one knew where we were. I sincerely hope there will be no future need for such gymnastics and that no one was hurt."

"Safer!" Hachisman's voice overrode other murmurs. "We could have been killed! That's enough. I've changed my mind. I want to go back to Healtha. I'm in a hurry, but I want to get to Mantra alive."

"I'm sure you'll get there alive fremale," Cyn soothed. "Unfortunately, it's now too late to return you to Healtha. That little boost took us out past the sixth planet. I'll be glad to put you down on Xiphe in three sdays, if you'd like. That's true for everyone, of course. Please, what's more important: is anyone hurt?"

Fortunately everyone had taken Cyn's advice to lie down while the gravity stabilized. Perhaps, Cyn thought wearily as he struggled to soothe and explain while establishing his new position and distance from the carrollpause and dragged out the charts that would give correction inputs for the travel time reduction, it would have been better if they had all been knocked unconscious. Finally, in desperation, he said he would join them for lunch and answer all their questions as fully as he could. It had occurred to him that he had to bring Niais down to the passenger section and explain her too. He might as well get it all over at one time.

The first thing Cyn had to decide was whether he was willing to trust the OM-puter button at all or try to work out his own course. The fact that the PP officer had had every intention of boarding Cyn's ship was so unusual as to imply strongly that the PP were involved in the ship disappearances. If so, who could tell how high the rot had risen? Cyn picked up the journey button and stared at it. There was no way for him to read it; perhaps the next stop was not Xiphe. Employees of Overstars were hired and paid through the Empress's Household, but the dirtside force were usually residents of the planet on which the office was, which could easily make them vulnerable to pressure from their own government and police.

Nothing might be what it seemed: The so-called raider might have been a drone set in place by the PP—which would eliminate the need for the fancy maneuvers Cyn had envisioned—and triggered to apply the tractor from one of their ships. Blowing it up was an expensive ploy, but the value of a mail ship would make irrelevant the cost of a hulk of some kind. There was no way to determine the truth about it, and it was a waste of time to guess any further. One thing was sure, Cyn was not going to trust the journey button he had been given on Healtha. When he got to Xiphe he could ask for a new navigation button.

The next few stus were desperately busy for both Cyn and the Pot's puter. Ordinarily journey buttons were prepared by the planetary office of Overstars, but all ships carried basic navigation equipment. Accidents did happen, buttons did get damaged or destroyed so that a ship arrived at an unexpected destination, and ships did get thrown out of Carroll's void by unexpected galactic incidents or internal malfunctions. It was necessary for the pilot to be able to navigate a ship diverted from its true course back into Empire space where help might be obtained. Of course, ship's equipment could not provide the kind of journey button an OM-puter could. A pilot could only set up a route from star to star. The complex trajectories that avoided or used intervening carrollpauses were far beyond the Pot's simple puter.

In the back of Cyn's mind was the uncomfortable knowledge that the other two ships had not disappeared from Healtha. That would mean that more than one Planetary Police force was involved, and that would confirm the information from Lystris that the Empire was in trouble. Cyn stared in despair at the mess of references around him. He couldn't compute a whole route. Then he snatched at the answers to the queries he had sent regarding the missing ships, which he had dropped back into the com bin. His memory had been correct. Both disappeared ships had also been making stops at Empire Star on Mantra—and that was the second port of call. He could compute that route during the sdays of travel from the carrollpause to Xiphe. There he would drop the whole problem into the lap of Patrol.

By virtue of his Free Trade background, Cyn did not love

the Patrol. Their prejudice that anything not federated into the Empire and any being not an Empire citizen was immediately worthy of suspicion and almost always dangerous and evil, made them unpleasant. Nonetheless he was in Empire service now and he had to admit that the organization fulfilled its purpose. In the name of the Empress, the Patrol controlled traffic and trade within the Empire with ruthless efficiency and impartiality.

Never for a moment would Cyn have considered joining that service. The men and officers were virtually incorruptible, but they were kept that way by a system of checks and balances, internal and external committees of investigation, and personal examinations by the Empress herself. The constant checks were not pleasant, particularly for the upper and middle echelon of officers who had just enough power to want more and were the most vulnerable to corruption, but it worked. Not that the members of the Patrol were required to be saints; they merely had to report any minor crimes or behavioral peculiarities that were "forbidden" by Empire rules or by the customs and mores of the culture to which they were native. What was already known could not make them subject to blackmail.

Originally Cyn had been thinking of stepping on the button and saying it had been damaged in the shakeup when the tractor grabbed and released his ship. Now he picked it up and put it carefully in his pocket. He would hand it over to the Patrol. Of course, it might be as innocent as his maternal grandmother—Cyn's mind checked and, in spite of his troubles, he chuckled.

That was a peculiarly unfortunate simile. His maternal grandmother was the craftiest Trader he knew. She was anything but innocent, and any being who trusted her before a Contract was made might lose its back teeth (if it had any and if they were of any value) as well as its credits. Suddenly his eyebrows shot up. Take away the silly hat and Fr. Rocam had a lot in common with his grandmother.

Cyn shook his head. He had been slinging numbers around for too long. The ship-puter was still mumbling to itself, and Cyn took the opportunity to get up, stretch, and walk around. He had drawn a hot caff from the rudimentary autochef on the desk when the chime of completed computation brought him back to his console. He keyed the puter to transfer the data to the navigation equipment and whistled as he watched the results appear on the screen. The passengers were going to have fits! The best the puter could do was ten jumps in and out of the void. They weren't much, just a little shiver when the ship came out and another to re-enter after the acceleration to get beyond the carrollpause. Unfortunately, the passengers would certainly notice the effect repeated ten times in about as many stus. He was going to have to do some very fancy explaining.

CHAPTER 5

"Pilot!" The voice had a crispness that made Cyn start. Fr. Aimie's face stared at him out of the av screen.

"Yes, frefem?"

"I don't know when you ordinarily eat second meal, but the time is long past for us. We would like to hear some of these explanations you promised."

"Uh . . ." Cyn cast a glance at the Healtha time chronometer which would be in use until they entered Carroll's void and sighed. "Sorry, I've been busy."

"And we have been worried."

The remark was unanswerable and the tone carried authority. Cyn recognized that Fr. Aimie must be a good deal more than a clothes horse who sold fashions. The authority had nothing to do with him and had little effect on him, but her protest was fair enough and there was no real reason— aside from the fact that he didn't want to listen to the complaints—to delay any longer. The one good thing about the manually calculated trip was that the hops in and out of the void might upset the passengers enough to make them leave the ship at Xiphe. Even the "pirate" might debark if Xiphe was not part of the conspiracy, because he would have lost any chance of seizing the ship.

He went to his bedroom to get Niais, pausing at the door a moment to enjoy the pretty sight of the child asleep. It was a shame to wake her, but she must be hungry too. "Niais," he said softly.

The blue eyes opened, dazed and a trifle frightened as they took in the strange place. Then she saw him and a smile broke like sunlight across her face. She held out her arms. "You took so long," she protested.

"There were things I had to do." Cyn was a little taken aback by the invitation in those open arms, but then he rebuked himself for having a dirty mind. Like the child she was, she was welcoming the one person she knew. "Come," he urged, "we'll go down to the passenger area now and find you a cabin."

Surprise took the place of welcome on her face. "But I like it here."

"You'll like it even better there," Cyn assured her. "Most of the time I'm busy, and you'd be alone here. There are six other passengers below. You'll have more people to talk to. Perhaps they'll even like to play some games. And there's a reader there with some nice stories in it."

"But I like it here," Niais repeated, smiling. "And I like you. Why don't you play some games with me?"

The sexual overtones of the invitation had not been in his dirty mind, Cyn realized. There was no mistaking the purr in Niais's voice or the sidelong glance under her lashes. Cyn was shocked. Despite the fem's loveliness, he felt not the slightest desire. He had never had the smallest inclination for molesting children. His preference had always been for fems who knew their way around—although, he thought wryly, this particular child seemed to know her way around pretty well. Nonetheless—

"Niais," he said sharply, "get up at once. You are very beautiful, but much too young for me. That's not the kind of game I was talking about."

"But it's such a nice game," she urged with a giggle while obediently getting out of the bed.

"Yes," Cyn agreed, and then, fearing to bruise her youthful ego—which might have been badly damaged already by her inability to qualify for full nymph status—he added, "but I can't play any games with you. There's been some trouble with the journey button and I have to run the ship manually, so I've got no time for any games, nice or not."

Niais blinked. "It can be a short game," she suggested hopefully. "Whenever you have a free moment. I'll wait patiently."

Although Cyn was stimulated enough by the conversation, it was not the way Niais intended. He felt more like strangling her than coupling with her. Once an idea got into Niais's head it seemed that only a crowbar applied to her skull would get it out. As long as she was conscious, it appeared impossible to divert her single-track mind to a new subject.

"Well, you can't wait here," he said, sidestepping the issue. "It's against the rules of Overstars Mail for anyone except an official mail-carrier to be in the control room without supervision."

He was annoyed, realizing he had been driven into using the same method to get her out of the cage. He felt a definite twinge of sympathy for whatever being on Ingong was going to get Niais—but better it than he. However, she nodded cheerfully, apparently accepting the rule, and came forward, clutching her package. Cyn's irritation diminished. She was really very good-natured. He picked up her travel bag and, thinking of the steep companionway leading down to the passenger level, reached for the package too. Niais flinched away, her eyes widening in alarm.

"No, please. I must carry this."

Cyn shrugged. "All right, but be careful and don't fall down the stairs."

Then he realized it was just as well he hadn't taken the package. He had no intention of facing that crowd unarmed, so he would need one hand for his stunner. It turned out, however, that Niais was the better weapon of the two. When they appeared at the head of the stairs, all the passengers were assembled in the central chamber. If any even noticed the unholstered stunner, it did not hold that person's attention. The brief astonishment all the faces displayed rapidly faded into expressions solely connected with Niais.

Fr. Rocam seemed both interested and mildly disapproving; Wakkin's eyes lit with a mixture of awe and desire that was almost laughable; and Hachisman and Demoson had almost identical expressions of appraisal—they had been there (and back again) several times. That was fine and to be expected, but there were two expressions that didn't fit the normal pattern and gave Cyn concern.

The simplest to interpret was the ungoverned and brutal look of lust on Mortchose's face. It sat oddly on that pink and rubicund countenance, but its naked ugliness was unmistakable. Cyn's hand tightened on the stunner's grip but he did not raise the gun. All he could do was warn Niais not to play games with that one—for whatever good warning her would do.

Fr. Aimie's expression was less easy to understand. Cyn would have taken as normal anything from utter indifference to active dislike, but what looked out of the older fem's eyes was cold calculation. The expression, however strange, made Cyn realize that he could not tell the truth about Niais's arrival on board. If the PP were not lying, she was an illegal piece of trade goods, fair game for anyone. To admit that was to invite ill treatment for her.

"This is Niais, another passenger," Cyn stated flatly. He handed her her travel bag. "Go put that in Cabin Seven. That will be where you will stay."

"Where did you get that from?" Mortchose breathed.

"From the same place I got you, Fr. Mortchose, an OM planetary office," Cyn replied coldly. "And it is not my business to explain one passenger's business to another—only to see that no harm comes to any of them."

Wakkin slid his chair back. "I think I'll help her put away her things. She may not know how to open the storage units."

Cyn's lips twitched. He judged Wakkin to be perfectly harmless. Even if his intentions were not strictly honorable, he would not force the little goddess into anything she wasn't more than willing to do. Wakkin, in fact, was the ideal person to play games with Niais. Only at the moment Cyn didn't want any passenger out from under his eyes.

"You may do as you like Fr. Wakkin, but I don't intend to repeat my explanations."

He had to pause to control his impulse to laugh at the way the young male's face fell. Maybe it would be safe to let him go. Cyn felt it would be virtually impossible for Wakkin to abstract his attention from Niais long enough to make any trouble. But before Cyn could suggest that some other passenger might transmit what he said to Wakkin, Niais trotted out of the cabin without her travel bag but still clutching her package. Wakkin jumped to his feet and slid a seat back on its runners for her. Her smile of thanks nearly lit the table and almost made Cyn forget her less endearing qualities.

"I am very hungry," Niais said in a small voice. "Is there somewhere I could get—"

Four male hands reached eagerly toward the autochef and four male voices mingled indistinguishably in attempts to explain what the autochef had to offer and how to operate it.

Cyn was rather proud of himself for sitting still and not joining the chorus—although privately he had to acknowledge that his hand had twitched in response to the enchanting plea. Fortunately he had remembered the autochef in the cage and immediately recognized the gambit—a favorite with Free Traders in any culture that failed to recognize the full capacity of their fems.

Wakkin had the advantage of being the closest and the most eager to be of service. While he obtained Niais's midday meal for her and explained how to open the self-heating containers, Cyn made his own choice and began to eat one-handed. The stunner lay, he hoped forgotten, in an easy grip on his lap.

"I don't wish to rush you, pilot," Fr. Aimie said, "but I'm sure you will wish to return to the duties you abandoned so reluctantly. Perhaps you could begin to explain while you eat?"

Cyn glanced around. "Right. First, I'm afraid I've been a little less than completely frank." He held up a hand and waited silently until the cacophony of protests died down. "Now just calm down. What I said about being safe was perfectly true. We are well ahead of pursuit and have reached a velocity at which no other ship, even one coming toward us, could do us any harm."

"About what were you less than frank, young male?" Fr. Rocam asked gently.

"About the cause of both shocks we felt. The first, I have good reason to believe, was the result of a traction beam applied by a drone of the Planetary Police, who then destroyed the vessel."

"Are you trying to tell us that you are prescient? Or that the PP announced this to you?" Fr. Aimie asked.

Cyn smiled. "Not really. The facts became fairly obvious

after they insisted on coming aboard."

Cyn was, of course, shading his story—as any good Trader would show his goods in the most favorable light to induce in his audience a readiness to buy. It was not dishonest. The facts were as stated; they were merely stated in such a fashion as to reduce any desire to examine them.

"Now, whether you know it or not," Cyn continued, "it is against Empire law for any planetary organization to tamper with the Overstars Mail. Naturally I was concerned that the PP had discovered a real source of danger to this ship and I suggested that the Patrol be alerted. By command of the Empress, Partrol has the right to board, examine, and remove anything or anyone on an OM ship. When the PP refused to call Patrol—"

"You see," Wakkin burst out, "where all these rules and restrictions guaranteeing planetary autonomy get you. All this nonsense about each planet being best able to decide for itself what its goals are. Every syr the power of the Emperor has been eroded. If he doesn't stop it, pretty soon no one will pay any attention to Empire law."

"I don't see that the personal power of the Emperor has anything to do with Empire law or authority," Fr. Rocam put in gently. "My husband was an Empire employee—an advisor to the Ecological Planning Department—and I'm familiar with the frustrations engendered by autonomy, but I still say it's the lesser of the evils."

"You don't understand," the young male protested hotly, even forgetting Niais in his concentration. "By the time the Council of Planets moves, all sorts of abuses have gone on for so long that they've taken on the aura of 'established custom.' And the members of the Council are so torn by their prejudices, mutual favor seeking, and yes, even corruption, that no decisive action is ever taken. When the Emperor rules as he should, wrongs will be righted at once."

"And wrongs will be committed at once, too," the old fem pointed out with a wry smile.

"Fr. Rocam, are you implying that the Council never makes a mistake?" Hachisman asked, his lips twisting cynically.

"Oh, no!" she exclaimed, laughing. "Only that there are so many people eager to point out those mistakes—every prospective Councilor seeking election points out the mistakes loudly and repeatedly. Tyrannies do not encourage the pointing out of mistakes."

"But there are horrible tyrannies inside the Empire, and their Councilors—whom no one would dare criticize—sit as equals in the Council. The Emperor wouldn't permit that. He would make sure that every Empire citizen is treated equally." Wakkin glared around at several sighs, then looked pointedly at Fr. Rocam. "The Emperor wouldn't permit planets to ruin themselves ecologically and become a burden on the whole system. He'll force them to—"

"He will enslave us all to set some free." Fr. Rocam's face crinkled into a smile as she broke into Wakkin's tirade—but the tone of voice recalled Cyn's maternal grandmother vividly to his mind.

Wakkin's mouth opened, but before he could reply, Demoson's deep voice intervened. "Maybe you belong in politics instead of the garment industry. Me, I like any government that guarantees contracts and doesn't interfere in other ways. Besides—"

"Besides, it seems far more important to me to hear what else the pilot has to say," Hachisman interrupted.

He was a nervous one, Cyn thought. He had been so scared that he tried to be first out of the shuttle. And he was white and sweating now. Cyn was annoyed with Hachisman.

He had been grateful for the reprieve, almost hoping that the passengers would forget to press him for more information once they got deeply involved in the political discussion. He had been interested too, hoping to pick up a hint about what had made his ship a target.

Personally, Cyn was opposed to any tightening of central authority; the more rigid the control, the less welcome the Free Traders would be. However, an Imperial tyranny was the least of his worries because he did not believe it would be possible to establish one. On the contrary, he was certain that any attempt to force the wildly divergent cultures and species that made up the loose federation of the Empire into a single pattern would cause the breakup of the Empire altogether. And since any Emperor who couldn't see the facts and tried to seize absolute power was too stupid to rule anyway, a tyrannical Empire had even less chance of being established. Tyranny or breakup, however, Cyn still could not guess what part the capture of mail ships could possibly play in the events.

"There isn't that much more to tell," he said, directly to Hachisman and then, with a glance around, making the remark and those to follow general. "As long as there was no immediate danger to my ship and cargo, it was clearly my duty to keep the Planetary Police off Overstars property. So I engaged the Carroll system—that's what caused the bumping around you got."

"That was dangerous," Hachisman growled. "Who knows where we would come out in the system?"

"Where we come out doesn't matter," Cyn said. "The only real danger is that the ship could come apart—but I know this ship, and the chance of that happening was vanishingly small."

He had answered somewhat absently, suddenly aware that

Fr. Aimie had glanced at him with a kind of grudging approval when he said he had hopped planets. The expression was quickly masked, which was more surprising than the approval.

"What do you mean it doesn't matter where we come out, you idiot!" Hachisman roared. "Don't you know that journey buttons are calculated from a particular planetary orbit?"

Recalled abruptly from his speculation about why Fr. Aimie should approve his avoiding the PP and why she should try to hide that approval, Cyn frowned at his troublesome passenger.

"Fr. Hachisman, unless you are a pilot, I can assume quite safely that I know more about journey buttons than you do. I can also assure you that mail-carriers are not given to getting lost in space. We are well provided with navigational aids and well trained in their use. Part of what I was busy with was calculating the corrections, but then I decided not to use the journey button at all."

He waited again for the cries of protest to wear away, then continued coldly, "It occurred to me that if the Planetary Police of Healtha were involved in trying to remove something or someone from my cargo, it was not impossible that pressure might have been applied to Overstars employees on the planet. If so, the route button might not send us to where we intended to go."

Aimie had exclaimed with the others, but with so little intensity that Cyn wondered whether she meant it. He had noticed that she blinked once when he mentioned the navigational aids and training—which implied she knew more about Overstars than a fashion salesfem should. No particular expression now showed, however, when she asked, "Do you have some reason to suspect the employees of Overstars on Healtha?"

"None," Cyn replied promptly. "Just what I've already said. I'm a cautious kind of person, though."

"I think you're a madman," Hachisman exclaimed.

"I'm sorry for your opinion," Cyn replied calmly, "but I was born in space. It's been my life and I don't like even a shadow of a doubt cast on my destination. The difference between using the button supplied and my navigation will be less than half a sday in time and ten small shocks when we leave the void, accelerate away from the carrollpause, and re-enter. And I will be sure—absolutely sure—of where I will come out."

"Yes, you'll be sure—but will we?" Demoson remarked. He shrugged his heavy shoulders. "How do we know one word of the story you've told us is true? Look, I don't know what's going on and I can't say I care much either. All I know is that if I don't get to Mantra in time to see what's being shown and put in my bids, I'll lose a fortune—maybe be out of business. I want a record. If I miss that GMA convention, I'm going to sue Overstars for all it's worth."

"If you miss the convention because of my navigation or my refusal to use the journey button, you will have grounds for suit. However, if this ship is attacked or otherwise tampered with from within or without—Overstars will not be responsible for your losses."

"That's like a sign saying 'Ride at your own risk.' " Demoson sneered. "If you get hurt, you still sue and usually you win."

"Fremale, you must do as you please. That is what I'm told to say in emergencies—and I've said it."

Another mixed babble arose, but Cyn didn't try to make out who was saying what. He was getting tired of the argument, specially since it was pointless. He wasn't going to be influenced by what any passenger said because he couldn't trust any of them. He glanced at Niais and had to hold back a smile. It just went to show how circumstances could change one's mind. A while ago he had been ready to strangle her. He was ready to bless her right now.

Without saying a word herself, Niais had also silenced two voices. True, Wakkin had broken her spell long enough to engage in one political outburst, but politics was easily as strong a passion as sex; it was to Niais's credit that Wakkin had dropped the argument in favor of looking at her. Mortchose too was looking at her—and he didn't seem even to have heard what anyone said. Cyn looked away, somewhat disturbed. There was a thin dribble of saliva trailing from one corner of the man's mouth. Still, Mortchose couldn't do any harm to Niais with five other people around.

Cyn slid back his seat and spoke loud enough to override the other voices. "Let me say again: I will not use an Overstars journey button on this route until I can get the button checked by Patrol—possibly at Mantra. Until then, I intend to set my own course so I can be sure we arrive at our proper destination. Anyone who likes can be landed at Xiphe and take the next ship out to Mantra. The delay wouldn't be long. Empire Star is a very busy port."

He rose then, the stunner swinging easily but clearly in evidence. Since he had chosen his seat just in front of the companionway, he had only a few steps to back to the stair, and he climbed that sideways, watching his passengers. As soon as he slipped through the door, he palm-locked it and sighed with relief.

The rest of the afternoon and early evening he spent on the routine duties he had neglected while working on the passage to Xiphe. From time to time Cyn listened to what was going on in the passenger level. He didn't like intruding on them, but he liked the idea that one or more was hatching trouble even less and compromised by keeping the vision panel off. If he had heard something suspicious he would have looked, but it didn't seem necessary.

Fr. Rocam talked to herself—Cyn frowned a bit over what she said, calling herself 'little old dear' and telling herself not to be frightened. Perhaps she wasn't as calm as she looked and sounded in public. She made funny flapping noises too; Cyn was just about to turn on the vision when they stopped and he decided she must have been uncreasing her clothing. Niais had found someone to play games with. Cyn couldn't tell who and didn't try to find out; they were obviously having a good time since Niais was giggling happily. Fr. Aimie was one paranoid bitch. She had a no-see-no-hear on in her cabin. Demoson snored. The others were silent. Cyn did switch on the vision in the quiet cabins, but they were dark. They had had a long sday; probably they were asleep. Suddenly Cyn yawned so widely he thought he would unhinge his jaw. Not long after, he was asleep himself.

CHAPTER 6

Cyn wakened with a startled jerk, his heart in his throat with an anxiety he had carried into his dreams, but the alarm was only his navigator, beeping querulously for attention. A single glance assured him all was well. At least they had reached the carrollpause without further incident. Cyn turned off the alarm and went to shower and depilate. When he returned, he used the av to check his passengers. Aimie and Demoson were talking amiably enough on one side of the rec table, the remains of breakfast in front of them. At the other side, Hachisman was earnestly explaining something to Rocam. Wakkin and Niais were in a bunk together; Cyn felt amazed that neither was precipitated from it, but he resisted the temptation to watch and found Mortchose, also in his bunk, but seemingly still asleep. All innocent as nuns' hens.

The old adage made Cyn's lips draw back from his teeth. He knew hens—nasty cackling birds that pecked at you—and as for nuns . . . There were enough of them in every starport. Cyn didn't mind paying for his pleasure, but having his credits lifted without any return annoyed him. And these passengers annoyed him. Why couldn't they let him get on with his job? The irritable question brought a brief chuckle. He'd better do just that before something else broke loose. He let the av run, a pattern of rec room and cabins regularly replacing each other on the screen, while he instructed the navigator to use the programs he had calculated the previous sday.

Later, however, while the Piss Pot was hopping peacefully from star to star toward Xiphe, Cyn began to wonder if he had not overreacted. He had spent most of the morning writing into the puter a detailed report of everything that had happened. He was not very happy with it; put in plain words after a good night's sleep, his actions sounded more like a kid acting out a Comet Joe book than a stable mail-carrier reacting to trouble.

The lingering feeling of embarrassment made him keep to his quarters, lunching on soy rolls and caff, and when Aimie asked to come to the control room to carroll a report to her employer, he agreed without hesitation. An instinctive grab for his stunner when she flipped open her shoulder bag and withdrew nothing more than some slips of plas, reduced him to red-faced paralysis until she shoved the slips at him and, brows lifted, told him to send the material, please.

He pulled out the keyboard and tapped in a code he had never seen before, which did not surprise him. All the time he was entering, he was also fighting a battle with himself, one part telling him he was a fool to send the message, that Aimie might be informing whoever wanted to steal his Pot where they were. The other part, the sneering adult who laughed at Comet Joe types, kept his fingers moving until he came to the address—that was in clear Universum, of course—which was Overstars Security. Cyn turned his head.

"Close your mouth, mail-carrier," Aimie said, smiling warmly at him—at least with her lips. "It makes you look stupid, and you certainly aren't that."

"I'm not?" Cyn swallowed. "I had just about decided that a Comet Joe chip had taken over my brain yesterday."

"Oh, no. I disagree with that, and I'm as suspicious about

the button you got at Healtha as you are." Then she was holding out a plas ident. "Can I put this in the reader?"

"Yes."

Cyn watched her walk around to the other side of his couch and slide the card in. If he had touched it, it would have sounded an alarm as soon as it was inserted. On the reader screen, Aimie's face and physical statistics appeared, together with her rank in Security. He nodded and she popped the card.

"As I said, I've agreed with everything you did. If I hadn't, you'd be sleeping sweetly and I'd be running the ship. Unfortunately, I do feel I have to check that the jumps you've been making are taking us to Xiphe. Can you prove it?"

"Yes," Cyn said. "Do you know anything about puters?"

"A little." Aimie smiled.

"Then ask the puter to display Healtha and Xiphe and plot the course the navigator is holding—unless you think I've had time to change all the programming so—"

She came closer, leaned over him, and tapped in a query, but it was for a planet unknown to Cyn. The image and coordinates that came up were clearly satisfactory, because she smiled at him again over her shoulder before she input the query he had suggested. On the star map that appeared, with Healtha and Xiphe color-coded, the course was direct, except for a single zigzag to avoid a dangerous O-type star. Aimie nodded and went to sit on the other recliner.

"If you'll type in this code—" her hand went into the rear pocket of shoulder bag and drew out another slip of plas "—you'll bring up a program that will translate what's in the com."

He looked at her blankly for a moment. The offer was a kind of additional proof that she was Security. Usually additional proof wasn't necessary; it was said to be impossible to counterfeit a Security ident. In fact, Cyn had never heard of a single case. Still in a situation where spaceships were expendable and Planetary Police suborned, the "impossible" might turn out to be something that just took a little longer or cost a little more.

If the puter held a program that would translate that code, he knew nothing about it and she could not have entered it since she came on board. That meant Security had implanted the program as part of the original imprinting of the Pot's puter, which had been done syrs before this crisis began. No one had been allowed to touch the "brain" of his ship since his assignment to her.

He called up the program, got a printout of the report in clear, and started to read, expecting some innocuous blather designed only to prove Aimie's point. Instead he found a report virtually duplicating the one he had filed—except that this one made him sound like the Galactic Hero instead of Comet Joe. First he was pleased, then annoyed. It was rather crude flattery and, of course, now that it had served its purpose of confirming the ident card's validity, the report would not be sent.

"I'm still sorry about all the bumping around," he said. "If word of it gets around, we'll lose passengers."

She wrinkled her nose delicately in a felanthrop signal of distaste. "I can think of a couple that would be no loss to society if they never traveled."

Cyn laughed. "Well, but if Overstars doesn't carry passengers who would be no loss to society, OM would soon be out of anyone who could afford to pay the fare. After all, we mostly carry politicians, planet buyers, fashion salesbeings—"

That broke Aimie's polished perfection and she giggled like a girl. "Such heretical notions!" Then she cocked her head at him. "What's the matter? Aren't you going to send my report? Don't be greedy now. I think it was quite laudatory enough."

"Laudatory enough?" Cyn echoed. "It makes me ridiculous. What you've got there is Bill the Galactic Hero, not me, Cyn the mail-carrier."

She cocked her head the other way and then laughed aloud. "I think you mean that. Tsk, tsk. You'll just have to bow with a red face when they start handing out the medals. Send it."

He was so surprised by the snap of the order that he pushed the SEND key without further argument.

As the com hissed, she smiled again and said, "You are a heretic, aren't you? Aside from salesbeings—whom you have maligned most unjustly because, as we both know, they exist only one orbit below angels—did you ever think about who would run the worlds and the Empire if there were no planet buyers and their tame politicians?"

"A new set of scoundrels," Cyn admitted wryly.

"You're embittered," Aimie remarked, her lips twitching.

"No, only constantly amazed at what people will endure to escape responsibility. They never seem to notice that if they 'let George do it,' inevitably, George will do them instead, sooner or later—and they deserve it."

"Did you leave Lystris because George was 'doing' you?"

For an instant Cyn felt surprised, then he realized Security must have checked him thoroughly. If they had put a Security officer aboard, they must have suspected an attempt to abduct the Pot was about to be made. He shook his head.

"There are no Georges on a Free Trader. It's so small, you see. Every crew member must carry responsibility and speak out as soon as possible. It's called pulling your own weight."

"You mean there's no designated leader?"

Cyn stared at her as if she were demented. Then he spoke clearly and slowly, as to a retarded child. "The Captain correlates the information input by each expert crew member and makes the decisions—yes. But the Captain comes up for review regularly and can be summoned to Meeting to explain anything a majority of the crew question."

She accepted that, nodding. "Could work in a small society. What happens when the Captain gets conflicting opinions from more than one expert? Is there more than one expert?"

"Always more than one. Can't have no one to pilot or navigate or handle your weapons if one crew member gets taken out. Consensus report goes to the Captain. Argument stays among crew members. But when you're talking facts like engine condition or levels of stores, you don't get much disagreement."

"And on matters of opinion? Don't tell me Free Traders don't have opinions."

"Only one that counts is the value of trade goods. You'll see knives out on that question sometimes. As far as everything else goes, opinions are pretty much the same. Don't forget, most of us are born on one ship or another, just as our parents were, and the ships are in close contact, even if they never see each other and do keep Trade secrets. As you direct the ion, so flows the plasma."

"Which were you, rebellious or bored?"

Cyn laughed. "Scared. You know, I almost forgot how scared I was a lot of the time until that business with the Planetary Police."

Aimie's brows rose. "Your behavior doesn't exactly confirm you as a timid soul. Timid souls obey Planetary Police."

"I never said I was timid, but things like that were too frequent on Lystris. It was more than that, too. Our landings were mostly in very uncomfortable places. Maybe the truth is that I'm a sybarite—a restless sybarite. I like sweet music, soft lights, and beautiful, willing fems, but I like them different each time."

"Is that a warning or a promise?" Aimie asked, her lips curving into a sensual smile.

Cyn was surprised, but not very. He had thought she had looked at him with considerable interest a couple of times the previous sday. And as Security, she probably wanted an excuse to be in the control room with him. Either way, simple interest or policy, he didn't mind. He stood up and she did, too. Since the space between the recliners was not large, they were almost touching.

"Take it any way you like," he said. "So long as you take me with it."

"But take you only temporarily?" Her hazel eyes were sparkling with amusement.

"No one wants me for long," he murmured, equally amused.

Her laugh was low and intimate, but as her lips parted to reply, the Pot shuddered into real space and Cyn's head swung toward his instruments. He checked the motion, but Aimie was already shaking her head.

"That's for when we're sure there isn't anyone inside the ship who would have welcomed the PP. Come down for the evening meal and when you go up, don't lock the control room door. Go to bed and turn out the lights. If you're sleepy, sleep." She smiled slightly. "I won't mind if you stay awake, but if there's a bug on your av, I want everything to look right. I won't let anyone get to your console, and I'll yell for help if I need it."

Cyn hoped he had managed to hide the shock he felt at the idea of using his control room as bait for a trap. To a Free

Trader whose ship was life itself, the control room was sacred. However bitter the hatred or violent the fight, everything ended at the control room door. Since he still liked his job, he didn't argue although he didn't intend to comply, and Aimie calmly picked up her plas sheets and left.

After a few smins Cyn recalled that groundlings felt differently about ships and as Security Aimie had the right to give orders. Nonetheless, it seemed to him she did not realize the danger of allowing an "enemy" into the control room when he was not there. He gave the matter some thought while arranging for the Pot to move from one jump to another as fast as possible. Finally he felt satisfied with his ideas and went to get his tools.

Cyn's lips twitched from time to time as he assembled what he considered a few fail-safe devices. Anyone who touched his console would get quite a surprise. He worked late, dividing his attention between the navigator and his new toys, but just about midnight, Lystris time, the Pot came out of its last transition at Xiphe's carrollpause.

Having reached his goal, Cyn accepted the fact that he was very tired. It was just as well, he thought, that Aimie was probably using the half-promise of sex to keep him docile and obedient—not that he'd refuse her if she weren't. Smiling, he shut down everything except life support, making the Pot indistinguishable from any other piece of space debris. There was no instrument that would detect his ship in that condition, so he could afford to rest. Finally he activated his new toys, which he had earlier attached in unobtrusive places—a bell that would wake the dead if anything so much as brushed the console, a loud buzzer that would go off simultaneously with every light in the top level of the ship flashing on and off at top intensity if the keyboard was switched ON, and several nasty but not fatal booby traps on the most crucial controls, like the one that opened the navigator slot—and went to bed. Although he had had a good night's sleep, he had put in a hard sday's work. And, since he no longer expected company, he slid quickly and dreamlessly into oblivion.

Just as easily, when a soft, lithe body slipped into bed with him, he roused into semiconsciousness if not full wakefulness. One did not, after all, need to be keenly alert to make love; in fact, a dreamy languor often improved his performance, allowing him to linger over their mutual pleasure. Nor did he need to be awake when murmuring endearments. Many syrs of practice in many, many spaceports had made him a genius at avoiding the use of a woman's name in bed.

Even when he came a bit more awake, he did not bother to open his eyes; it was very dark in his bedroom and he knew who she was. The fact that she had come soothed away a half-remembered anxiety, implying her talk of watching for a hostile act was only an excuse. Very soon he became alert only to his own pleasure and his partner's body language, his one need to be sure she was satisfied with his performance—and she gave ample evidence that she was. As they settled to sleep with her arm still around him as if to cling to what they had had, Cyn was vaguely aware that there seemed to be an extra pillow behind him. If she had brought that up with her, she hadn't needed it. He smiled slipping into a second oblivion even deeper and more dreamless than the first.

"Cyn."

The urgency of Aimie's whisper brought him instantly awake and fully alert. But there were no alarms and none of the booby traps had gone off. Nightmare, he thought, and his hand went out to reassure and comfort. The body beside him was still, relaxed, inert. The tense whisper could not have come from it.

"Cyn, wake up."

The whisper had not come from the bed. It was above him.

"Space her!" Cyn exclaimed in a bitter undervoice.

"I'm sorry to disturb your beauty sleep," Aimie hissed, "but I've got—"

"Not you," Cyn growled. "That little—"

He hesitated, seeking in his wide store for an epithet that would satisfy him, but he could find none in any of the several languages besides Universum that he spoke. He gave it up and sat up carefully, sourly grateful that her arm—hand still clutching her package—was no longer around him. He loosened the blanket so he would not uncover Niais and a handlight flicked on, then off. Aimie recoiled, apparently only then realizing there were two bodies in the bed. He heard her gasp and then move away.

Cyn dragged on his coveralls, casting a single fulminating glance at the peaceful huddle under the blanket, before he ran after Aimie. If Niais had been awake, he would have turned her over his knee—not, probably, that it would have had the smallest effect on her, but it would have made him feel much better.

The control room was now partially lit by the desk lamp Aimie had switched on. She was feeling and peering intently inside her shoulder bag and her eyes were wide, her lips turned down by some strong emotion. Cyn stopped short with a sinking sensation of shock. How could he have guessed that hard, polished exterior covered such an easily bruised ego? He would kill that Niais!

Seeking the words that would most quickly make his point, he said, "Look, I don't voluntarily molest children."

Her head lifted and the anguish on her face was temporarily eclipsed by laughter. When she saw Cyn's indignation, she gasped, "Sorry, but that 'child' is the living end! I've never in my life seen anything as funny as the way you looked when you realized I was standing up, not in bed with you."

"Funny! I'll kill her! I was half asleep and thought—"

"I know what you thought." Aimie chortled. Then she remembered, and her eyes grew hard. "No, you're right. It isn't funny at all. She got by my sensors. How?"

Cyn held up a hand, walked back to the door, and shut it softly. Then he said, "I have no idea why your sensors didn't pick her up, but she isn't trying to take the ship."

"Isn't she?" Aimie's eyes met his. "She got on the ship without being listed as a passenger, and the Planetary Police tried to use her being on the ship as an excuse to board."

Cyn frowned. "I didn't say she wasn't working with Healtha's PP—I don't know about that. All I said was that she isn't trying to take the ship. I never heard her come into the control room—I didn't call out or anything—but she didn't go near the console anyway."

"Did she convince you of that in bed?"

"Don't be ridiculous," Cyn said, smiling. "She's good in bed, but I've just come away from three sdays with a nymph."

He went on to explain about the alarm he had set if anyone touched the console. He did not mention the lights and buzzers and booby traps. Aimie had been warned enough to stay away from the controls and, though he knew she was Security, there were such things as double agents. And he told her, too, of Niais's earlier invitation to him.

Aimie shrugged. "I still don't trust her."

Cyn smiled again, very sweetly. "I don't trust anyone."

She looked startled, but said only, "You're right. Someone has set up a homing caller somewhere on the ship."

"Shit!" Cyn spat. "So there is someone aboard who wants

this ship captured." He turned and looked speculatively toward his bedroom. "Maybe you're right. Maybe she came up to keep me in bed so I wouldn't pick up the signal. Do you know how long the homer has been running?"

"It started to work about ten smin before I came up—I wasted some time trying to find it on the passenger level, but it isn't there."

"Then Niais didn't set the homer," Cyn said. "We were—in her terms—playing games for a lot longer than ten smins, so she couldn't have put it in place—"

"She didn't have to put it in place tonight," Aimie snapped. "That could have been done any time. All she had to do was give it a signal to start sending."

Cyn nodded. "Right. And she had that precious package of hers with her. I thought I was keeping her—well, I thought it was you, actually—but she certainly seemed absorbed by what I was doing. Still, if signaling the homer to start sending just needed a squeeze on something . . . I was pretty busy myself. I might not have noticed."

"I think I'd like to see what's in that package," Aimie said grimly.

"Me too," Cyn agreed, "but not now. The first order of the sday is to get that homer or we'll have unwanted company. Will that thing guide you?" He gestured toward her shoulder bag.

"Like a treasure hunt—hot and cold. I know it isn't in the passenger area, and the response is even fainter up here, so it must be in one of the lower levels."

"Cargo—but I've got the life support off there."

"No one took a suit during the sday." She shrugged angrily. "But if Niais got past my sensors, maybe someone else did too."

"Will that gadget work for me?" Cyn asked.

"No," she said. "Everything is locked into my DNA and skin secretion patterns."

"Shit," Cyn repeated with even more heartfelt fervor. "We don't have time for me to dismantle my alarm, set up life support, and then wait for air and heat to build up in the cargo levels. Could you search down there in a suit alone?"

"Any idiot can use a suit, but it might take me a lot longer to search the cargo area than you. Why shouldn't you come with me?"

"Because of that nitwit in my bed," Cyn pointed out.

"Lock her in," Aimie suggested. "Or can she get at something in your quarters that would be dangerous?"

"Not that. You can't run the ship from the bed, although she could call up visuals. That doesn't matter. There's nothing much to see. But the door only locks from the inside. Overstars wasn't figuring on keeping prisoners—Wait, I'm pretty sure I can just jam the handle on this side so she won't be able to pull the latch back."

While he attended to that, Aimie found the storage cabinet that held individual life support gear. She looked at the space armor and shuddered, but that would not be necessary. It was impossible for any passenger to have placed the homer outside the ship so the heavy-duty gear could stay where it was. Instead Aimie dragged out Cyn's well-worn light-duty suit and the stiffer spare. Next she adjusted her telltale so she wouldn't have to touch it again once her hands were gloved.

By then, Cyn was finished with the door. He helped her into her suit, pointing out the most necessary controls. She listened, but from the efficient way she closed her faceplate and nudged on the speaker, Cyn thought she was more familiar with the suit than she had implied, which probably meant she didn't trust him. That made them even. He made quick work of getting into his own suit and they entered the lift.

At the top cargo hold, he held the lift door open while she watched her indicator, walking forward, turning from side to side, and eventually coming back to him. "It's stronger than in the passenger level, but change of position doesn't affect it, so I'd say we should try the lower hold."

A repeat of what Aimie had done on the level above, except that she walked farther into the lower cargo hold, brought her back signing "negative" with her gloved hand. "Nothing," she said. "The only thing I got was maybe a little fading as I walked deeper into the ship."

"Fading?" Cyn repeated slowly, and then sharply, "I'm an idiot. The damn thing must be in the shuttle." He gestured her out of the lift and toward the cargo hold lock that connected with the shuttle. Inside, as they waited for the lock to fill with air, he said, "Anyone could have slipped down that corridor and into the shuttle any time yesterday or even the sday before, and whoever it was wouldn't need a suit. You know the rules are never to cut off life support in the shuttle when the ship is carrying passengers."

As soon as they stepped into the shuttle, the telltale registered more strongly. Both broke open their helmets and a moment later Aimie slipped off her glove to turn down the indicator intensity, which was peaking. At lower intensity, the telltale led them through the cargo area and up the ladderway, past the empty end seats. Near the top, the intensity of response fell off again, and Cyn started down, searching carefully. He soon found a small dark cube on the underside of one of the steps about the middle of the ladderway.

He regarded the innocent looking little box with disfavor. When Aimie reached toward it, he slapped her hand away. "Booby trap," he explained.

"I don't think so. There would be a double pulse of some kind, I think, and there isn't. Besides, it needs a fair-sized power cube to send a signal any distance. This whole thing is too small to hold much other than the power supply. If you don't touch it, how will you turn it off?"

"I'm not going to turn it off," Cyn said. "It's possible that whoever put it there would be alerted."

"But even if we're not yet near Xiphe, we are in real space. Isn't it possible that someone could pick up the signal?"

"We're right in Xiphe's system," Cyn said. "That's why I daren't turn off the signal. If it's been heard and suddenly stops, whoever is heading in on the beam will know we're aware of them. They'll start to search for us in other ways. Probably the Pot can outrun them, but my sensors aren't any better than they need to be to avoid collisions, so they could be on top of me before I knew. And there's always the possibility that they'll be using one of the previously captured OM ships. If not, I'll bet power cubes against waste cases that they'll have some way to stop me from running. Everyone in the galaxy knows OM ships can outrun anything."

"Well, what? I know you aren't going to sit here and let anyone steal this ship."

"I guess the best thing is to leave the target or send it off at a reasonable trajectory and get ourselves well out of the way."

"You're going to abandon the shuttle?" Aimie's voice scaled upward. "But it's our only emergency vehicle."

"Don't be an idiot. I'm just going to leave the little box and the stair tread to which it's attached—in case it gives a warning when detached from the surface on which it was placed."

Aimie had climbed down to look at the homer. She stepped aside, in front of a tilted up seat and asked "Leave it where?" sounding exasperated. But her question was addressed to Cyn's back as he jumped down into the cargo section. When he came back with a case of tools, she pointed out caustically, "The ship is all one piece and enclosed."

"Sure," he agreed, dismantling the stair, "but all I have to do is go out—"

Cyn hesitated over the word, bending closer to what he was doing to hide his expression. To a spaceman, his ship was his home, his womb. To leave it and expose himself to the empty immensities of space was traumatic. To those like Cyn, bred to resist claustrophobia, wide open spaces could trigger the opposite complex. Cyn himself was not among those who were made so helpless by agoraphobia that they could not even walk dirtside, but he did not like to be out in space.

"You can't go out in that light-duty thing you're wearing," Aimie protested.

Cyn began to wonder whether she had set up the homer. No, that was ridiculous. Why should she warn him about it if she had set it up? He loosened another join and said, "There's space armor. It's right here on the shuttle near the emergency hatch. The cubby's marked—in case you should need it."

"Powers forfend!" Aimie exclaimed.

Cyn turned his head toward her as the stair came loose. He left it in place while he stood up, replaced his helmet, and then refastened his gloves.

"I hope you won't need space armor, but the way things are going this trip someone might. Anyway, I don't need to bother with it. I'm only going to be outside the hatch for a few smin, just long enough to throw the homer away. The acceleration will be the same as the Pot's, and the tiny bit my toss will add won't be distinguishable, even with the finest instruments. Then I'll speed up the Pot. By the time anyone gets to the homer, I hope we'll be far enough away not to show."

"I don't like being outside of a ship in space," Aimie said, her voice suddenly thin. "I don't even like to think about it."

"I'm not too fond of the idea myself," Cyn said with vast understatement as he refastened his helmet and then added, as calmly as he could, "Please watch your instruments and see if you can spot an alarm going off when I move the homer."

She looked into her bag and made some small adjustments, then nodded. Cyn bent and picked up the whole stair he had detached. She shook her head. "Nothing."

Cyn nodded without answering, climbed down the ladderway more carefully so he wouldn't jar his burden, and went to the back wall of the cargo section of the shuttle. The emergency hatch opened smoothly and he got down into it, sliding his feet forward until he was lying on his back—at least he told himself he was lying on his back. Actually, his back did not touch the "floor" because ship's gravity was not transmitted outside of the shuttle.

The lock was not a particularly tight squeeze. There was at least the thickness of his body above him and room for him to stretch his arms out to either side or for another suited figure. He laid the stair on his belly and attached it to his belt with a clip. A light touch on the control above and to his right at about waist level caused the hatch to shut. A second touch started the evacuation of the lock. While the air was pumped into the reserve tank, Cyn carefully fastened the line coiled in a tension-activated container attached to his belt to an eye bolt near his left hand.

When the air was gone, the panel below his feet and the emergency hatch in the body of the hangar both slid open. Cyn grasped the handholds in front of him and very carefully pushed in the direction of his head. He began to float out of the lock. He could slow himself or increase his motion or turn by pressure on the handholds and he retained his grip on them until his helmet cleared the lock and the outer hatch beyond it. Then he bent his body and legs until the magnetic plates in his boots fixed on the hangar of the shuttle. When a gentle push forward with each foot did not move his legs, he straightened up very slowly, hearing in memory the voice of Lystris's captain.

"Remember that the difference between maneuvers in free-fall inside a ship and those in space armor depend on the greater mass of the armor. Whatever acceleration you apply will be magnified by that mass. Since your mass is constant and cannot be controlled, your motions when in armor must be much slower than in the ship."

Nervously he touched the line at his waist. It was safely taut and he pressed the lock that would prevent it from unreeling farther. Keeping his eyes on the stair attached to his waist, he unclipped it, turned so his back was to the Pot, set the stair flat, and gave it a good push. Concentrating on shoving stair and homer away at as close to a right angle as possible, Cyn thoughtlessly bent his knee sharply. One foot came loose. He nearly screamed, but the line at his waist held and he had enough self-control to lower the free foot slowly, not slam it down so that he jarred the other loose too.

Breathing like a long-distance runner, he twisted around and bent to grip a handhold in the lock again. Twenty thousand subjective syrs later, the inner hatch closed behind him and he was safe. Without excuse or explanation, he allowed himself to slip down to the floor.

CHAPTER 7

Cyn might have been more flattered by Aimie's anxiety about how he had withstood his adventure if she had not pointed out that she might be Security but wasn't a pilot. Moreover, he was becoming so paranoid that the remark seemed gratuitous, which made him wonder whether her denial meant she could pilot the Pot. How truthful Aimie was, was of relatively minor importance, however. Now that the homer was free of his ship and on its way, he had to get the Pot as far from it as possible.

Leaving Aimie to struggle out of her suit as best as she could, Cyn disabled his alarms, doing his best to keep his body between her and what his hands were doing. As far as he could tell, she seemed to have no interest in his activity. But when the console was usable again and he fired the real space engines, setting the controls for the highest acceleration, she swung around and asked sharply what he was doing.

"Getting as far away from here as I can," he replied.

"But once the ship is active, it can be detected."

"True enough, but it could probably be seen for what it was on visual as soon as the detached homer is found. It would take a tenth syr for the homer to drift far enough away to prevent that with the tiny acceleration I've given it."

"Oh." She smiled apologetically. "I kind of forgot that. Where are we going?"

Cyn stared at her, brows knitted, for a moment before answering, "Xiphe. Where else?"

"We're asking for trouble if we go near Xiphe. Don't you think someone will be waiting?"

He didn't reply immediately, shucking his suit off in silence. Then he said, "Maybe, but I have mail to deliver." His jaw stuck out stubbornly. "I told you before, I like this job. And I'm not going to break my contract by skipping a scheduled stop. Even if you have the authority—"

Aimie shook her head. "I don't. I just thought—"

"And I've got another little problem, too," Cyn interrupted, jerking his head in the direction of his bedroom. "Niais's passage wasn't booked correctly. I have to take care of that."

"How did that happen?" Aimie asked.

She had identified herself as Security and Niais was a pest, but Cyn still found himself reluctant to betray that she had been shipped as a "beast, caged." He shrugged. "I don't know, but it's my right as a mail-carrier to have the official at my next port of call make a determination about any item that I think presents a problem."

Aimie smiled at him, lifting a brow. "My, but you have studied the rules and regulations, haven't you?"

He shrugged. "I've got plenty of time, why shouldn't I? I've also studied the guts of this ship until I can take her apart and put her together again in the dark."

"If that's what you like," she said, still smiling. "Suit yourself." She looked down at the bag by her side for a moment, then said, "So you're going to run for Xiphe."

"*I'm* going to run until the Pot won't blip an rs screen on any ship that reaches the homer. Then I'm going to yell for Patrol."

"Are you sure which side Patrol is on?"

"I'm not sure which side I'm on," Cyn pointed out. "But I intend to keep my ship. I can't believe a Patrol ship would let an OM ship be taken within its jurisdiction. And if I'm wrong, I've got the Carroll system running. If I have to, I'll hop. Once should be enough. The second hop will take us to the carrollpause and into the void and we can disappear."

"Do you think you can get away with playing the same trick twice?" she asked doubtfully.

"How can anyone stop me? I can hit the Carroll button faster than anyone can get close enough to blast me. I don't think they want to blast us anyway." He looked at her, allowing his suspicion to show, and asked, "Do you know something I don't know?"

"I wish I did." Aimie sighed. "I wish I knew anything of value."

She sounded very sincere, Cyn thought, and wondered how good an actress she was.

After a moment, she asked quietly, "What if there's no Patrol ship around?"

"That I'm not worried about," he said. "Every system anywhere near Mantra must be lousy with Patrol, and Xiphe Overstars must be screaming bloody murder. Even if they're rotten to the core, they'd have to report us as being a sday late. Remember, two ships have already disappeared in this sector. Besides, Xiphe isn't a homo sap planet. I think they'd prefer less rather than more interference from a humanoid-dominated Empire, which means status quo. More likely to be indifferent to Niais too."

Aimie laughed. "She'll have a fit if you leave her on Xiphe. I've heard her talking to Wakkin about having to go to Ingong."

"She won't know anything about it until after I'm gone," Cyn said. "I'm not even hinting that she might be held. Let the local OM agent explain it to her. If I remember the port info right, Xiphans are something like crabs decorated with patches of feathers. They hear but don't talk. You have to read a screen. That ought to mess her up. I don't know if she can read."

"Cruel, that's what you are." Aimie smiled, then sighed. "I'm dead," she said suddenly. "I've got to go down and get some sleep. Be careful."

When she was gone, Cyn palm locked the door behind her, sat down, and flicked on the av. He saw Aimie cross the darkened rec room and enter her cabin, but she did not set up the no-see-no-hear. He watched as she fiddled inside the shoulder bag, set it on the inside of her bunk, and dropped into the bunk herself. A brief scan showed all the other cabins still dark and quiet. Cyn checked the velocity, keyed a query into the puter, and, when he had the answer, set an alarm for when he thought it would be safe to call for help. Then he let his eyes close.

They seemed hardly to have shut when an insistent thudding brought him erect with a stunner in his hand and his heart in his mouth. The control room was empty. No reason for the sound that appeared on his control board. Then he realized the noise was coming from the locked door of his quarters. Groaning, he rose, removed the wedge, and slid the door aside.

Niais looked at him with wide eyes. "You don't have to lock me in," she said, gently reproving. "I like being with you. I'll come any time you want to play games with you, but I have to eat. I'm hungry."

"I didn't—" Cyn began, and then swallowed "want to keep you for that purpose." It would be stupid to tell her the truth. "I'm sorry," he went on. "I didn't lock you in. The door just stuck." And then, his voice rising, he added, "Don't you have any clothes?"

"Certainly," Niais replied, looking puzzled. "I was

wearing clothes when I came aboard," she added gently and distinctly, as one might remind a backward child of a fact he had forgotten—again.

Cyn swallowed. He would not, absolutely and positively, he would not lose his temper.

Niais smiled kindly. "One doesn't wear clothes when one plays games. They interfere. Except—" a thoughtful frown creased her alabaster brow very slightly "—some people like one to take them off slowly, or—"

"One wears them when walking around the ship." Cyn's voice grated.

"Yes, but I didn't walk around. I came directly up to play—"

"Don't say it again!" Cyn exclaimed forcefully.

Bitterly, bitterly he regretted the ignorance of Niais's character that had induced him to use that phrase. He had said the words in all innocence, believing one or more of the other passengers would partner her in some of the games provided in the rec room puter to while away the dull stus of transit.

"You are so shy and nervous," Niais marveled, blinking her beautiful eyes. "But really, you have no need. You are very good at—at—well, at that, and nice looking too."

Cyn put a hand over his face and gripped tightly. He hoped it would keep his burning eyes from falling out. At the least, momentarily he had blocked out the sweet vision of that tormenting child. Well, Power willing, he would be quit of her soon.

"You know," Niais said, her voice lilting suddenly with the thrill of a great discovery. "You are alone on this ship too much. It isn't good for you to be embarrassed about . . . ah . . . doing what is so natural. You should be able to talk about it, and—"

96

"And you should be able to talk about something else," Cyn roared.

Niais lowered her head and looked up at him under her long lashes. "Yes," she agreed, but doubtfully, as if she had heard this before but could not really believe it. "That is what my—"

The alarm Cyn had set began to beep, and he drew a deep breath. "I have some work to do now," he said. "Use the autochef on the desk and get yourself some breakfast."

"Shall I go away?" she asked rather sadly.

About to utter a relieved "yes," Cyn recalled that it might have been Niais who had set that homer and then crawled into his bed to keep him occupied. He told her instead to take her breakfast into his bedroom, explaining where she could find a clean coverall to wear.

"It will be too big," she protested.

"Put it on anyway," Cyn said with careful gentleness. "I find it unsettling to think of you dressed in nothing but hair and a package."

He could see the lighting of her eyes and shook his head firmly before she could speak. "I said I was busy. You get something to eat." He stopped and watched as she operated the autochef. When the containers were in her hands he said clearly, "Now go right back into my quarters. I have no time to play games, do what comes naturally, or any other euphemism you can think up. Go into the bedroom at once and wait until I have time to deal with you."

"Oh!" Niais smiled blindingly. "Oh, good. You deal very nicely. I'll wait."

Cyn refrained from groaning with only a slight effort, and activated his com to squeal his prepared appeal to the Patrol. Oddly, he found himself somewhat less irritated with Niais's latest misunderstanding. Apparently, what one said to Niais mattered very little. She was capable of interpreting remarks

97

in only one way. Myrrha, he recalled, had nothing like that singleness of mind. She had been willing, eager, even insistent about coupling, but in the intervals she was interested in and knowledgeable about a wide range of subjects. And when he had made that point to Niais, she had said, "Yes, that was what my—"

The alarm had prevented her from finishing the remark, but it seemed to Cyn that the child had looked—well, stricken was too strong a word. Probably she didn't have enough brains to be "stricken." Still, she had been moved by as much emotion as she was capable of. "That was what—" failed her as a nymph? Cyn had a sudden flash of sympathy for the unfortunates who had tested Niais. Then he grinned as he wondered whether they were still at large or whether extended investigation of Niais's thinking processes had resulted in the examiners being confined afterward to a "home for the bewildered."

A moment later he felt ashamed of himself. Niais could be infuriating, but she was only a child, after all. Surely the punishment of being banished for life to a distant planet where she might never see another of her own species was too harsh.

The com unit began to hiss, and Cyn forgot all about Niais. He read what was coming off the receiver with a growing sense of relief. It looked good. Ship and captain were identified in the standard patrol pattern and—glory be—the captain was an urso. They were a warrior culture, much occupied on their own planet with clan wars. The urso were most unlikely to look kindly on any attempt to enforce Imperial notions of peace and justice on their worlds.

In a surprisingly short time the vocal com chimed for attention. Cyn flicked on voice and image, studying the fur-covered face that stared out at him with relief. He smiled, recalling that as a Free Trader a similar image had usually made him curse subvocally. Now the teardrop and infinity symbol on the uniform collar was most comforting. Nonetheless, he kept one eye on his rs screen as he transmitted a squeal of his report and Aimie's and gave a succinct vocal resume of the Pot's adventures. All the time, one hand, out of range of the visual pickup, hovered over the jump control.

"Recorded and filed," the Patrol commander stated. "Now, pilot, what can we do for you? Take your passengers off?"

Cyn's hand trembled over the jump switch. "No, sir," he replied. "An Overstars paid fare is a valid contract to deliver to a stated destination, and I intend to deliver them as per contract. Now that I'm warned, I can maintain security aboard my ship—or the passengers can voluntarily debark at Xiphe. I request from Patrol protection against outside inter-ference."

There was a moment of silence while the commander con-sidered the request. Cyn wished he could read anything in the countenance on his screen but the alien features told him nothing. All he could do was hope his own tension was as un-readable to the Patrol officer. There was nothing on his rs screen, but he knew that Patrol carried far more powerful de-tection apparatus than the Pot. No other vessel could have punched through a vocal and visual image beyond rs distance or have picked up his much weaker signal.

"Very well," the Patrol commander agreed. "Proceed on your most direct course to Xiphe. We will keep you in range. Off."

Image and voice disappeared promptly. The Patrol did not waste anything, particularly power, which they might need for other purposes. Cyn sighed. The answer he had re-ceived was so exactly the correct answer and the one he wanted that he was swept with suspicion. It was completely wrong for anything on this trip to go right.

That was just what happened, however. Once, the Patrol

vessel opened contact to report that Cyn's Pot was outdistancing it and Cyn had to struggle with his suspicion again before he slowed down, but the Patrol vessel did not try to creep up on him. And once as they passed the fifth planet of the system, a blip did appear on Cyn's screen. Before he could react, the Patrol was warning the vessel off. It was a little slow to respond, which called forth a blast of destructive energy into the space between the Pot and the intruding vessel. It altered course then. After that, Cyn, who had been awake again for more than a whole sday with only two brief naps, felt confident enough to send Niais back to the passenger level so he could tumble into his bed and sleep.

An alarm woke him, sounding loud from the panel above the bed, but it was only to warn that the ship was approaching orbital distance of its target. The alarm was for most distant orbit, so Cyn had plenty of time to wash, eat, and contemplate the idea of landing on Xiphe to deliver the mail—and he hoped Niais—and leaving the rest of the passengers in the ship.

He did have safeguards—all unknown to Overstars—to prevent anyone but himself from using the Pot, but he was not at all happy about what might be done to his puter, his console, and his ship in an attempt to circumvent those safeguards. The solution, almost equally unpleasant when he considered the passengers' reaction, was to take them all with him. Cyn stared at his av, which presently displayed the whole group eating the midday (now Xiphe time) meal. His order would certainly be unwelcome and cause complaints, but it would have two advantages: he would not need to explain to Niais why she was being singled out and taken to Xiphe alone, and it might expose any person who welcomed the opportunity to be on the ship in the absence of its pilot.

The latter advantage failed to materialize. The moment

after he announced that, because of the attempt to take the ship in Healtha's system, he wanted all passengers to come to Xiphe with him, half the passengers exploded into protest. Rocam and Niais seemed indifferent, and Mortchose seemed scarcely to have heard; he was too busy staring at Niais. The others shouted and waved their arms—including Aimie and the usually calm Demoson, who said angrily that Cyn had no right to make them leave the ship and he, for one, would not.

"Suit yourself, Fr. Demoson," Cyn said. "I'll gladly freeze you down if you prefer. With the ship dead, the freezer can operate on the same backup system that keeps the shuttle-hangar sensor alive. Patrol will have charge of the ship while I'm dirtside, and it will be easier for them to watch her if even the life support is off."

"Patrol . . ." Demoson said thoughtfully. "So you felt you had to yell for them. Why? Has there been any trouble since we cleared the Healtha carrollpause?"

Cyn shook his head and smiled. "I've told you all before, I'm a very cautious person. Patrol, specially an urso ship, gives me a real sense of security. And I'm not going to argue with you people. I'll give you adequate warning to get to the shuttle and then I'll shut off life support in the ship. If you want to stay behind under those circumstances, I won't try to force you to board the shuttle—but you're likely to be pretty cold and blue before we get back."

"You've got no right to do this," Hachisman complained, but with more of a whine than his usual abrasiveness.

"Safety first is an OM rule," Cyn said. "After due consideration, I could see no way to ensure the safety of any passenger left aboard when I shuttled down to deliver the mail. Nor could I see any harm coming to any passenger from one extra landing and liftoff in the shuttle. That's my decision. I've recorded that and this exchange and it will be squealed to the OM office on Xiphe as soon as we orbit."

"What if someone tries to grab the shuttle?" Aimie asked.

"Anyone who comes near the shuttle is going to be vaporized by Patrol," Cyn pointed out. "A Patrol ship can look two ways."

Wakkin bit his lip. "We're a sday late already, aren't we?"

"Yes, but this won't make us any later. I have to land to deliver the mail anyway."

"Got an answer for everything, don't you?" Demoson sighed. "Can I send a com to Mantra, pilot?"

"I have a com to go also," Hachisman said.

"I suppose I should let my niece know that I'll be a sday late," Rocam twittered, "but you can wait and send word to her during our next transit if you are too busy now."

Cyn would have liked to refuse and might have done so if only one person had asked to send a message, but with Patrol on their tail he couldn't see that refusal would be worth the argument. "I'll send the messages with my squeal," he said. "The OM office will transmit them. I'll come and pick them up in a few smin."

He reactivated his alarms and booby traps and left the control room, ostentatiously palm locking the door as he came out. When he had accepted the messages, he looked around at the passengers and said, "In view of the general dissatisfaction with this passage, maybe you would like to reconsider going to Mantra on this ship. I'm sure another ship will be leaving from Xiphe for Empire Star very soon, perhaps even later today."

"But I have to go to Ingong," Niais said. "I had to wait two swiks before a ship could be scheduled to Ingong. I—I don't think I can wait another two swiks. I'm expected."

Cyn's heart sank, but then he reasoned that if the OM agent decided to keep her to get clearance, it would undoubtedly let those expecting her in Ingong know. Wakkin was also shaking his head and muttering something about being late already. Rocam laughed gently.

"I'm an old woman," she twittered, "and I've lived a very dull life since my husband died. I've had more thrills on this trip than in syrs. And if the next . . . ah . . . excitement should prove fatal—well, I have very little to lose."

Before Cyn could protest, Aimie said, "Us fems must stick together. I'll stay aboard with Pilot Cyn."

The glance she cast at him was as suggestive as any expression Niais could achieve. Cyn was momentarily shocked, mostly because it was completely out of character for Aimie to show any private emotion. Why expose her interest . . . But the answer was so obvious that he didn't need to finish the question. Cyn flushed slightly, inadvertently supporting Aimie's excuse for remaining.

Demoson's voice followed hers immediately, as if he had been waiting for her to declare her intentions. "And us fashion folk must stick together too." He made a grimace of dissatisfaction and looked toward Aimie for corroboration. "The garment trade always runs on the edge of disaster. If I do business at the GMA, good—I'm in business. I might even make a killing. Even better. Then I'll be rich. But if I don't do business, I can't wait for the next conference—I'm ruined."

Cyn didn't bother to comment that being dead was even more final than being ruined.

Hachisman looked around at the others and sighed. "I wanted off in the beginning, but I've changed my mind. Partly, time is getting tighter, but mostly—" he smiled wryly "—I think the trouble is over. Even if it isn't, you seem remarkably skillful at wriggling out of holes, Pilot Cyn."

"Thank you all for your votes of confidence," Cyn said, barely suppressing an impulse toward sardonic laughter.

Apparently his voyage was right back on track; everything that could go wrong was starting to go wrong again. He looked around at the faces, wondering bemusedly if they were all agents who had somehow got their signals mixed and all boarded his ship by mistake.

"But I do hope," Hachisman said, "that we can use a direct journey button from Xiphe. I hate getting waked up and having my caff slop out of the cup when the ship jumps."

"I hope so too, Fr. Hachisman," Cyn said with more emphasis and sincerity than he had intended. "I'm not exactly thrilled needing to do all those calculations, you know," he added quickly to cover his gratitude for the reminder about the Healtha journey button.

The journey button might be pure and uncontaminated, but if it was not, Patrol was a far safer depository for it than an OM office. When he could free himself, Cyn went back to the control room and called the Patrol ship again. He explained about the journey button. Expressionless as usual, the commander approved Cyn's foresight and said he would let Cyn know before he earthed what Central Command wanted to do.

Relieved, Cyn looked at the messages. Rocam's was in clear; and said only that there had been a short delay and she would be a sday late but she hoped in time for the wedding. Demoson's was addressed in clear to a factor at a hotel, the remainder in code; and Hachisman's was all code and very short. Cyn looked at it doubtfully, but the use of a single code word that expanded to a full address was a common way to save transmission charges. And a passenger could sue Overstars, claiming heavy losses, if he refused to transmit a message. He shrugged and keyed them into the com one after the other. With Patrol virtually breathing down his neck, he could afford to be a little less cautious.

CHAPTER 8

As it turned out, Patrol was actually breathing down Cyn's neck. The vessel took an orbit just beyond his and before he launched the shuttle, he was informed that he would have an escort down to the landing field. Central Command had requested that Cyn hand over the Healtha journey button to Patrol. The hissing of the com, carrying hard copy of the order and the commander's signal, was Cyn's receipt for "lost" OM property.

Well content, Cyn took his time descending, making one last orbit low enough to get visuals of the planet, which he displayed on the screens in the passenger compartment. His last hope was that a lush and beautiful world might tempt one or more of his passengers to a change of opinion, even at this late time.

Xiphe did not cooperate. The visuals showed a rocky desert covered irregularly with a dusty grey-green growth. If water existed at all, it was not the sparkling blue or green of most oxygen worlds but mud, indistinguishable from the dull soil. The cities were repellent: broad mud domes set randomly in ugly clusters here and there on plains that shimmered with heat. During the early part of the descent, Cyn had occupied himself with working up a little speech describing the joys of a sday or two exploring the lovely world and marvelous culture of an alien species. He did not make the speech and was rather surprised when Fr. Rocam almost leapt from her seat as soon as he gave permission to unstrap after grounding the shuttle.

"There's a kind of port city," she said eagerly, heading for the still-closed door. "Maybe I can find something really unusual for my niece."

Mortchose and Wakkin both looked toward Niais, but Cyn said quickly, "Niais, you'll have to wait and leave with me. There's an incorrect entry on your passage permit. We have to clear that with the office." The light showing the ramp was extended came on and he said, "Shuttle ramp comes up at 32:41 Xiphe time or 4:15 Healtha evening, if any of you are still using Healtha time. I won't wait if anyone is late, but I'll leave his or her baggage at the OM office in Empire Star, Mantra."

He watched all except Niais rush to leave, and wondered what their hurry was to get out into the uninviting environment shown on the visuals. Shaken by a momentary distrust of the shuttle's instruments, he walked back to look out the door. He sighed. The mud-colored world hazed with mud-colored dust was there. The screens had not lied.

In the next cradle, the Patrol shuttle that had escorted them rested upright. It had earthed a few smins after his shuttle, but several of the urso crew were already standing outside; their landing procedure took less time because the cradle did not need to bring the ship flat. Cyn patted his pocket to make sure the Healtha journey button was there. He was already looking beyond the Patrol vessel toward the transports that were swallowing his passengers when a moving figure behind the group of Patrol crew caught his eye.

The figure disappeared around the body of the Patrol shuttle almost instantly, but there had been a flash of dull gold like Aimie's travel garb and a familiarity about the movement. Security and Patrol? Well, why not? Someone had to keep an eye on Security, and who better than Patrol? From the beginning he had felt she was not telling him everything. But why hide her association with Patrol? Or could she have walked around the Patrol ship to escape the others—or to deceive him? Cyn sighed again. He seemed to have developed a full-blown case of paranoia in the four sdays between Healtha and Xiphe. He hoped he would not be babbling and drooling and stunning the lights on his console before they reached Mantra.

He started nervously and whirled around when Niais spoke. "Everyone is gone," she said, from the seat where she was still obediently waiting. "And the chair-bed in my cage is very comfortable. You never did deal with me on the ship, so . . ."

Cyn closed his eyes, then opened them slowly. She was breathtakingly lovely, dressed now in the gauzy tunic and underskirt she had been wearing when he first saw her. "No," he said firmly but quietly. "I have to deliver the mail."

He had to deliver more than the mail, he remembered then. He had to hand over Niais to the OM agent for a correction on the bill of lading. He glanced over his shoulder out of the door toward the mud-colored domes that made up the port buildings. Could he bear to leave the poor child here, without even human companions with whom to play games? His lips twisted. On the other hand, could he bear another seven sdays of Niais's company—three sdays to Mantra and another four to Ingong?

Four? Ingong was a long jump, but it was only three sdays to Mantra and in Empire Star Niais could name her own price—if she had sense enough to name any price. More likely she would—But he was no fool and for her own good he could think of her as an article of Trade. He could make contract with a good broker in partners. But he would be gone from Mantra in a sday. Well, he could figure out how to enforce the contract on the way to Mantra.

He found himself staring at Niais, who was looking expectant again because of his long silence. It was unfair not to try to explain. "Why are you going to Ingong?" he asked.

"I have to go there," she replied simply.

"You don't have to go anywhere you don't want," he pointed out. "It will be easy to prove you are not a beast. There is no indenture on you. All you have to do is debark at Mantra, and you will be free and independent. Niais, Ingong is a very long way off the main routes and the people there are not like us. You are very beautiful. I can arrange with a broker to get you any terms you like as a life companion—"

Her trill of laughter was equally a joy to the ears and a trial to the spirit; it was almost the delicate bell chime of a nymph but implied lack of consideration of the proposal.

"But I don't wish to be a life companion," she assured him earnestly. "I must go to Ingong."

Cyn sighed. The conversation had come round to the beginning again, as it always did when one talked to Niais. He patted her absently and told her to wait a little longer while he got the robos to collect the mail and packages for Xiphe. When that was done and the robos had been sent off to the OM office—unmistakable because of the service symbol set in bright tiles in the dull roof and walls of one dome—he collected his delivery record for the OM clerk and the manifest and bill of lading, listing Niais as a "beast, caged."

"I have to stop in the Patrol ship," he explained, gesturing to her to follow.

The heat enveloped them as soon as they stepped out and Cyn sealed the shuttle. The air was like that of a warming oven, not searing but hot and still. Fortunately, it was also so dry a perceptible cooling could be obtained from evaporating sweat. Concomitantly, Cyn could feel the tissues of his nose and throat drying. He was therefore annoyed when the guard at the Patrol shuttle would not admit Niais; however, the climate was not dangerous, as long as she didn't exert herself, and he expected to be with the commander for only a few smin, so he left her near the foot of the ramp with the urso who was guarding the ship's entrance.

He was delayed considerably longer than he had expected by the commander, who asked several questions about the homing caller Cyn had ejected from his ship. Cyn answered the first few quite willingly, but then remembered Niais and said he would have to take the fem who had been with him somewhere out of the heat unless she could wait inside the Patrol shuttle. The commander gave the order at once, apologizing politely for the restriction, saying he had expected Cyn to come alone and that tight security was necessary in a Patrol ship.

Having acknowledged the apology with equal politeness, Cyn put Niais out of his mind. He was surprised, however, when the commander's next questions were about his passengers. The questions were sufficiently penetrating to make Cyn doubt an urso could pose them, and brought to his mind that glimpse of a gold jumpsuit. Had the questions been posed during Aimie's earlier visit to the Patrol ship and the urso commander merely relaying? Cyn felt a little hurt; she could have asked him herself. In the next moment he was amused; he didn't trust her any further than she trusted him. But it was his Pot that was in danger.

"Commander," he said, "who wants my ship? Why? The Postmaster sent me a crazy warning about pirates, but you must know that pirates are impossible. I've never, in five syrs, carried more than three passengers, yet I have six aboard, seven if you count the fem who was shipped as cargo. Now you're asking questions about those passengers. Why?"

Fur rippled on the urso's head. Cyn knew it was an expression of emotion, but he couldn't read it and the commander's voice told him nothing as he said, "I ask about your passengers because of the doubt you named. Central Command can get the facts I ask for from Overstars, but it might take three sdays. I hoped CC could obtain significant information about them while we were still in contact before you jump into the void. As to who wants a mail ship and why, I wish I could answer your questions but I cannot—not by order but by ignorance. We have been warned specially to protect any mail ship passing through our assigned area that will stop at Empire Star."

Cyn shrugged mentally; he had thought the appeal worth a try, although he had not really expected enlightenment. And then he realized he had got more than he expected. The danger was to ships scheduled to land at Empire Star. No general weakening of Empire control was causing the attacks on mail ships but something specifically to do with Empire government.

There was something else, too, but he couldn't pursue the thought because he needed his wits to answer the commander's questions. He tried to keep to simple fact, but the commander repeatedly prodded for his speculations. Eventually he yielded them, but under protest, and he insisted on finishing up his statement—which found suspicious the behavior of every passenger, including Aimie—with a warning about his growing paranoia.

The urso made a very strange noise and hung his long, purple-tinged tongue out of his mouth to flop around for a few ssecs. Cyn was startled, and showed it. With the tongue flapping, somehow the urso said, "I am laughing, male. It is

110

not common among my people, but we can laugh. If you are earnest in your pursuit of this paranoia, you will soon be a fit recruit for Patrol."

"Power forefend!" Cyn exclaimed so passionately that the urso's tongue began to gyrate wildly, smacking his nostril flaps and cheeks.

"I thank you," he said when he had his mouth under control again. "I have not enjoyed an interrogation so much in a very long time. In the name of the Empress, the goodwill of my service."

"And the thanks of mine," Cyn said, getting up.

He was pleased and relieved, until he got down to the outer lock and realized that Niais was no longer waiting. "Where is the person whom the commander ordered to be allowed to wait here for me?" he asked the guard.

"Before the commander's order came, one she named Wakkin arrived in a transport," the guard replied. "She complained of the heat. The Wakkin person said he would take her to a cool place, and she left with him."

Cyn groaned. He was annoyed but not alarmed. Niais was safe enough with Wakkin. For a moment he stood indecisively, wondering whether he should try to find her immediately or attend to his chores first. Would he need her as evidence to have the bill of lading changed? Possibly he could manage without her presence just then. All the clerk was responsible for was making out the form for his complaint. He could then offload the cage and leave Niais and correction of the shipping orders to the local Postmaster.

Another point: He was already late in presenting his delivery record, and the mail couldn't be sorted until it was checked against that. The clerk would be annoyed enough about that, but probably wouldn't complain when he said Patrol had held him up. If he wandered around looking for

Niais, however, he would surely have more black marks on his record.

Cursing himself under his breath for not having made clear to Niais that she must wait for him, he set off for the OM office. The clerk accepted his delivery record without any curling or lifting of the appendage Cyn was pretty sure would sign irritation, and Cyn found himself thinking that the description in the Overstars list did not do the Xiphans justice. Neither in disposition nor appearance did they really resemble what he thought of as crabs.

True they had broad carapaces and seven thin limbs; the hind central one, which Cyn suspected was modified into a sting or piercing weapon, was the one he had been watching and it never quivered as it would if the Xiphan were angry. The two limbs adjoining a smaller domed structure, which apparently could be pulled back into a slot in the great carapace, were well endowed with manipulators. But both larger and smaller shells—if they were shells—were gorgeous. The larger shell was covered not with "patches" but with elaborate patterns of brilliantly colored, gleaming feathers through which the bare portions of the carapace sparkled; the smaller had no feathers, but was as lavishly patterned in what appeared to be polished jet and bronze.

When his delivery record had been accepted, entered, and his copy stamped, Cyn showed the clerk the bill of lading for Ingong and described the problem, ending, "She's a person, not a beast. I think it's illegal for a sentient being to be labeled a beast for shipping."

The small screen Cyn had been handed showed a rush of words, the manipulators working a keyboard and bringing out the Universum letters as quick as speech. "Very likely, because the cost of shipping is less than the fare for sentient passengers. Who will pay the difference? However, I have not the authority to change the bill of lading."

"I didn't suppose you could do it yourself," Cyn replied. "I have the cage and the fem. You make out the forms and I'll drop the whole problem in the—" Cyn swallowed the word 'lap,' which would clearly be meaningless to the Xiphan and went on, "—into the manipulators of the local Postmaster."

The carapace bobbed back and forth. "Amusement," the screen said. "Xiphe is not a major port. No Postmaster. This third is all the OM staff on the planet."

"I'm glad I'm making everyone so happy," Cyn muttered.

Query marks appeared. "Talking to myself," Cyn said. "My species does that when they have a lot of trouble. So, if you don't have the authority to change the bill of lading, and there's no Postmaster, what should I do?"

Out from under the smaller carapace came two slender stalks bearing at their ends brilliant blue eyes. These intertwined gently near their base while the free ends began to clap together in a measured beat. Cyn watched briefly, but the peculiar activity had no effect on the rapidity with which the manipulators worked the keyboard and he had to return his attention to the reading screen.

"If this third were you," Cyn read, "s/he would forget all about the problem. You say the person wishes to go to the place named in the bill of lading and wishes to be delivered in the cage. It seems to this third that you are not damaging the person even if you deliver her as a 'beast in a cage.' You will save this third a great deal of trouble if you act in this way."

"Sure," Cyn said, "and I'll be making a lot of trouble for myself if I deliver goods under a false bill of lading."

The eyestalks stilled, unwound, and withdrew under the small carapace. "You can register a complaint—for that you will need a statement from the person and two other witnesses; this third is required to serve as one witness if you so request. You must make out the standard 'mislabeled' form and a second form that states you felt it necessary to transfer the problem to the next suitable port because there were no facilities here for maintaining the integrity of the kind of cargo involved."

The screen cleared and immediately began to fill again. "This is true," it said. "The only facility for your species is a small waiting room. Few species homo come here aside from those who have business and therefore have quarters prepared—and there are not many with business on Xiphe. However, if you make such a complaint you will cause this third much labor in the making of files and submission of reports"—Cyn tightened his lips against a grin; the very type on the screen looked reproachful—"but you will doubtless escape reprimand."

Cyn shook his head, about to apologize for the extra work he was making for the clerk, when the Xiphan suddenly drew the small carapace under the larger and squatted flat on the floor. Cyn was so surprised that he almost missed a new burst of words on the screen. "**ANGUISH**. This third cannot prevent you from leaving the cage and the person here. This third will then be forced to register the complaint with the Postmaster General and, in its own good time, perhaps after this third has been driven to a cracked braincase by the forms and reports required, the Postmaster will no doubt make a decision about whether to alter the bill of lading or return the person to Healtha."

Cyn had to bite his lips hard to keep from laughing. The clerk didn't know the half of the trouble that would descend on her/him if he left Niais. However, such cruelty was completely out of the question. To leave her for a swik or two until another ship could undertake her transport was one thing; to abandon her indefinitely in such a place was impossible. The clerk's original idea about carrying her to the next port, which would be Empire Star, protected by a registered complaint was best.

"I can't leave her here without adequate facilities," Cyn assured the Xiphan.

Then he had to choke back another laugh, when it promptly rose from the floor and the smaller carapace came forward. The screen lit with words again. "This third is glad you realize the person might be damaged by remaining here with no cold rooms or special liquids. These are costly and this third has no permission to provide such."

"All right," Cyn said. "I'll chase her down and get one of the other passengers so I can register my complaint." He put the bill of lading back in his pocket with the manifest and said bitterly, "I hope Overstars gets whoever shipped her this way and sues for the additional fare."

The clerk rocked back and forth in the manner that s/he had identified as amusement earlier. "Do not fear. Doubtless they will and wring out a penalty as well. Overstars does not miss such opportunities."

Cyn smiled and started to hand the screen back to the clerk, but shook his head sharply. "Damn and blast, I almost forgot! I had to turn over the journey button I got at Healtha to the Patrol. I have a receipt from them, but I guess it isn't going to do me any good. I'll bet you have no puter for making journey buttons here."

"Right, no puter," the screen stated. "But journey buttons are available. Prepared for one place only—Empire Star."

"Why Empire Star?" Cyn asked, his skin crawling.

The eyestalks popped out, the blue orbs at their ends rising and falling in what had to be understood as amazed examination. "Not clear to you that if a journey button is damaged or destroyed, the central office at Mantra would want to know why?"

The logic was good, and Cyn, rapidly reviewing the material he had given the OM clerk, suddenly felt better. Nowhere on the delivery list or the bill of lading for Niais was any mention of his route after Xiphe except, of course, the stop at Ingong. He hadn't presented the manifest and his pickup was for "all mail, all ports," so the clerk couldn't know he ever expected to stop at Mantra—unless the Pot's route had been betrayed, or even prearranged, at Healtha so that Xiphe, the only other stop before Empire Star, could also be corrupted. In any case, Cyn preferred not to expose his suspicion; he could use or not use the journey button as he pleased once back on the Pot.

"Good," he said. "Empire Star's on my route anyway, so I'll take the button."

By the time the clerk was finished filling out forms and entering serial numbers, Cyn was almost certain "this third" was not involved in any plot to abduct mail ships. Too many trails now led to this office if Cyn's ship did not arrive at Empire Star. The clerk even, after popping its eyes out to examine him again, allowed Cyn to pick out his own journey button.

Having put the button carefully in a pocket that opened only on the inside of his coveralls, Cyn asked, "If you're the only OM employee, how much longer will this office be open? I could see the port city wasn't very large, but it could still take me quite a while to find my 'beast' and another witness."

The screen came alight. "Only a few places cold enough for species homo and similar cold climate beings, so search should not take long. However, this office, like other OM posts, is always open. The first and second are on call when this third is resting. Pull **INQUIRY** at the entrance and one will come."

Cyn thanked the attractive creature, who promptly awakened all his suspicions again by offering to summon transport for him and direct it to the largest place that maintained cold rooms for aliens. He was soon pleasantly reassured when the clerk informed him, with the same charming self-centered helpfulness, that the driver coming was, "This third's first's sib/sib/kin second. He will not cheat you," the clerk added, "and will take Empire credit chips."

This time Cyn let his grin loose, since a smile would be appropriate to the thanks he was offering. He wondered how much the clerk made in kickbacks for providing transport—or, depending on the culture, other types of profit—but he was a lot more comfortable in his mind knowing that the Xiphan was not acting out of pure altruism.

Thus Cyn entered the transport through a rear hatch with a clear mind. The driver, whose patterns were different but just as attractive as the clerk's, was settled in a sunken section at the front; the rear, much too large for Cyn, was a round area of sand confined by a low lip, into which Cyn guessed four Xiphans could squeeze themselves.

In the event, his confidence was justified. The transport carried him swiftly past the domes closest to the landing field into some inner area, where it passed two domes and circled a third, coming to a stop near the tunnel-like entrance. The driver then pointed toward the opening, held out one manipulator and tapped twice with the other on the lip that divided his section from the sand. Not cheap for a short ride, but not outrageous either. Cyn had no inclination to argue; he exposed two credits on his palm, then pointed to himself, to the ground, and added two more credits.

"Will you wait for me?" he asked.

One credit was gently picked up by a manipulator and the rear hatch sprang open. It did not close when Cyn got out, so he assumed he had been understood and said, "Thanks," as he brushed the sand from his "seat" out of his clothes. At the tunnel entrance, Cyn stopped, surprised. There had been no door at the tunnel into the OM office or anywhere else inside the Xiphan structure. He had assumed they did not use doors. However, the short tunnel was well lit and there was nothing in it. Still, he touched the hilt of his stunner, supported by a loop under the flap of his thigh pocket, as he started forward. When he reached the door, he lifted the latch. It swung open immediately, emitting a blast of what seemed ice-cold air. Cyn hurried inside and closed the door behind him.

He was now in a short inner tunnel and he paused to shake his head at himself. He was beyond simple paranoia if it had not occurred to him that a door was needed to keep the cold air inside. In the few paces he took to reach a chamber larger than the OM office, the air no longer felt cold at all. But he did not step inside. He stopped short, momentarily stunned.

As if to make up for the drab world outside, the walls and ceiling were painted in large and small circles fitted together. Each circle contained what seemed an entirely different, intricate, brilliantly colored pattern. The floor, of polished stone, was also patterned, and it was dotted with low, round tables surrounded by cushions, all gleaming and glittering with color and sparkling plas.

Cyn had to close his eyes and swallow. When he looked again he found that the monochrome garments of those he sought leapt out of the warring colors and designs. The first that caught his eye was Demoson in a neat grey jumpsuit, kneeling on a pillow and eagerly talking to a native whose feathers were fluffed against the cold. Near Demoson's hand was a reading screen much like the one Cyn had used in the OM office. On the table before Demoson and the Xiphan was a spray of feathers; its brilliant pattern, warring with that of the table, did odd things to Cyn's eyes.

He looked away, glad to fix on Hachisman in a dull brown tunic and tights, who was directly across the room, leaning against a perfectly ordinary-looking bar. Mortchose was not far away, sitting on a pillow at the table nearest the bar. He had a glass in his hand, his back against the wall; his eyes were closed—Cyn could sympathize fully with that—and his face was perfectly blank.

"I'm glad I found you all," Cyn said, walking toward the bar. "Has anyone seen Niais? She took off with Wakkin while I was busy, but I still need her to thumbprint that report about the mistake on my bill of lading."

Demoson looked up, smiling. "She was here with Wakkin, but when First Phiilaas came in with his samples she went crazy—in her own way." He chuckled. "She couldn't work her usual charm on Phiilaas, though. He wouldn't agree to give her any feathercloth, but there was a male in here who said he knew where she could buy a cloak or some lengths of the stuff."

"Is that what you're doing?" Cyn asked.

"You bet your life. I'm trying to buy every length that isn't already bespoken before Fr. Aimie gets here." Demoson grimaced. "But she's probably at one of the offices outbidding me already."

"Can Niais buy anything?" Cyn asked. "Does she have any credits?"

Hachisman laughed. "Don't worry about that. Wakkin went with her. He'll pay if she can't."

"Do you think she'll be gone long?"

The dour man laughed again. "She hasn't been gone long,

and it does take a fem a while to pick and choose."

Cyn sighed. "Does anyone know where she went?" he asked. "I'd better go after her. Sometimes these reports of mislabeling take time to complete."

The Xiphan with Demoson extended a manipulator and tapped the reading screen. Demoson nodded, levered himself to his feet, and brought the screen to Cyn. The symbol on it was meaningless to him. He looked at the Xiphan and asked, "Can I show this to my transport driver outside?"

The Xiphan tipped forward, which Cyn took to be agreement. Out to the driver, who acknowledged the name or address or whatever it was with a similar forward dip; in to return the screen. Cyn gritted his teeth against the hot, cold, hot contrasts as he climbed back into the transport. He was almost glad when the showroom—for it clearly was a showroom—to which the transport delivered him was not cooled.

The entrance tunnel was much longer and led to a relatively small circular area pierced regularly with openings to other rooms. Between each opening the wall was painted, but with a single pattern. With the mud-colored background, the effect was very lovely. Below each painting were cases containing small rounds set with patterns and rainbow sprays of feathers, which Cyn guessed must be trade samples. His eyes lit with an acquisitive gleam. Was Xiphe far enough off the routes of the Trade Combines to make it safe for Lystris to stop here? He would surely com a suggestion to his mother ship.

A peculiar gurgling whistle drew his eyes to the Xiphan approaching him and he realized it was asking a question he could not understand. He realized too that he had been so distracted by the trade possibilities for Lystris that he had not noticed Niais was nowhere to be seen—and he had no way of asking for her. To his infinite relief, that problem was solved before he had to face it; the Xiphan was already extending a reading screen, which implied a familiarity with Universum.

"I am looking for a fem and a male of my kind," Cyn said. "Were they here?"

"Two males," the screen read. "The fem took a wryyzelt cloak. One male paid. The other invited them to his place where it is made cold and there is such liquid as you ingest. That male left his direction in case any others of his kind should desire similar refreshment."

Cyn was relieved and didn't question why a stranger would leave such direction. He accepted the plas slip the Xiphan offered and eagerly brought it to his driver. It seemed perfectly reasonable to him that anyone on a world like Xiphe would welcome company of his own kind. Thus, after he had tapped on the door that shut in the cold and had been told to enter, not suspicion but his regard for the energy costs of cooling in the Xiphan climate made Cyn virtually leap inside. The thoughtful gesture saved him from being struck by the blow aimed at him, but the weapon glanced off his back with enough power to send him staggering, and he tripped on a cushion and fell.

A male voice cursed. Cyn rolled, struggling to draw his stunner and face his attacker, and Niais's voice cried out, "What are you doing?"

"I was going to put him to sleep," the male voice snarled, "but now I'll have to burn him. I need his ship."

Cyn twisted frantically, but the wrong hip was on the ground and he could not draw his stunner. As he struggled, he caught a glimpse of Niais—again dressed in nothing but her hair and her package—beside the male who had struck at him.

"But I have to go to Ingong," she was saying anxiously.

"You'll like the place we're going better," the male said, laughing.

The weapon leveled. Cyn caught a glimpse of Niais shifting her package. He flattened behind the cushion that had tripped him, praying she would throw it, praying the cushion would absorb some of the weapon's energy, digging a knee into the floor to lift his hip, reaching for his stunner, knowing the effort was hopeless.

The blast of sound and the screams that followed shocked him nearly witless but fortunately did not impede the actions already programmed into his brain. He had his stunner out and responded to a male shout of alarm—separate from the screams—by firing in the direction of a doorway he had not consciously noted. Someone fell out of the opening. Cyn fired again at the twisting form to make sure and then swung the stunner toward the male who was screaming, only to drop it and leap to his feet. Blood was pouring from what had once been a hand and lower arm as the male crumpled to the ground.

"I'm sorry," Niais wailed. "I'm sorry. I didn't know that would happen."

Cyn pulled his belt knife and ripped a strip from the male's already blood-soaked sleeve. Having tied off the arm so that the blood flow slowed, he retrieved his weapon and made sure his attacker was really unconscious. He then rushed to turn over the male in the doorway, but his face was as unfamiliar as that of the one who had struck at him. He secured the second one, simply but effectively, by tying his thumbs together behind his back with another strip of the first male's sleeve, removing his shoes and foot-pads and also fastening his big toes together.

Then Cyn breathed. When his lungs felt as if they had air in them again, he turned to Niais. "Where's Wakkin?"

"I'm sorry," she whispered. "I'm so sorry. I only wanted to pull the stunner away from him. I have to go to Ingong."

Resisting an impulse to scream, which Cyn knew was generated by tension rather than her single-minded purpose, he went and put his arm around her, drawing her with him to where he could cover both the door and the archway.

"Yes," he said. "I promise I'll get you to Ingong. Don't worry about what happened. That wasn't a nice male." Cyn had to suppress a mental wince at the word 'nice,' but he felt he had to use language that was most familiar and thus most comprehensible to her. "You don't have to be sorry about him. Just tell me where Wakkin is."

"Oh," she said, the trouble lifting from her face. "Wakkin went with the one you stunned to get drinks for us. I did think it was taking a long time, but the one you said isn't nice wanted to—" She blinked, then sighed in a long-suffering way. "I don't know what you want me to say, but do to—that, and it isn't nice to bring up . . ."

"Let's not worry about what's nice for a while," Cyn said. "Right now it's not important. You stay here. If you hear any noise outside or the door starts to open, you yell for me. Yell loud! Never mind whether it's nice or not. If you want to get to Ingong, you yell as loud as you can."

"All right," she said, sounding very doubtful, "but I can't wait right here all the time. I have to get my feather cape."

"You have to get more than that!" Cyn exclaimed, realizing that he was so accustomed to seeing Niais stark naked that he had forgotten it was inappropriate. "You have to get dressed. Where did you leave your clothes this time?"

"Over there, on that cushion." She pointed.

Cyn sighed. "Go get dressed," he said wearily. "Then pick up your cloak and come back here and do what I told you—listen and yell if you hear anything."

CHAPTER 9

Cyn stared blankly into the blank screen of his com console aboard the Pot. The Patrol commander had just given him a final report on the two prisoners he had delivered to them on Xiphe. Cyn couldn't believe that after all that had happened, he had no more idea who had put the homer into the shuttle than before he had landed. He didn't even know whether the attack on him on Xiphe had anything to do with the homer or the disappearance of the other mail ships.

The man who had lost a hand was in the Patrol ship's freezer and couldn't be questioned. The one he had stunned had been questioned—as soon as he had wakened in Patrol custody, he had agreed to answer under truth drugs. He seemed to be a pilot who had lost his Imperial license and was now so far down on his luck that he had agreed to the other man's plan for "borrowing" an Overstars Mail ship. More information might be gleaned from both men, the commander had said, but he didn't have the equipment. Deeper scanning would need to wait until Patrol transshipped them to a messenger boat, which would take them to Empire Star.

I might as well have saved myself the effort and the money of dragging them back to Patrol, Cyn thought irritably—and then started to chuckle. That whole business had been rather funny.

Fortunately, only the two men seemed to be involved. At

least, there had been no occasion for Niais to choose between niceness and the necessity of screaming. Cyn had found Wakkin stunned and bound in the farther chamber. Having cut him loose, he carried him out to the waiting transport and dumped him in, ignoring the gurgling whistles and waving mandibles of the Xiphan driver. When he came out with the second body, the gurgles and agitated mandibles stilled. The third produced the Xiphan's eyes—bright orange rather than blue—extended to a remarkable degree.

The eyes stayed fixed on the prone forms, not lifting to Niais, who had followed Cyn out, until she got into the transport. Then they seemed to examine the cloak. Cyn remembered wondering whether those cloaks were a luxury item on Xiphe and Niais's possession of one would raise the transport fare. He couldn't see why any Xiphan would want one, since every Xiphan seemed to have his own grown-on model, but then he dismissed the thought. It was true he was short of money, but this was no time to worry about it. He could get a receipt from Patrol, and probably Overstars would pay.

The fun had begun when Cyn pointed to the OM symbol on his breast and pointed down the road—if it was a road and wasn't a front yard or back yard of one of the nearby domes. The Xiphan had withdrawn his eyes by then, but he extended the three credits he had already collected, and began to tap each of the credits four times.

"Twelve credits!" Cyn exclaimed, outraged. "You only charged two to take me from the OM office to—"

Before he finished the Xiphan was pointing to the three bodies and Niais. Cyn saw the logic of it. The driver was only charging two credits for the trip, but two credits for each of the riders he carried. Cyn remembered that he owed the driver a credit which had not been collected at the first stop. He wasn't sure what the last credit was for, but was cynically certain there would be a good reason.

Once they had started Cyn grew less cynical. The vehicle moved much more slowly than it had when he was the only passenger, seeming to strain against the load. Possibly the system of propulsion used was not efficient and the energy required, and thus the cost of running the vehicle, was acutely sensitive to weight. By the time they reached the OM office, Cyn was so grateful to have arrived—he thought several times that the transport could struggle no farther and that he would have difficulty in getting another to accept the load—that he was willing to forget all about the extra credit. He didn't have to. Some time during the confused period that followed, after he tried to explain what had happened to the Patrol commander who had finally agreed to pick up Cyn's prisoners, the clerk had explained.

The extra credit, it seemed, was to pay for the sand removed from the transport on his clothes and that of the others. Cyn remembered laughing about paying for sand on a whole planet of it. The OM clerk had been very indignant— no, hurt—at the idea that his first's sib/sib/kin second would ask for payment for ordinary sand. Cyn learned how the sand was cleaned, treated, and graded to provide comfort for passengers and readily apologized for his lack of understanding. He laughed again now, thinking that the Xiphans were very nice people.

Ursos, on the other hand, had warped senses of humor— or, at least, the urso Patrol commander did. He had arrived in a Patrol flitter with a guard to investigate Cyn's allegation that the two men had attacked him without provocation. His voice had been flat, his questions suspicious. He wanted to know why Cyn had been armed and why he had been pursuing passengers who had a right to freedom of movement.

Cyn began to laugh again. The Patrol commander had

probably learned a great deal more than he wanted. First the OM clerk had explained, at considerable length, about the necessary forms for mislabeled cargo. Then he had heard Niais's distracted and rambling description of the events in the wounded man's rooms—ending in wails of, "I only touched that thing he said would burn Pilot Cyn, only touched it. I didn't know it would blow up and hurt him." Finally Wakkin had been revived. His amazement at facing a Patrol investigation when his last memory was of reaching for a cool drink would have been hard to fake in his dazed condition. Clearly Wakkin had not been stunned for any cause he had given.

By that time, various passengers had begun to arrive at the OM office—Rocam looking strangely disheveled but clutching several packages; Aimie, as polished as ever, and with the smug expression of a cat that had licked out the creampot and got away with it; Demoson, also looking smug until he saw Wakkin's condition, then worried and concerned; Mortchose, blank until his eyes fixed on Niais; and Hachisman, the last in, who stopped in the waiting room archway, clearly shocked by the crowd there.

Each arrival, except Aimie and Mortchose, had caused some interruption of the commander's investigation with exclamations and questions, turning to Cyn for satisfaction and reassurance. He did his best, realizing that none would be willing to stay on Xiphe even if he tried to frighten them, until Hachisman began to rave. He pointed to the wounded male and said that Cyn attracted disaster. He demanded a new pilot from the OM clerk, but thrust away the proffered reader, which explained that there was no pilot available and the clerk had no authority to make the substitution anyway.

Cyn remembered silencing Hachisman by telling him coldly that Niais, not he, had vanquished the male that attacked him and that, if Hachisman wanted a new pilot, he would be perfectly delighted if he would wait on Xiphe for the next ship. That seemed to stun Hachisman, who apologized weakly and almost wept as he added that it was so important that he get to Mantra, so important. To which Cyn had replied at first with moderation that he was doing and would continue to do his best; but then he had lost his patience and snarled that the single most desired goal in his life at this moment was to get them all to Mantra and never lay eyes on them again.

For some reason, that struck the Patrol commander very funny. When Cyn turned to face him again, he was having another tongue waving fit and said that Cyn was surely in the wrong service and belonged in Patrol rather than Overstars.

"Oh, no, I don't!" Cyn had replied forcibly. "I left Free Trade because I was tired of being shot at, and if I can't have a peaceful life, I'm going back to Lystris."

The memory made him scowl at the blank com. That was the point: Was he going to be shot at again? All seven passengers were still aboard, and he hadn't the faintest notion which of them truly wanted to arrive on Mantra and which wanted the Pot or something the Pot was carrying. He couldn't even exclude Niais, who had saved him. If the down-and-out pilot and his crony were simply an unlucky coincidence, she could have saved him because she wanted the Pot for another purpose.

Crazy as it seemed to envision Niais as part of any plot, there remained the question of how she had saved him. Blasters did not disintegrate when they were touched. And if this one did, why hadn't Niais's hand been destroyed too? Could it have been a faulty weapon that detonated when the male tried to fire it? Another coincidence?

Cyn rubbed his burning eyes. This was getting him nowhere. He looked carefully around at his console. They would be at the carrollpause in a stu or two, but he did not need to be awake for that. The navigator had all the information it needed to take the ship over the jumps he had already calculated from Xiphe to Mantra. Despite his conviction that the Xiphan clerk was honest, he had not been able to bring himself to use the journey button. After Mantra, he told himself, yawning.

Aboard Lystris a standard time cycle of dark and light had been maintained, and Cyn kept the pattern aboard the Pot when he traveled alone because he was used to it. He did not necessarily work during light stus and sleep during dark ones, but the circadian rhythms of his ancient phylogeny were soothed by the recurrent pattern. From now on, however, he intended to keep his waking and sleeping stus the same as the passengers. Wearily Cyn turned from the com screen to that of the av. He breathed a brief prayer of thanks to the Powers that Be. All the avs in all the cabins gave back nothing but heavy breathing. Cyn levered himself off the pilot's couch and finally headed for his own bunk.

He was asleep before he hit the mattress. Until he stepped out of his coverall, Cyn had not yielded to his fatigue. The continued excitements and anxieties of the sday and the need to check and recheck his calculations had kept him going, but when the need for alertness was gone, Cyn responded like a bludgeoned beast. He slid deep into unconsciousness, his body totally given over to cleansing and repair. Dreaming would come later, after the toxins were removed and the worn cells restored.

Even if he had been awake in his bed, however, he would not have heard the silent shadow that mounted the steps of the black companionway without hesitation. A delicate manipulation of a small instrument opened the supposedly foolproof palm lock and the shadow slipped through the door. No sooner was that door drawn closed, but not fully shut, than another, which had shown a bare crack, opened—only wide enough to allow a second, even more furtive shadow to slip out. It crept up the companionway and listened at the door, breathing so carefully that cims away the sound was imperceptible. Then it peered in through the crack the first shadow had left to avoid the click of the latch. Finally, with infinite care, it slid back the door and slipped inside.

A few moments later, a third door opened, this one without any hint of furtiveness. Niais made a moue of dissatisfaction when she saw the rec room was totally dark and all the cabin doors were closed. Leaving her own door wide open to light the way, she tripped across the room and climbed the companionway stair. Clad only in her ever-present package and her cornsilk hair, she made a fetching picture. It was not a picture that invited rejection, and Niais was not fearful. She trod firmly on each stair of the companionway and slid the door back with confidence, indifferent to the whirr of bearings on the track and the distinct click it made as the latch that would hold it open caught.

Four ears perceived the sounds. One head flung up sharply from an intent perusal of plas sheets drawn from Cyn's desk. The movement showed clearly against the console telltales, and their dim glow was reflected in the darksight lenses that masked the upper half of the face. In the next instant, head and body disappeared as the shadow crouched down beside the desk.

The other head had jerked and turned just a fraction, but the movement gave nothing away. The shadow was crouched low where a protruding portion of the console created a shelter from the telltale lights. The only effect of the movement was a brief, dull gleam from the barrel of a weapon as it shifted to a position that would better cover the door and the snooper.

Niais paused uncertainly on the threshold. In the dark she had become just a trifle disoriented. Her head swung right, then left, then right again. Both forms tensed and the weapon pointed more directly at her. Then Niais uttered a small wordless sound of satisfaction and started off toward the partition that closed off Cyn's private quarters from the control room. When she pushed open that door, Cyn stirred uneasily.

"Good," Niais exclaimed, "you aren't busy now. I played games with Wakkin, Demoson, and Hachisman. And now I'd like you to deal with me when you're awake, as you promised."

Cyn struggled upright, forcing open sticky eyelids and fumbling for the light switch. Momentarily the all-too-familiar sight of Niais in one piece of slightly hair-veiled skin drove out what little sense sleep had left him. However, even his instinctive sexual response could no longer block his sense of self-preservation. His sleep-dazed mind recorded the vision confronting him as a sign that something was wrong—very wrong.

"What?" he mumbled.

"I did as you told me when I first came," Niais repeated patiently. "I played games with the passengers, and then I waited until I thought you must be finished with your work so you wouldn't be too busy to deal with me. When I came up, I saw the big room was all dark, so—"

That penetrated the fog of sleep and incipient lust. She could not have got in! The door was palm-locked. No matter how tired he was, he wouldn't have left it open considering his distrust of the passengers. He remembered locking it.

"How did you get in?"

The light now streaming from Cyn's quarters into the control room revealed nothing. In the few ssecs between the time Niais had opened the door and Cyn had switched on the light, the plas sheets had been returned tidily, the drawers closed, and the intruder who had been occupied with them had disappeared. Entrance into the control room and close inspection of the walls would have revealed one unaccountable shadow moving without reference to any light source. Cyn's mumbled, "What?" made it pause and then move more swiftly and with less care toward the dark haven of the companionway.

The light induced no movement in the crouching second shadow beyond a mouth tightened over a flood of unvoiced obscenities. Things weren't going right, and he wanted to kill to relieve his tension. But his master had bid him obey the mouthing maniac, and that fool had said no killing. The mouth pursed a bit tighter. Well, the new one was mad, but maybe not a fool about the killing. They needed the pilot to land the shuttle, and even his master did not know which of the others it was—or whether the one on this ship was only another decoy. He had to bring them all back to his master. So—no killing.

But when they arrived he would demand the young blond one as a reward—she couldn't be the one his master wanted; she hadn't been on the passenger list. His mouth grew wet and spittle formed in the corners as he imagined the point of a very sharp knife scoring a thin, red line all around those high, young breasts. Then they could be peeled like ripe fruit . . . and the screams . . .

The shadow his eyes had sought all the while his mind made pictures, slid around the curve of the pilot's couch. His weapon rose smoothly. The shocked incredulity of Cyn's, "How did you get in?" made the first shadow jerk around. Without thought, the second pressed the firing stud. The mouth tightened with chagrin, but there was no time to wait for that slow creeper to get out the door. The weapon remained correctly aimed as the shadow rose, but there was no need to fire again.

Swift as thought the patient waiter sprang into action. He darted across the band of light coming from Cyn's bedroom so swiftly that, even had Cyn been watching instead of staring stupidly at Niais and asking how she had opened the door, he would have seen only a flickering change of intensity in the light. The shadow's teeth bared at this success. He would manage without that crazy "electronic genius" his master had forced him to partner. He had watched, and the thief, now lying unconscious, had opened the door for him. He had not needed the madman's devices. And the thief would believe the pilot had done the stunning.

Niais blinked at Cyn's stupid question, then said kindly and slowly so that Cyn would be sure to understand her. "I slid it back. All the doors in the ship open the same way."

The clear young voice was both a curse and a blessing to the shadow that now hung over the navigation console. It covered the faint click as a journey-button was pressed into its slot, but it also told the pilot what would galvanize him into action. Still, the meddler needed only thirty ssecs and the pilot was half asleep. The fact that he had never done this before did not trouble him. His "genius" partner, who was so clumsy it would have taken him ten smins to perform, even though he knew exactly what he was doing, had built a mockup for him. He had practiced on it until he could perform the necessary actions swiftly and correctly, even when drugged or drunk.

Only, the shadow suddenly realized, it was impossible to do what was necessary with a weapon in his hand. Reluctantly, snarling with impotent rage, he laid his weapon down on the console. He had wanted to stun the pilot before he began to change the route, but the "genius" had forbidden it, insisting it would be much better if no one knew what they had done until they arrived at their destination. That way the other passengers would be perfectly docile and five people, three of whom might be very dangerous, would not need to be watched or confined. He had to accept it; he himself knew it was impossible to keep everyone stunned until they arrived. They needed the pilot conscious in case of emergency—space was not kind to the ignorant—and repeated stunning of the others could end in death or brain damage, which the master would disapprove.

One did not flirt with the master's disapproval. Punishment or death was the result of that. His lips moved as he recited what he had learned by rote and his fingers moved over the switches and buttons of the navigation panel. With his left hand he pushed up and held a toggle switch to release a lock and with his right he keyed the command that not only cancelled but erased the present instructions to the navigation equipment. The released toggle went back down. Again fingers and lips moved, another lock was released, a single key depressed. The navigation system was now bound to the new journey button.

An audible breath sighed out of the shadow. Now that his purpose was accomplished, he was less concerned about being caught. Unlike the "genius," he was quite sure of his ability to control five people. The relief he felt about locking in the new course made him give one more moment to take a deep breath and glance at the console—and undid him. Just as his hand reached out toward his weapon, the Pot, obedient to its new commands, shuddered—with near violence because of their proximity to the carrollpause—into Carroll's void. Thrown off balance a step back and another to the left, his groping fingers touched the console cims for the weapon they sought. At that moment, a human missile hit him, driving him sideways into the band of light. He was a shadow no longer.

Mortchose was a professional killer and at the top of his field because he enjoyed his work. He could kill efficiently—swiftly or very slowly—with almost any weapon in existence. But he was a killer, not a fighter; to fight without killing placed constraints on him that greatly diminished his efficiency. Cyn, on the other hand, had brawled his way out of most of the low-class drinking houses on half the planets of the rim. He had fought humans with and without weapons, spiders who threw webs, multipods with tentacles (with and without suckers and/or weapons), amoeboids that enveloped, worms that stung—if it lived and breathed oxygen he had probably tangled with it. He knew no niceties of technique, no refinements of blows. He fought with nails and teeth, with fists, elbows, and straight fingers, with knees and heels and toes.

They were not unevenly matched, the trained killer and the experienced brawler—except for one thing: Cyn was naked as a jaybird. The momentary advantage surprise had given him evaporated quickly. He got in one good bang of Mortchose's head against the edge of the console, but missed breaking his nose. Then the little round male was able to twist away and straighten up. Cyn gouged at eyes and nostrils. Mortchose tried to chop, but remembered they could all be dead without the pilot and pulled the blow so that it had little effect. He ducked in close to grapple where Cyn's greater height would hold no advantage. Cyn knew some good holds himself, but his bare feet suffered too much in infighting. And his shoeless state was a serious handicap in other ways. As he broke free, he launched a kick that connected with

Mortchose's knee. Had Cyn been shod, he would have broken the kneecap and that would have ended the fight. As it was, the killer shrieked with pain and spat filth—but he did not fall.

"Lights!" Cyn shouted. "Turn on the lights."

The words terminated in a gasp. Mortchose had not been slowed as much by pain as Cyn expected. He had aimed a blow at Cyn's middle that would have felled him had he not turned so that it glanced off his side. Cyn kicked and caught Mortchose again, but only on the shin, not on the already sore knee. The move brought him too close and he took another glancing blow on the ribs, countering with a roundhouse swing that clipped the side of his opponent's head. The lights went on.

Cyn caught a single glimpse of Niais, standing at the entrance to his quarters, with her arms wide apart—the package held firmly in her right hand. He caught a glimpse of something else, something moving—then reeled from another blow on his left side, staggering to the right. As he dodged the follow-up attack, he realized Mortchose was trying to drive him away from the console.

Ducking straight down beneath a chop at his head, permitted Cyn to see the stunner lying near the navigation panel. "Get the stunner," he yelled as he launched himself up out of his crouch, driving Mortchose back, away from the console.

He almost missed that time. Little, fat Mortchose was a lot faster than his rotund form hinted but not quite as fast as Cyn. The pilot's long arm did catch Mortchose as he was in the act of dodging sideways, and when Cyn's desperate fingers gripped, the added momentum dragged the killer down.

The maneuver was Cyn's undoing, however, because he went down too—underneath. As he fell, he saw Niais, her package back under her left arm, obediently inching toward the console. She would never make it, he thought—and what did it matter? That child had no more idea of how to use a stunner than the stuffed bird on Rocam's hat.

Sobbing with effort, Cyn forced a hand upward, groping for Mortchose's nostrils, but it was already too late. One of the killer's hands had found his throat, a knee was pressing into his groin. The lightnings and fireworks of pain were starting to dim as Cyn whirled down toward unconsciousness when a singularly unpleasant wet "thunk" touched the edge of his receding awareness.

The lancepoints of agony in throat and groin withdrew abruptly to be replaced by a heavy sensation of suffocation. Instinctively, Cyn heaved. A weight rolled off him. Air whistled into his lungs.

Applying an ungentle foot to Mortchose, she continued, "I'm sorry I can't say the same about the damage to this whatever-it-is."

Cyn's vision cleared to show Aimie, hair lacquered to its usual perfection and clad in a dead black, but still quite exquisite, jumpsuit, staring down at the weapon she had used to subdue Mortchose. It was an oddly shaped, soft/hard plastic object filled with a viscous fluid that, in ordinary circumstances, moved continuously to display beautiful, ever-changing, coruscating colors. Just now the liquid was oozing slowly from a deep dent, becoming colorless as it came in contact with the air.

"Thank you," Cyn croaked, putting a hand to his abused throat.

"I'm sorry I can't say the same about the damage to this whatever-it-is," she continued, applying an ungentle foot to Mortchose.

With considerable effort, Cyn rolled over and levered himself to a sitting position. Dazedly he looked around. Niais had reached the stunner and was holding it. Aimie was examining him with detached interest. Mortchose was snorting on the deck. He passed a hand over his face, which for once had not taken much damage. He knew he had palm-locked the door and yet there was nearly a convention going on in his control room.

"How did you get up here?" Cyn asked Aimie.

"My sensor box recorded someone in the rec room, so I got up to look. I saw the control room door was open, but earlier I had seen you palm-lock it—so I came up." Her eyes met his squarely as she spoke, holding no shadow of the flat lie she had told or that she carried an override for any lock on an OM ship. To distract him, she thrust the object she held nearly into his face. "What is this thing?"

"A book," Cyn replied, after swallowing experimentally. "At least, we think it's a book of children's stories. Perhaps it's a reading primer or some other elementary text. But for all I know it could be a pair of shoes or a portable stove. It's very difficult, from what the White Worms say, to figure out what anything they have is. They don't mean to be obscure— I don't think. It's simply that the way they think is so alien— though they understand Trade quite clearly."

"The White Worms of Kyssyssk?" Aimie breathed. "Artifacts from their world are costly. I'm very sorry to have broken it. I had no idea."

"It doesn't matter," Cyn said. He had got to his knees and was busy removing Mortchose's clothing, which he had slit from neck to crotch with a knife pulled from the killer's belt. "Lystris can pick up another for me next trip." He looked up at her and smiled. "It's a cheap price to pay for being alive. I was fond of it, but I'm fonder of breathing." He pried open Mortchose's mouth.

Aimie had quirked a questioning brow at his mention of

the Free Trader ship, but she was distracted. "What are you doing?"

Cyn felt around, extracted two teeth with circumspection, ran his fingers through Mortchose's hair, hissed with satisfaction, and removed a small coil of wire that looked remarkably like the hair.

"I'm disarming him, I hope," he replied. "From what I've found so far, I'd say he was a professional killer and he probably has ten more toys hidden or implanted in him." He found another knife, clear as glass, in a skin sheathe and he sat back and sighed. "I'm kidding myself. I'll never find everything." He looked over his shoulder. "Niais, bring me that stunner."

She came forward, holding out the weapon, a distinct expression of disapproval marring the normal exquisite blankness of her face. "I wish," she said plaintively, "that you would stop fooling around with all these other people. You promised to deal with me when you weren't busy."

Aimie raised a brow, but Cyn merely blinked. He had learned his lesson. He was not going to get involved in another argument with that lovely nitwit, especially not about so slippery a concept as whether what he said when he sent her out of the control room a sday?—two sdays? he was losing count—earlier had implied a willingness to entertain her at some other time.

"I wasn't fooling around," he said severely, taking the stunner and checking the adjustment. He subdued a brief temptation to scramble Mortchose's brain permanently. The authorities might want to question the killer in the future. "He was trying to kill me," he added.

The disapproval deepened on Niais's face. "A lot of people try to kill you," she said. "That isn't nice."

Aimie made a small choked sound. Niais looked at her

questioningly. "You're quite right," Aimie said hastily and with commendable gravity. "But Mortchose isn't a nice male, and he might try to kill someone else too."

"But you aren't going to burn him or kill him back, are you?" Niais asked anxiously. "That wouldn't be—"

"No," Cyn interrupted, feeling that if she said "nice" again he might kill *her*. "I'm going to put him to sleep for a while." Having adjusted the stunner to the maximum that would do no permanent damage, he suited the action to the words. Then he looked up at Aimie. "I wish I could be sure he hasn't been conditioned to resist these things."

"If you want to lock him up, you can put him in my cage," Niais suggested brightly. "It's quite comfortable and strong too."

"Cage?" Aimie asked.

Cyn shrugged. Aimie would figure it out by herself in a smin or two. "Niais was the 'beast' shipped in the big cage you saw brought onto the shuttle."

A ssec's widened-eye disbelief was followed by an equally brief expression of unholy amusement and an almost subvocal mutter of, "I can see why." Then Aimie regained control of herself.

"It might work," Cyn remarked thoughtfully. "The cage has a fairly large mechanical lock. He might have micro weapons or tools concealed in his body, but I would have found anything big enough to pick a mechanical lock. And I'll turn him over to the authorities on Mantra." Then he frowned and shook his head. "No, I can't be sure he's traveling alone and I don't dare lock the shuttle from the inside. It's the only escape craft. That means if he has a partner, whoever it is could get in, pick the lock, and let him loose."

"Freeze him down," Aimie suggested. "He can't be conditioned against that."

"I suppose I'll have to." Cyn still looked troubled. "There isn't any way to lock the medic compartment, but an alarm will go on up here if the freezer goes off once it's been set. I'd be able to get down there and stop anyone before he could be revived; that takes time." He nodded. "The freezer it is."

He started to bend to grab Mortchose just as the automatic navigator emitted a beep, the ship came out of Carroll's void, and the real-space engine warning sounded. But acceleration did not follow; the engines did not fire, a plaintive, repeated beeping came from the navigation panel, and a red light began to flash. Cyn turned to stare at the console.

"I don't believe it!" he exclaimed. "I went over those calculations three times and had the navigator make a map for confirmation."

He got to his feet, groaning softly as his maltreated body complained, and limped over to look. Then he spat an oath as he remembered the position of the stunner. Mortchose had not come up to kill him and take over the ship—all he had in hand was a stunner. Mortchose had been working at the console!

In ssecs Cyn's practiced hands had exposed the journey button Mortchose had inserted. He swallowed, keyed a query, and stared hopefully at the display screen. It remained stubbornly blank. Cyn swallowed again. The fool had wiped out the navigator's memory rather than storing it. Cyn rubbed his eyes, stared at the blank screen chewing his lip, then keyed another sequence. The single word NUL appeared.

"What's wrong?" Aimie asked from the other side of the pilot's couch.

"We have accomplished the impossible," Cyn snarled. "We're lost in space."

CHAPTER 10

"That's ridiculous!" Aimie said, suddenly slapping open a pocket Cyn would never have suspected in the tight jumpsuit, and pushing a thin card the size and shape of an ident into the reader.

"Don't—" Cyn began warningly, then went white.

He didn't move, however. There was something small but very dangerous looking in Aimie's hand. To Cyn's surprise, for he had assumed—Security or no—she intended to steal his ship—an identification picture flashed onto the screen. The puter clucked and whispered. The screen went blank, the card popped out of the slot. Cyn drew a breath. Now he knew what she was, though he had never actually seen one of those programmers before. The device worked through the reader; it was duralloy, not plas, and word was that those little items had really nasty self-destruct mechanisms, which were almost equally destructive to anyone who was not its DNA-keyed owner and tried to handle it.

"In the name of the Empress," she said, "this ship is mine."

The screen went blank, the duralloy program card popped out of the reader slot, and the single world **CONFIRMED** flashed on and off. Cyn trembled with rage; his Pot had been brainwashed and would now respond only to commands given when the duralloy card was slotted, and it was timed to eject randomly.

"It's impossible to be lost in space," Aimie repeated. "You are in trouble, pilot."

Cyn burst into angry laughter. "Frefem, if you don't like the word 'lost,' that's fine with me. Let me put it this way. I don't know where we are. If you do, all you have to do is set a course for anywhere you like. If you don't but you can navigate and run this ship, you are in trouble and I will cheerfully take to my bunk. If you can't navigate, then *we* are in trouble."

"You have," Aimie said, "a remarkably nasty point."

Cyn met her eyes levelly for a moment, adding up that phrase, "In the name of the Empress" with the near-admission that she could not navigate. His rage began to fade. The combination almost precluded her being involved in the ship disappearances, which meant, despite taking over the ship, she was not the one trying to steal it, and he could still trust her—within reason.

"But how did we get lost?" Cyn muttered. He turned quickly, having completely forgotten the weapon Aimie held, then froze with his hand stretched over the button and looked back at her. The short, ugly snout was no longer peeping from her fist. "Is it possible that that fool didn't know a journey button is only good from one particular system? Could the button he had have been programmed from Healtha and jumped us clear out of Empire space?"

"Can you find out?" Aimie asked. "The puter showed me a star plot from Healtha to Xiphe."

Cyn stared. She really didn't know anything about navigation. "Those were jumps I calculated. The puter can't read a journey button. If it could, I'd have checked the OM buttons and saved myself a lot of work."

He wasn't really thinking about what he said by the time

he finished. He was wondering what purpose there was to giving Aimie a device that would control the ship if she couldn't pilot it. It was barely possible that the problem of navigation might never have arisen before. Overstars Security was concerned with cheating, with illegal use of OM ships. Perhaps Aimie could get all kinds of information from a puter; she had certainly known how to read and check the Healtha to Xiphe route. Normally her inability to pilot wouldn't matter. Anywhere in Empire space she could just call for help; there were rescue crews, there were beacons, the Patrol would come—and as far as Cyn was concerned something still stank to fill space.

Part of Cyn's process of thought must have passed through Aimie's mind while he was speaking because instead of responding to what he said she suddenly asked, "We are still in Empire space—aren't we?"

"How could we be lost in Empire space?" Cyn retorted. "Didn't you see me try for a beacon—any beacon—and get nothing?" He was staring at the console, trying to figure out where to start. "How long did that fight last?" he asked, turning toward Aimie. "It seemed like a thousand years to me."

"What in the world does that matter?"

Cyn blinked at her ignorance. "It matters because that's how long we were in Carroll's void. Travel between carrollpauses is theoretically instantaneous, but because of certain parameters I don't understand, it actually takes a finite time. If I knew how long we were in the void, I might be able to calculate—"

"What do you mean, we're lost?" Niais asked suddenly.

Cyn had forgotten her completely. "It's all right," he soothed, forcing a smile. "We're in no danger. I'll find out where we are eventually. It's just—"

"But I have to go to Ingong!" she exclaimed.

"Yes, yes," Cyn assured her. "You'll get to Ingong. I'm only trying to make sure you get there on time." He turned his attention back to Aimie. "Now, it couldn't have been more than five ssecs or less than two between the time we entered the void and the time I jumped him. That's—"

"How do you know when you enter and leave this void you keep talking about?" Niais asked.

Her alabaster brow was slightly creased and Cyn thought she must be trying to figure out whether or not it was important to arrive on Ingong at a particular time.

"The ship shivers—shakes itself, sort of," Cyn replied absently, and lifted his hand to look at his chrono. He was not wearing it, but the bareness of his wrist suddenly brought to his attention the bareness of the rest of him and the fact that, though he had been warm enough while fighting, standing still and thinking was much chillier work.

"Sorry," he said shortly to Aimie with a gesture at his bare body because he had no idea whether nudity was taboo in her cultural background. Certainly, he thought with an untimely spark of humor, it would be abhorrent to her in her cover identity as a fashion salesperson. "I'll go get some clothes on."

A slow smile, different from the practiced, polite rictus that often appeared on her face, curved her lips. "It would be safer and warmer," she agreed, "but I was enjoying the view."

"Thank you," Cyn said gravely, but he couldn't help grinning as he turned away. He had found the answer to one question often propounded in drinking-houses patronized by OM employees. He was sure now that Security was not totally staffed with robots. He had plenty of evidence that Fr. Aimie was a living fem.

Before he had reached the door of his quarters, Niais said,

"The time between the two shivers was seventeen Healtha mins and a little less than half a min more. I cannot come closer than that."

Cyn and Aimie both turned and gaped at her. She looked from one to the other, her eyes vacant of thought, smiling, eager to please.

"Honey," Cyn said softly, "don't make things up. It could be dangerous. You aren't even wearing a chrono."

Niais blinked and a vague trouble misted her eyes. "I never make things up," she said, her voice flatter than usual. "It is a failing in me. I have no imagination." Her gorgeous smile wiped out the trouble. "But I have perfect pitch and perfect time sense and perfect directional sense. You can check me. It is now three forty-two Healtha time."

Bemusedly, Cyn came back and glanced at the ship-time chrono. Before he had to ask, Aimie had slipped her card into the slot—but the weapon had appeared again in one hand and the other hovered over the reject button of the reader. Cyn asked the puter for Healtha time; 3:42:27 appeared. Considering the delay, that was close enough.

"Good for you, Niais!" he exclaimed.

At least he had a point from which to work. A seventeen-smin sphere from Xiphe's star was a more reasonable area to consider than the entire galaxy. Cyn took a deep breath, pushing away fatigue and the aches of his misused body. First clothes, then the disposal of Mortchose, and then, if Aimie was willing to trust him—Cyn eyed the navigation console with a jaundiced eye—more calculations.

When he returned to the control room with his coveralls and boots on, he went directly to the console.

"It won't work," Aimie reminded him.

"The av will," he said, calling it to life.

She made no effort to stop him as he began a scan of the

146

passenger level. "What are you looking for?" she asked, as the screen showed only darkness and silence.

"To see if anyone is awake. I'd just as soon not have the others notice where I store Mortchose—unless you want to keep him here and hit him on the head again every time he stirs."

She didn't answer, waiting patiently for him to be satisfied. Cyn was surprised not to feel more resentment, but Aimie's manner was so neutral that he found himself accepting her right to check what he was doing. In fact, as his muscles stiffened and his aches increased, he resented far more being unable to permanently scramble Mortchose's brain. He reminded himself that it might be important for the authorities to probe that brain, but even after he sent Niais firmly back to her own cabin, dragged Mortchose to the lift with Aimie's help, and got him frozen down, an uneasy foreboding hung over him.

He soon discovered that the "impending doom" did not arise from their position in space. Although Overstars provided only the crudest star maps outside the Empire—marking either inhabited or dangerous planets so that a ship with a malfunctioning navigation system or journey button would know what to head for or to avoid—Cyn soon found that their position probabilities were limited. On three-quarters of the seventeen-smin sphere there was no position in which his beacon finder would give a NUL response.

Even one-quarter of the sphere was a very large area, but at least they were still well within the galaxy and he was not faced with the fear of jumping the ship into the intergalactic void. No matter what heading he chose—if Niais was correct in her time estimate—some carrollpause would bring the Pot back into true space. Cyn manipulated the map so that the ship was the center point of the most probable quarter and requested jump time to each nearest star.

He was in luck again. The only jump times that corresponded to within one smin were those for a planet in a two-sun system populated by highly civilized chlorine breathers and a giant red sun where the one planet habitable by oxygen breathers was filled with beasties it was better not to meet. Cyn wasn't worried about either the chlorine atmosphere or the beasties because he had no intention of landing in either system; he was simply pleased that the systems couldn't be confused. Each of the other carrollpauses was sufficiently time differentiated so that no matter when the ship came into true space, he would know just where they were.

Not that one jump was likely to take them to any of the systems shown on the Overstars map. Overstars listed only systems that could be helpful or must be avoided at all costs, even in an emergency. Many stars with no planets or with dead or uninhabitable planets, or even unrecorded stars, might intervene between his position and any of those shown, but again, the jump times were unlikely to coincide; and if they did, he hoped he would know from the system characteristics that he was in the wrong place.

Cyn tucked the printout of nearest-star jump times under a paperweight, sighed, and started the whole process over for fifteen- and nineteen-smin spheres. It should make no difference, of course; nearest stars to the center—in this case the Pot's position—should remain nearest stars for any size sphere, but it was a good check on his earlier calculations and the nineteen-smin sphere still showed them reassuringly distant from intergalactic space. The main reason for the effort was less any doubt of Niais's time sense than a rigid training in an "I tell you three times" philosophy.

Aimie had been watching from the second recliner, rising to reinsert her ident whenever the card was ejected without any comment, but when he compared all three results, patted the console kindly—as if the puter were a sentient creature that had behaved very well and deserved reward—she said, "You really can navigate, can't you."

Cyn, who had almost forgotten her, except for cursing her abstractedly every time his console shut down, swung his seat around. "I got from Healtha to Xiphe."

"Yes, you did." She lifted one delicately arched brow. "But I'm afraid I don't believe you learned what you were doing in any Overstars training class."

He laughed. "Well, no, but it only takes a little common sense and really listening to what they say in the training sessions."

"Really? I'm not a complete fool and I assure you I listened hard, but I couldn't have done it."

"Yes you could, anyone could," Cyn said irritably. "It's tedious but not difficult." Then in response to her cold stare, he shrugged. "It might have taken you a swik to dig the equations and methods out of the puter—which I didn't have to do—but they *are* there and our class was told they were there. I was quicker at it because my training was shuttle pilot on Lystris, and that made me responsible for the escape craft and emergency ship's pilot—as well as maid-of-all-work, of course."

"Ah, yes. Your record said you were bred a Free Trader, and you've spoken about Lystris." Her voice was cold, then suddenly she blinked and cocked her head to one side. "Have you kept up your contacts with your old ship?"

Cyn's eyes opened wider. "Of course. My mother and father, my whole family, are Lystris."

"And you, are you still Lystris? Can you prove it?"

All expression was gone from Aimie's face, and her voice was so neutral that Cyn couldn't guess whether he would be clearing some doubt or confessing to some "crime" if he admitted he was still part of Lystris. Then rage flashed over him again. Loving Lystris was no crime; he would not deny he remained her son.

"You bet I can prove I'm still in Lystris."

He got up and walked to the desk. From a drawer he drew a folder of plas sheets—the same ones Aimie had extracted earlier and had no time to examine. These he shoved at her. Like all carrolled messages, they were time, date, and place stamped. All were the kind of personal messages one keeps for sentimental reasons—birthday greetings, notices of life matings and the birth of new shipcrew, thanks for gifts received. The last message was stamped less than two swiks earlier, from Baltor, Cyn's port of call before Healtha—a notice that Fersis, sib/kin, had transferred from Lystris to Sotoyna for mating.

Aimie shuffled through the pile and saw that they went back the full five years. There was even a farewell and good luck in your new ship from the entire crew of Lystris on the date that Cyn completed training and was assigned a ship of his own. She looked up at him, allowing puzzlement and a touch of amusement to show on her face.

"Do you mean to tell me that you really did come to Overstars because you wanted secure employment?"

More puzzled than angry himself, now that she had not leapt accusingly on his bond with his mother ship, Cyn frowned and said, "Yes, of course it's true. I told the recruitment officer that I was tired of wondering which of my clients would try to eat me. I just hated working in full armor in poisonous atmospheres. And I wanted to be able to enjoy myself when I did get dirtside. What's so strange about that?"

"Overstars Security didn't believe you," Aimie said. "Free Traders are a small group among our mail-carriers, but they are well known and fairly predictable. You seemed to fit the pattern well. Overstars psychological testing determined that you were of a 'loner' nature. That type is known to get into serious trouble in the close interpersonal conditions of Free Trader ships, but is often perfect for Overstars duty. After OM determined you weren't a criminal, Security's conclusion was that you had been exiled from your ship for—"

"Exiled!" Voice and expression showed Cyn's panic at the thought. "No!"

His horror did as much to convince Aimie of his continued attachment to the ship Lystris as the evidence of family fondness in the plas sheets, which he had snatched back from her as he exclaimed against what she suggested.

"I do like being alone," he admitted, his voice shaking, holding the folder of notes tight against him, "but I never got in trouble on Lystris. I'm not a quarrelsome type." Then he cried, "What the hell is this all about? What does Security want with me? I thought you were aboard because of the mail ships that disappeared. Is this personal? Am I in trouble because of my Trade deals?"

"Trade deals?" Aimie echoed, sitting up straighter.

"It's no crime to order Empire goods for my family and arrange for them to ship in goods from out of the Empire—like the artifacts from Kyssyssk—when I can find a dealer to take them. And it's nice for me because I make a commission both ways. I know damn well there's no rule in Overstars against what I've done. I researched that carefully." Watching Aimie's expression, Cyn began to relax.

"So that's the answer," Aimie said thoughtfully and nodded. "You're still a Free Trader, just taking a free ride in an OM ship."

"I do my job," Cyn said indignantly.

"I think you do," Aimie admitted. "But you're the first

case we've had where the bond wasn't broken with a lot of bitterness. No one ever checked because you did seem to fit the normal pattern—" she laughed aloud "—aside from being a little too honest. That was noted repeatedly on your record. You know, it's rare that a mail-carrier whose been in Free Trade doesn't carry illegal goods—"

"I don't!" Cyn snapped.

"No, you don't. No snooper's ever found a whisper or a smell of contraband on your ship." She paused and stared and went on slowly. "Then mail ships began to disappear and all of a sudden you were rich enough to pay for three sdays in the nymphs' Garden. To Security it was a foregone conclusion that you were spending the down payment you got for your ship."

"Me?" Cyn howled. "Me give up my Piss Pot?"

"Piss Pot?" Aimie repeated, sounding stunned. "Who cares about where you take a leak? I'm talking about this mail ship."

Angry as he was, Cyn had to laugh. "Didn't you ever look at an Overstars ship? Turn her upside down and you have—"

Aimie hiccupped. "A cradle for a titanic ass!" Her eyes widened, and then she shook her head. "Damn you! I'll never think of the ships as anything else and I'm sure to say it to just the wrong person." She lifted a brow and looked at him measuringly. "That was very funny, but the money for three sdays in the nymphs' Garden had to come from somewhere."

"Sure it did," Cyn said. "Doesn't Overstars check their own bank? I've had an account with them for five years."

"In Overstars Credit Central?" Aimie shook her head. "We did check, of course. There was about a thousand credits in that account."

Cyn laughed. "As of my takeoff from Baltor. That was

when everything went into a reserved account in the Healtha Banking Union."

Her expression didn't change, but she lowered her eyes and didn't answer immediately. Finally she said, "That's easy for you to say when there's no way for me to contact the Credit Union. Anyway, you couldn't have saved enough, even in the full five years, to pay for a visit to the nymphs."

Memory lit a brief flame in Cyn's pale eyes. "I didn't have quite enough," he admitted. "I'm in debt to Lystris right up to my eyeballs. But you can check. The records of all my Deals and my accounts are all in hard copy off the com. I never kept my personal accounts in the puter—because it wasn't mine, not because I knew you probed its brain. The plas are in the third drawer—and even you'll have to admit I didn't have time to fix those." A gesture toward his desk made her free of the contents. "Investigate away. All trading was in my own free time, and I've never carried cargo for Lystris on the Pot."

She reached down, but before she opened the drawer Cyn asked, "Do you want me to start looking for a known planet or should I go to bed while you check on me?"

"One smin," she said, and pulled a fire-resistant plastel box out of the drawer. "Key?"

"Why should I lock it?" Cyn asked irritably. "I don't expect to have Security checking my personal expenditures."

"You should when they're on nymph-Garden scale." She laughed. "I'm beginning to think Security needs to keep an eye on you to protect you, not Overstars. You're an innocent."

While Cyn stood openmouthed, she flipped the box open, looked at the top sheet, dug in and glanced at several randomly distributed through the substantial pile, then found the very bottom sheet with her fingers and pulled that out.

After that she examined the Credit Central statements, her eyes running over the numbers with a familiarity she had not shown with the puter. When she laid those records carefully down in the box, she stared out into space for a time. Suddenly her nose wrinkled in that felanthrop gesture of revulsion.

"Something stinks," she said.

"To fill space," Cyn agreed.

He had recognized the way she examined his accounts; she acted like the margin estimator on Lystris. So what was she doing with a puter-control card?

Aimie pushed the box a little way, got up, and went to the console where she carefully keyed a long string of numbers and symbols. The screen showed **WORKING**, then **QUERY**, to which Aimie responded with another string, which she keyed in very slowly and with what Cyn felt were timed pauses. The screen recorded **ACKNOWLEDGED** and the duralloy card was ejected. Aimie waited, watching the chrono, then reinserted the card, pushed the query key, and was rewarded by **RESTRICTED USE CANCELLED**.

"I didn't know you could do that," Cyn said, smiling.

She let out a long breath. "I wasn't sure I could, either. I've never done it before—either taken over a ship or returned it to normal use. That's what stinks. I'm trained for Security work, but mostly I'm an accountant."

Cyn whistled. "What happens if it doesn't work?"

Aimie laughed. "The ship doesn't blow up anyway. I think it sets off a kind of all-stations alarm for the Patrol."

"Maybe it would have been better if you messed it up," he said, and then added, "Can you set off an alarm—" and shook his head before he finished the sentence. "That would mean sitting here and waiting on the chance that some Patrol ship would pass close enough to pick up the signal." He sighed.

"Well? What do we do? Start searching for a known planet or try to yell for help?"

"You know more about out-of-Empire space than I do. What do you think?" she asked.

"I don't believe the com aboard this ship is strong enough to reach a Patrol vessel even on the rim of the Empire. But if the alarm taps other sources of power—"

"I have no idea. I doubt it. I suspect the program is designed to use the ship's ordinary com system for foiling a hostile pilot." She smiled suddenly. "I don't find you at all as hostile as I expected."

Cyn grinned. "I'll get mad later—again. Right now I don't have time. We try to find ourselves then?"

"Yes—because I don't have the vaguest idea how to trigger the alarm to Patrol anyway. It's supposed to go off by itself."

"Why did Security send you?" he asked. "If I had been paid to 'lose' the Pot, what could you have done about it?"

"I don't think—" she began, and then said, "Damn! We've been assuming that the journey button Mortchose put into the navigator didn't work—but what if it did? Ships can be boarded in space. Get those screens working! Is there a ship in the area? Maybe Mortchose expected to meet someone right here."

Cyn shook his head. "The puter being frozen doesn't affect the proximity alarms. Those are separate idiot circuits, like life support. There's nothing close enough to board us."

Still, to pacify her he set up an rs scan and showed her what to look for, but he was sure nothing, except possibly a piece of space debris, would appear. Cyn knew they had not arrived at the journey button's destination because of the 5.27-degree skew he had entered into the navigator. That was an override to all navigation, not part of a program, and therefore had not been erased when Mortchose wiped Cyn's calculated jumps from the navigation memory.

Though Aimie seemed trustworthy herself and apparently had decided to trust him, he was not in the least tempted to confess his corruption of the navigation equipment. Partly this was because she was OM Security and might take a dim view of his tampering with the navigator, partly because he had the uneasy feeling that their troubles weren't over. His star card in the hole was that the Pot would never arrive at any programmed destination, and he didn't want anyone else to be able to explain why.

Still, Cyn thought, a 5.27-degree skew shouldn't have taken them so far out of Empire space that a beacon would not show—unless Aimie was right and Mortchose's destination was outside the Empire. But why would anyone go outside Empire space? There were enough nonfederated planets inside Empire space, and enough federated planets with sufficiently corrupt governments that criminals were welcome. Criminals that stole mail ships? Possibly not, because that would be an Empire offense and bring Patrol or even the Navy to investigate.

While the thoughts ran through his mind and Aimie scanned the screens, Cyn completed his instructions to begin the jump to the nearest star. Space near them was still comfortingly empty when the ship quivered into Carroll's void with a gentleness that implied considerable distance from any solar system.

Aimie went back to the desk and sat with the open box of records before her, but she did not look at them. She watched Cyn attend to the readouts on the console and when he relaxed back into the recliner said, "What I started to say earlier when you asked why Security had sent me, was that . . . I don't think I was supposed to be successful at stopping the takeover, only at stopping you from interfering with it."

He swung around to face her. "What?"

"Look, I was told you had only about a thousand credits in your account. The implication was that a thorough investigation had been carried out and that the money used to buy you three sdays in the Garden was from a payoff."

"But that means that Security—"

"Is tainted," Aimie finished grimly. "Maybe only Security on Healtha, though. The clerk at Healtha recorded a 'suspicious action' warning. He didn't think an ordinary mail-carrier would have enough credit to pay for three sdays in the Garden. Usually that would have been forwarded to Security Central. Someone would have been assigned to check you and find out whether what you were doing to get the credit was detrimental to Overstars." She smiled. "We do overlook a peccadillo or two that aren't dangerous."

"But ships had been disappearing, so . . . Wait. Healtha Security could be innocent as babes. They couldn't take a chance on the ordinary slow process of notifying Central. They had to get someone to investigate the suspicious situation immediately."

Aimie nodded. "It would work either way. I was there. At Healtha, I mean. And the complaint was a question of unexplained funds. So I might have been assigned in all innocence. In fact, that was why I never questioned the assignment, although I was surprised when that puter-controller was issued. But I don't believe it!"

Aimie stared past him at the lights on the console, and Cyn turned quickly to scan them even though he suspected she was just thinking hard. When he looked back at her, her eyes had refixed themselves on the plastel box, which she slowly replaced in the open drawer. But Cyn was now acutely aware that the jump was unusually long for a single star-to-star hop.

He examined the Carroll system instruments, but progress through Carroll's void—if that wasn't a contradiction in terms—seemed to be normal. Seemingly they had emerged from the void not only outside the Empire but in a galactic hole of some kind.

"The orders I got," she went on thoughtfully, "aside from finding out where the credit came from—were, quote, 'to regard Pilot Cyn as a suspicious person and to prevent any unorthodox action that would interfere with standard operations.' Rightly, considering my ignorance, I should have stunned you in the shuttle, the smin you started yelling at us. And that would have put us right in the hands of the Healtha Planetary Police."

With half his mind on the long jump, the other half fixed on the implications of what Aimie was saying, Cyn just blurted out what was foremost in his mind. "And you should have taken over the ship before we got out of Healtha's carrollpause, right after I planet-hopped." He cocked his head to the side. "It was you that opened the palm lock, not Mortchose, wasn't it? He didn't have anything on him that could scramble the control."

CHAPTER 11

Aimie was saved from having to reply by the Pot, which chose that moment to shudder itself into real space and bleat for instructions. But Cyn had already realized her answer didn't matter, and he applied himself to his console, checking that all the programs were functioning properly. A small program called jump-chrono was counting ssecs of jump time. This stopped at the instant the Carroll system was cancelled, and the puter was comparing jump-chrono time against jump times for the entered list of nearest stars. When the NEGATIVE Cyn had expected appeared, he entered the brief code, which called up another series of programs—one of which negated the 5.27-degree skew—that started the jump procedure again. This would first move the ship in real space until it was sufficiently clear of the carrollpause to re-enter the void. Jump-chrono was set to start counting again automatically as soon as the Carroll system was engaged.

When he swung back to face Aimie, she shrugged. "I opened it. I wanted to have a look around and see if the puter would spill out anything. Most people use it for computations even if they don't store records in it. I see why you need to know. If Mortchose couldn't open the lock, it means he must have a partner aboard who could do it for him."

Cyn shrugged. "Not necessarily. Maybe other pilots don't lock off the control room, or Mortchose expected to get me to let him in on a pretext like sending a message and substitute his button for the one I was using. The thing that has me completely baffled, though, is that he's not a pilot."

"Are you sure?" Aimie asked.

"I'm getting so I'm not sure of my own name," Cyn said, "but I'll swear Mortchose is a hired killer and not too high class. First I thought that he had come up here to kill me and steal the Pot. But that can't be true. All he had in hand was a stunner. Admittedly he could have scrambled my brains with it—but he didn't even try. He never came near my bedroom. If he intended to pilot the Pot himself, it makes no sense for him to be fooling around with the navigation before killing me. Once I was dead, he'd have had all the time he needed to take the Pot anywhere."

"He didn't try to kill me either," Aimie remarked. "I saw him and didn't get the full charge, but I revived so fast he had to have the stunner set on low. But he didn't even stun you, so maybe he didn't want you even partly addled. Why send a man who can't pilot the ship he steals?"

"Pilots don't grow on trees," Cyn said. "If they're making grabs at many mail ships, maybe they're running out of pilots?"

Aimie snorted a laugh. "In an operation as expensive as this, buying pilots would be the least of the problems."

"I'm not so sure of that," Cyn said. "Most pilots prefer to look forward to years of legitimate work. This kind of job can't last very long. They'd have to find renegades. And even renegades like to know where they're going. Pilots aren't comfortable sticking in a journey button without being given a destination—and they tend to check up on where they are. Also, like your assignment, this whole thing may have developed in a hurry."

"What whole thing?" Aimie sighed. "That's what I want to

know. What are we mixed up in? What does anyone want a mail ship for?—let alone three or four mail ships."

"And every one of them headed for Mantra," Cyn muttered. "You're Security. You should know better than me."

"Every one headed for Mantra?" she repeated.

Cyn nodded. "I checked."

She didn't answer at once and then said, "I am beginning to get an idea. No, it's so impossible I'd rather not say just yet. But one thing's sure. I smell a triple set of books."

"Books?"

Aimie smiled at the complete puzzlement. "I don't know why, but the sum total of financial records of a business's activity—or a person's for that matter—is called a set of books. Legitimate enterprises keep only one set of books. Bent ones keep two sets—that's mostly what I deal with. And really crooked Deals are said to be covered by three sets."

"Why are we talking about business records?" Cyn asked somewhat plaintively. "Are you back to thinking about whether I'm honest?"

"No Trader is honest," Aimie said, grinning at him. "But I'm sure without doubt that whatever you sold, it wouldn't be the Pot. You're out of it. The lack of a pilot is beginning to make sense, though, if you consider that what Mortchose did might have been a second, third, or even a fourth backup plan."

"I don't like that."

She paid no attention to his remark. "I smell credits, exponential numbers of credits. Add it all up. First there was the tractor ship. Are you sure that was a drone?"

"No," Cyn admitted. "I just gave the simplest version. The other was more complex: Two PP ships were following us. Why two? It's possible that only one had been suborned and the other vaporized the tractor ship, so to speak, by ignorance."

"All right. That's the simplest attempt to grab the Pot and doubtless there would have been a pilot aboard the tractor ship to take over. If that failed, there was the first backup—the PP ship with dopey little me to force you to let them board. I'll bet a pilot would have been in the boarding party. That's two pilots."

"And there was the pilot on Xiphe," Cyn said.

Aimie giggled. "Someone is going to suffer for this. Do you realize the mountain of credit you've vaporized by always being one step ahead?"

"Very funny." Cyn's mouth twisted. "It's my balls they'll be readying nutcrackers for."

"No, this is too important. You and me they'll shoot dead as soon as they've got what they want. But I think that's why Mortchose is just an experienced thug. He was only supposed to keep us under control while the Pot was being taken over. The journey button was a last resort, to be used if all the other backups failed. And with two successes behind them, I don't suppose they thought it would get to that."

Cyn stared at her unhappily. "No one could afford to do that for every ship bound for Mantra. You're saying this particular ship was the target. But why? There's nothing aboard that anyone would make that kind of effort to get—" he hesitated and made a disgruntled moue "—except the passengers. One of them must be what they want. I swear," he sighed, "if I knew which one, I'd set him or her adrift with a beacon on."

"A passenger isn't the only possibility," Aimie pointed out. "You might be carrying a certain message going as plain ordinary mail so its importance wouldn't be suspected." She hesitated, then asked, "How much of what's going on in the Empire do you understand?"

"I'm not feebleminded," Cyn said.

"I never thought you were," she retorted smiling, "but Free Traders are notoriously indifferent to Empire politics."

"I'm not," Cyn admitted, then grinned. "I told you I liked my job. No Empire, no Overstars Mail. I know it rattles and creaks a bit, but I'd like to see the Empire hang together a while longer."

"Me too," Aimie said. "Did you know that the Emperor or Empress can be replaced by a vote of the Planetary Council if a challenger appears?"

"Challenger?" Cyn repeated. "You mean I could go before the Planetary Council and say I wanted to be Emperor and they'd have to listen to me?"

"Yes, but it wouldn't take them more than five ssecs to vote 'No' unanimously."

Cyn burst out laughing. "I don't believe that. Even an issue as open-and-shut as a challenge from a total misfit without experience, background, or any other claim would take them at least a year to decide—and even then the vote wouldn't be unanimous."

Aimie's mouth twisted; the Planetary Council was notable only for shilly-shallying, bribe taking, and histrionics meant for the home planet of the representative. "I meant they had to listen formally to the claim and formally deny it. There are qualifications, and the first is that as long as one of the current Empress's children is living, no one else's claim can be considered before that claim."

"But no member of the Imperial family is on the Pot," Cyn protested, suddenly realizing where Aimie's seemingly random change of subject was leading. "They all look so much alike, the Empresses could put on their makeup by looking at each other's faces."

"They don't look alike at all," Aimie retorted. "All you—or anyone else—ever sees is a solidograph of the first Emperor and Empress dressed in modern clothing." She laughed at his suddenly wide eyes.

"What an idiot I am," he said, shaking his head. "I should have noticed that they never got any older."

Aimie laughed. "You probably haven't been interested in them long enough to note changes of age." Then she sighed. "I guess they don't teach Empire history on a Free Trader. If they did, you might have remembered that the dynasty has changed a number of times. There have been successful challengers, even from nonhumanoid species, when no heirs were willing to serve."

"Nonhumanoid—" Cyn began, but Aimie shook her head.

"Not now," she said. "Right now the dynasty is homo sap."

Cyn groaned. Despite what Aimie had said about the Imperial family not looking much alike, he had been hoping there would be some hint of the distinctive image familiar to him—very tall, very slender, hairless, with ethereally delicate and beautiful features, the male hardly distinguishable from the fem. But if the current dynasty was homo sapiens . . .

"Powers that Be!" he exploded, "Fr. Rocam could be the Empress, and no one would know."

Aimie smiled. "It's not as bad as that. Lots of people must know what the Empress and Emperor look like. I doubt the solidograph is used in the privacy of the Imperial residence; carrying the projector around must be a nuisance. So the Imperials can't count on true anonymity and must travel with some guards. That leaves out Rocam."

"That's a relief," Cyn said sardonically, but before he could follow up with a question about Aimie herself being an Imperial sibling intending to challenge the Emperor, the ship came out of the void again. Aimie got up to look hopefully over Cyn's shoulder, but the screen showed **NEGATIVE** when the comparisons were run. Instead of going back to the desk, Aimie slid into the second recliner and raised it. And when Cyn turned away from the console after restarting the process of the search, she asked, "How long is it likely to take to find a known star?"

The slight amusement that had lingered on Cyn's face at the idea of Fr. Rocam being the Empress disappeared. "I wish I knew," he admitted. "From a couple of stus to almost a sday and a half standard. Why?"

"Because it seems to me I'd better get back to the passenger level and keep an eye on the medic compartment. It occurred to me that getting Mortchose stashed away quietly isn't a total solution. That little nitwit Niais heard us say we would put him in the freezer. What do you want to bet that the first person who mentions his name won't hear the whole story?"

"I hope she waited that long," Cyn said in a resigned voice. "I did tell her to stay in her own cabin until everyone was up, but I would take odds that she's hopped into someone's bed. There's no need to worry, though. The freezer alarm will wake the dead. We wouldn't be able to miss that going off. In any case, I'd rather you stayed here."

She met his eyes, one brow lifted. "Why?"

"Two reasons. I'll give you the nasty one first. I'm ninety-nine percent sure you want to get this ship safely to Mantra, like me, but if that freezer alarm goes off when you're down there, either you'd be dead or that one percent doubt would grow. If you stay up here and no one tries to revive him, we're home free. And if the alarm does go off—well, at least you and I will know we're on the same side—whatever that side is—and that we're in this together."

He looked at her challengingly, but got an approving smile instead of a burst of temper, which was a relief. "Anyway," he went on with a sigh, "I'm just about done in. Either you'll have to nurse the navigator for me or I'll have to put the search on hold until I get a couple of stus of sleep."

"How complicated is the navigation job?"

"Not at all. I'll set the console to state that it has reached a carrollpause instead of just beeping. When it does, you check to make sure the jump-chrono is off—if it isn't, you just get me. If it is, you wait until **NEGATIVE** comes up and you key in the Batch." He pointed to the symbols on a scratchboard beside the keyboard.

Aimie looked at the symbols and then at the keys and nodded. "What does it do?" she asked.

He smiled tiredly. "The Batch tells the navigator to start the jump procedure. First it fires the real-space engines and boosts to a distance from the carrollpause where entering won't jostle us too much, then it engages the Carroll system and restarts the jump-chrono simultaneously."

"That's a lot of instructions for a few symbols."

Cyn rubbed his face with both hands, pulling at his eyelids in the vain hope of relieving the feeling that his whole eyeball was coated with sharp grains of sand. "You know better than that," he said. "Each symbol calls up a whole program—and I didn't write the programs. They're standard navigation programs stored in every ship-puter and are listed in the OM manual. I know them by heart, but the manual's around somewhere and you can check."

He was so tired that he had forgotten one of the symbols was for a program he had written himself—the correction of the 5.27-degree skew. As it was, his weary indifference carried perfect conviction.

Aimie nodded. "Anything else?"

"If you get a **POSITIVE**, don't touch anything. Just call me."

He started to slide the console over to her couch, stopped it midway, and pointed out the av panel with its own screen and a small, separate keyboard. When he flipped the ON switch, the screen showed the rec room. He began to show her the controls.

"Don't bother," she said, smiling. "There isn't any av I can't handle. I may be mostly an accountant, but I was trained in Security techniques."

Cyn nodded acceptance; Security should be expert with av systems. "Oh," he said, gritting his teeth over a yawn, "I fixed the av so it couldn't be turned off anywhere." Aimie grinned without comment and Cyn realized she had noticed—that was why she had had the no-see-no-hear on in her cabin. "You might want to monitor," he suggested.

She laughed aloud at that. "It's right up my line."

With considerable relief, Cyn allowed himself to fall back on the recliner and stretch out as it unfolded. His head was turned toward the console though, and he saw the door of the medic compartment slide past as Aimie manipulated the videyes. As his eyes closed, he muttered, "Freezer alarm . . . loud bell and light on top . . ."

"I found it," she said. "Go to sleep."

An insistent hand and voice forced Cyn to unglue sticky eyelids. The expletive drawn from him as he moved his stiffened and bruised body to sit up was not fit for a lady's ears, but Aimie did not blanch. She said only that she couldn't keep awake any longer and told him that he had had six stus of sleep. When he had dragged himself back from the fresher and got himself a caff and a sweet roll, she pushed the console back to his couch.

"The passengers started asking questions during the second meal," she said, putting up a hand to smother a yawn.

"I identified myself as Overstars Security and told them that Mortchose had attempted to take over the ship and had been placed under restraint. Believe it or not, no one knew a thing and Niais sat there with her eyes and mouth open as if it were the biggest surprise to her. Do you think she's mind-damaged and has no memory or is a lot smarter than either of us?"

"Maybe neither," Cyn replied, almost echoing her yawn. "The nymphs never pass information from one client to another—I suppose they might use what they were told for their own purposes, but I've never heard that anyone else could get intelligence information from a visit to the Garden. Not passing information may be ingrained in Niais. If so, we're lucky and the others may not know where we've stashed Mortchose."

"Nice if we had one piece of luck this trip. I haven't been monitoring much—too nervous about getting the inputs right and not missing some danger signal—but no one seemed to be doing anything unusual when I did check." She sighed and pointed to the scratch pad lying on the console. "I wasn't sure whether you'd need that, but I made a list of the jumps and the travel times between jumps."

By the time Cyn had examined the list out of curiosity—the number of jumps they made before they reached a known star was not really important—she was fast asleep. Over the next seven stus, Cyn made fewer jumps, extending the time of real-space travel so that the Pot could slide into the void with almost no vibration. Whether it was the smoothness of the transits, which avoided sharp reminders that the journey was not normal, or whether Aimie's explanation and authority had cowed them, Cyn had no trouble with the passengers. They did not try to call him on the av, and when he scanned the rec room and cabins, they were all engaged in innocent—if one stretched the meaning of the word as applying to

Niais—and normal activities.

The only thing that troubled Cyn at all was that he felt almost as sore and tired as if he hadn't slept. He caught himself dozing off several times, when the navigator had to beep repeatedly for his attention, so after Aimie woke and they had eaten, he asked if she could manage alone again.

"I'm sorry," he said. "I wouldn't be much company anyway."

She frowned at him. "I don't mind punching the keys or my own company, but are you sure you shouldn't step down and let the medic run over you?"

"Maybe later, after everyone's asleep," he said, then smiled as her frown grew more intense. "And I'm not being a tin-badge hero. I know nothing's broken and I don't have the deep kind of pain that might mean internal injury. Remember, I didn't get any sleep after we left Xiphe. I was working out jumps to Mantra."

Aimie chuckled. "Oh, yes, and before that three sdays in the Garden and a night with Niais. No wonder you're worn out, poor thing. By all means, go take another nap."

More at ease with her navigation duties, Aimie spent some time going through Cyn's desk and records, which confirmed what she expected. She spent considerably more time looking for hiding places, but she found no secret panels or drawers— not surprising because there weren't any. She did see the extra relay box, but since it was indistinguishable from all the others behind that panel did not recognize it as significant (which was what Cyn had intended) and thus did not find the High Code decoder. She was thorough and efficient, even though she liked Cyn and did not expect to discover anything. Periodically, to keep herself fresh, she interspersed her search of the control room with monitoring the passengers, attaching to the av several different instruments from her shoulder bag, which she had brought up from the passenger level after she had helped Cyn put Mortchose in the freezer.

When the passengers had their third meal, she drew hers from the desk autochef, watched their faces, and listened to their conversation. It told her nothing new. Hachisman was a nervous Nelly; Fr. Rocam was altogether too calm for an elderly lady on a space flight that had already provided a number of unexpected thrills; Wakkin seemed utterly absorbed in Niais, who still clung to her package—which Aimie thought she would like to examine more closely; and Demoson appeared to be a workaholic totally devoted, in the privacy of his cabin, to a small puter, which she would also like to examine.

She continued to monitor even after everyone retired to bed. Once, she almost woke Cyn: Rocam's door opened surreptitiously, the old lady slipped out, and there was a brief dark flicker in the av. Aimie's eyes flew to her own instruments, but no sign of electronic disturbance showed. And Rocam only walked around the rec room in the dark for a while, waving her arms and whispering to herself. She touched nothing, not even the autochef, before she went back to bed. Still, for a while Aimie watched the av screen alertly, shifting from the rec room to each cabin, but she could detect nothing wrong so she decided let Cyn sleep. And then the Pot shivered itself out of Carroll's void.

Within ssecs of the gentle shiver, another door opened, but Aimie was busy checking the chrono and starting the program again. She had no eyes for the shadow that slipped along the wall, across the corridor to the shuttle, and clapped a device over the door control into the medic compartment. Inside, the shadow moved toward the faint in-use light on the bottom freezer compartment.

A different device was fitted over the control panel and a very faint whine sounded momentarily as thin wire probes passed along the sides of the **ON/OFF** switch and linked so that the warning device was caught in a loop that said the freezer was **ON**. More probes reached from the device to the temperature sensors and accepted their feedback, sending a steady repeat of their original signal to the output failsafe of the freezer. Now the shadow reached for the **REVIVE** controls. Its hand dropped once, but then reached out again and began the process of warming Mortchose into life.

Almost sixty smin later, the Pot shuddered again as it left real space and re-entered Carroll's void. There was no sign now of any tampering with the freezer; the in-use light glowed and a fine mist of frost obscured the vision panel. However two shadows now occupied the medic compartment. One, bending over, urged the other to his feet the moment the vibration began, muttering intensely, "Come now. You can rest in my cabin, but we have to go while the pilot is checking that we're safely back in the void."

The door of the compartment slid only wide enough for a hand to emerge and press a button on the device over the door control. For the few ssecs it took to get to the cabin door, every electronic device on the passenger level repeated the signals it had been giving before the button had been pressed. Mortchose was pushed roughly inside the cabin, and the shadow retraced its steps, pressed the button again, and lifted the device from the door. For the instant of detachment, everything went dead. When the device was loose, normal operation of the electronic systems began again. The shadow slid quickly back to the cabin.

"Into the bunk."

Mortchose was shoved, then rolled to his side so the other could slide in beside him. It was a tight fit but the av in the room would show only the outer body.

"I've told you everything I know." The voice was so low it could not carry past Mortchose's ear, which the lips nearly touched. "You'll have to find out where we are and get the pilot to take us to the base. And you don't know me. No matter what happens, you don't know me. And I won't try to help you. That way, if something else goes wrong, we'll still have a chance. Understand?"

"You haven't been that much help to know." The words slurred, but Mortchose's voice was no louder than the other's.

"I got you out of the freezer as fast as I could. They're watching, and I had to patch together that circuit baffler for the freezer. You won't be able to get to the control room through the door this time. You'll have to get in through the lift. As soon as we drop out of the void again the pilot will be busy for a few smins and we can get into the shuttle. I can cover that and give you something to open any locks, but the only weapon I have is a blaster I've assembled. It—"

"I'll manage the rest. Don't worry."

"No killing. Remember, we don't know which one it is, and Fr. Aimie is Overstars Security so she'll have information we need. No killing."

Mortchose made a wordless sound and the other shuddered, but finally the killer nodded.

CHAPTER 12

Right after the Pot came out of the void again, a flicker of darker in dark drew Aimie's eye to the av. Almost simultaneously **POSITIVE** appeared on the navigation screen. Aimie wasted no time staring at what she thought must be a malfunction. Instead she looked at the total time on the chrono, grabbed for Cyn's list and then for the manual that lay near it. Her eyes widened, and she went to shake him awake.

This time when Aimie shook his shoulder, Cyn sat up, quickly alert. "I'm glad you're wide awake," she said. "Wait until you see what the nearest star is. I've looked it up."

Cyn pulled the console to his position. As he locked it in place, his eyes went from the **POSITIVE** to the jump-chrono time. He shook his head as he took in the total. From what Aimie had said, he was sure he could guess where they were, but he flicked on the external vision screens. Dim, but huge in the screen despite the distance, hung a swollen red orb. Somewhere not very far from its primary, although it was still invisible at this range, spun a doomed planet. What life remained on it hunted by heat seeking in the lurid light that gave no warmth, preying on each other.

"Par for the course," Cyn said.

"What does that mean?" Aimie asked, looking anxiously at the console. "Equal for what course? That doesn't make sense."

Cyn turned from the screen and smiled. "Old Free Trader cant. I think it comes from some ancient game. What it means is, 'I expected no better'—which is true with the luck we've been having this trip." He rubbed a bristly cheek and his tongue roamed his foul-tasting mouth. "Is there anything urgent or can I go wake myself up?"

"Nothing urgent," she replied. "At least the freezer alarm didn't go off."

"But something else?"

Aimie nodded. "Go ahead and clean up. I didn't think it was worth waking you about, so it can wait until you're ready."

"Right," Cyn said when he came back from the fresher, "let's hear the next installment of bad news."

"The first part you suspected already. Mortchose must have a partner aboard—or someone else isn't at all that he or she seems to be."

"A White Worm calling a slithian legless." Cyn laughed. "No one is what he or she seems to be this trip."

Aimie lifted her brows but didn't answer directly, merely saying, "Someone has bugs in all the cabins, and it isn't me."

Cyn merely nodded. He didn't ask how she knew, having seen the array of little boxes plugged into the av.

"The other thing is weird," Aimie continued. "I almost woke you, but . . . Rocam came out of her cabin. I saw her for a smin silhouetted against the light from her door before she shut it. She didn't turn on the light in the rec room, just walked around waving her arms and whispering to herself. There was an odd flapping noise, maybe her sleeves? And I thought that twice a shadow that wasn't her passed one of the pickups."

"Maybe you should have waked me," Cyn said, frowning.

Aimie shrugged. "She didn't touch anything. There was

174

no electronic activity at all. As far as Rocam herself, I thought she was just working off a fit of nerves. She's like solid rock when the other passengers are around, but a lot of people feel they have to put on calm in public. As far as the flapping and the shadows—they were gone so fast you wouldn't have seen anything anyway. And I'm not even sure now whether it was my eyes playing tricks—watching a shadow flapping its arms in a room lit by emergency buttons does tend to makes one see things. I am sure, though, it wasn't the shadow of a second person."

"How can you be sure of that?"

"I said weird. Whatever it was, if it was anything, was at the level of the pickup or above. Now those pickups are about head level on the wall so that the clearest view you get out of them is faces. I was watching the lower levels of the room, of course, to make sure no one was smart enough to come out of a cabin in a crawl. Then there was this—this black flick. Well, you know how the pickups are correlated through the puter to give one image—I could still see the floor clearly, without any shadow, but one area, high up, went dark for a split ssec."

"We can keep a close eye on Rocam."

"I guess so." Aimie sighed. "But let's not neglect anyone else. I'm not even sure the flickering shadow had anything to do with Rocam anyway because I think it happened again just after we came out of the void. Something caught my eye, but the **POSITIVE** came on the screen and I got kind of excited. When I looked again there was nothing. I may have seen that blacker flick again on the av out of the corner of my eye, or maybe the whole room went darker for a ssec, or maybe I imagined it."

Cyn frowned. "Could be a malfunction."

"I did glance at my instruments as soon as I was sure where we were and the av was working fine, but you know how intermittents are. If you don't catch them while they're happening . . ."

Briefly Cyn checked the system, but the av seemed to be functioning perfectly and he had no time to waste chasing down an intermittent malfunction that might not exist. Now that he knew where he was with respect to Empire space, he had to calculate a course that would take them back as close to Mantra as possible. His worst problem was that the crude charts he had did not indicate how many, if any, carrollpauses intervened between the stars displayed. He fed data to the puter, muttering irritably at the complication of the 5.27-degree correction he had to apply each time.

Aimie had curled up on the copilot's recliner and fallen asleep. Now and then she moved restlessly. The sounds she made faded into a familiar background as Cyn became more and more deeply immersed in his calculations. Then a sharper 'scritch' drew his eyes to her, but she was not moving and he swung around to look at the companionway door, which he had dogged shut when he and Aimie returned from freezing Mortchose the previous "night." Because he had set the lift not to respond to signals from the passenger level at the same time, he glanced toward it idly—and then sat frozen. The doors were half open, and a space-armored and helmeted figure, blaster already aimed, was stepping into the control room.

Ice filled Cyn's veins. Because of his spacer contempt for earthers and the absence of life support in the cargo holds, he had assumed those areas to be safe against trespass. He hadn't given a thought to the emergency suits in the shuttle, which could provide access to the lift through the cargo holds. Worse, he had overlooked the fact that the suit of space armor would make its wearer almost invincible. And any passenger could have got into the shuttle. Who? Cyn stared, but the face was indistinct, shadowed behind the plas faceplate.

Blaster unwavering the helmet speaker rasped softly, "That's right, space hero, you sit still till I tell you to move."

"But—" Cyn swallowed his protest as the blaster jerked.

Mortchose! Although the voice was distorted through the helmet's speaker, it was Mortchose's. But the freezer alarm had never gone off. Even if Aimie had not tried to wake him, he couldn't have slept through the alarm. And the lift had been palm-locked—but so had the companionway door last night. He had been sore and tired when he locked the lift, but that was no excuse for forgetting that Mortchose had had no electronic baffler on him. Mortchose was the hands; his partner, who could play with electronic locks, must be the brains . . . All thought dissipated as the blaster lifted higher threateningly.

"Get up slowly." Mortchose used his free hand to detach a line from the suit's belt and toss it on Cyn's couch. "Take that and tie her up."

Cyn might have taken his chances against a stunner, but the results of a blaster bolt were too permanent. The helmet was an additional curse. He couldn't see Mortchose's face to gauge its expression, nor could he tell when the killer's eyes shifted from him momentarily. Obediently he picked up the thin coil and looped it over Aimie. When he bent over her to catch the end, her eyes opened, flicked down toward her chest. Cyn saw her shoulder shift and the fabric of her jumpsuit gaped showing a dull gleam. He could only shake his head, but Mortchose himself supplied the explanation that wiped out the disappointment that had flicked across her face.

"I know she's Security," the killer said evenly. "Whatever she's got on her, it won't work through this suit, so don't think about it."

Aimie's body appeared to droop in defeat, but Cyn could feel the slight arching of shoulders and back, the tensing of muscles that would permit him to tighten the rope around her enough to satisfy Mortchose. He was relatively sure that when she relaxed the coils would become much looser—but what good that would do Cyn couldn't guess. About the only way to fight a man in a suit was with a blaster or to cut off his air. Air . . . the idea was lost as a hollow laugh came from the helmeted head.

"You think you're so smart, but you're a stupid mutt."

Cyn's heart sank at the snarling fury in the voice, which came through the speaker's distortion. Professional killers didn't usually get angry, but he had hurt Mortchose's pride. If it hadn't been Aimie, even more vulnerable than he at the moment, who had hit Mortchose on the head, he would have tried to soothe the killer by reminding him that he had actually won the fight between them. As it was, Cyn made no reply, merely tying the line at the foot of the recliner.

Behind the plas plate, Mortchose's eyes might have glanced at Cyn's knots, but he made no attempt to examine them for slipshod work. A small hope stirred to life in Cyn. Freezing could leave a person disoriented, and Mortchose had seemed slow to give his orders. If Mortchose was confused, possibly . . .

Before the thought was complete, another made Cyn sick and wish he had actually made Aimie more helpless. What if Mortchose simply didn't care if she got loose? She had hit him. What if he would welcome the chance to blast her? Cyn tried to warn her, shaking his head again slightly and glancing from her to the weapon. She lowered her lids, then raised them. Did that mean acknowledgement or defiance? The armor creaked and Cyn dared not hesitate any longer. Cautiously he straightened up and turned to face Mortchose.

"You stupid mutt," the killer repeated. "You didn't even notice I put a new journey button in your navigator."

A new chill coursed through Cyn as he realized that it was very likely whoever was abducting mail ships—or something they carried—would choose the dead planet of a red giant as a safe hideout. Such planets were often too cold to support life, but not usually as cold as space itself. And, when they did host living organisms, those were most often small and inoffensive.

"But I did notice," Cyn protested, realizing that Mortchose believed they had arrived at the destination programmed by his journey button. "For Power's sake, look. The button is on the console, not in the navigator. The sun you see on the screen isn't the one you were aiming for."

Mortchose laughed again. "Oh sure, but I'm not stupid even if you are. So the button isn't in the navigator. You took it out when you arrived and saw you weren't in Mantra's system. I see the numbers on the screen. You've been trying to find out where we are. Don't bother. Just get this ship moving toward the planet."

"Listen to me," Cyn cried. "The planet here is dangerous. All I've done so far is my job. I'm not looking to get killed. I wouldn't argue with you if it weren't important. I tell you what lives on the planet of this sun is death."

"For you maybe." Mortchose's voice held a grim satisfaction. "Not for me."

"For everyone," Cyn insisted. "Let me take the ship back to Xiphe's carrollpause. You can put in your journey button and get us into the void long before anyone could stop us."

"I told you twice that I'm not stupid," Mortchose snarled. "Just because you once caught me off guard, you think you can con me into anything. The Patrol's around Xiphe."

Cold sweat slimed Cyn's body. Reason would not pene-

trate Mortchose's hurt pride. His surprise attack had succeeded, and Mortchose's main business was not being caught
by surprise.

"I didn't catch you," Cyn said desperately. "The ship
lurched and—" He stopped and caught his breath. The
blaster had moved threateningly.

"Stupid mutt! You think I can't blast you because you're
the only one who can run the ship, and you think I can't blast
the smart bitch because she's one they want information from
at the base. But you're not quite right. I can't kill her, but
there's no reason not to soften her up a bit. I can burn her feet
off, for example . . . slowly." His voice softened lovingly over
the words, and he added consideringly, "That wouldn't
damage her ability to talk."

"She'll die of shock," Cyn cried. "Don't hurt her. I'll do
anything you want."

He started toward the console, terrified that to encourage
his obedience or simply for the pleasure it would give him,
Mortchose would give Aimie a sample of what he could do.

"Wait," the killer ordered.

Cyn stopped and stood rigid. He was beginning to fear
that the freezing had addled what brains Mortchose had and
that he wasn't rational. If the killer turned the blaster on
Aimie, he would have to try to jump him and tear his air hose
loose. Yet if Mortchose killed him by reflex action, he would
have doomed all the passengers aboard because no one else
could run the ship. But Mortchose did not use the blaster
and, as far as Cyn could tell, was not even looking at Aimie.

"Get that little blonde doll up here," Mortchose said.

"She's only a little girl," Cyn whispered.

Mortchose took a step backward so that when he aimed at
Aimie the arc the blaster would have to travel to get back to
Cyn would be shorter.

"All right," Cyn said. "I'll move the ship anywhere you want, and I won't argue about anything. I won't talk unless you tell me to."

Mortchose took another step back.

"I have to move to get to the av," Cyn said, his voice shaking. "I'll get Niais up here, but I have to call her. She's asleep."

"Stand right where you are."

"Please—" Cyn pleaded.

"Stand still." Mortchose's voice rasped.

He moved slowly backward, feeling his way so nothing would trip him. Cyn bit his lip. Mortchose was now too far away for him to reach by a leap and he would be dead before he had taken two steps. But when the killer reached the best angle between Cyn and Aimie he didn't stop. He began to sidle to the left. Cyn let the breath he had been holding ease out. He knew he was trembling with relief and made no effort to control his shaking body. He hoped Mortchose would enjoy that symbol of weakness enough to do nothing more violent. Finally the suited figure stopped. Cyn tried to keep all expression from his face, but despair was bitter in his mouth. Mortchose wasn't confused at all, and he knew his business. He had placed himself so that Aimie, the av, and the door Cyn would have to open to let in Niais were all very nearly lined up.

"Now sit down and call the doll."

Cyn pushed the av button and wet his lips. He had thought of allowing his distress to show to warn the passengers that something was wrong. But if they were already under the control of Mortchose's partner, that would do no good; and if they were not under control and tried to help, that might give Mortchose a good excuse to indulge his sadism.

"Niais," Cyn called. "Niais, wake up."

The lump on the bed stirred.

"Wake up, Niais," Cyn repeated.

The light in the cabin came on and the girl sat up, blinking her beautiful eyes and putting her right hand up to push back her tousled hair. Her other hand still clutched the package she clung to so persistently. Tears rose in Cyn's eyes. A baby with a security blanket—and he was calling her to torture or death. He did not pretend to himself that Mortchose could have any more normal designs on the child.

"Who's that?"

Niais's voice was sweet, her expression hopeful as she quickly pushed the control to speed the air circulation in the cabin and looked toward the door. Cyn hesitated a bare instant, his mind leaping from Niais's wish to have a fresh-smelling cabin for a new lover to the fact it was air circulating.

"It's me, the pilot."

He spoke slowly, hoping Mortchose would think it was because Niais was sleepy and he wanted to be clear, but he was willing to take a chance because he had suddenly realized that every moment's delay was important. Air! The idea that had come to him and slipped away when Mortchose's blaster threatened. The recycling unit in the suit was limited. If it took long enough to get to the planet, Mortchose would pass out.

"Put on some clothes and come up here," Cyn added when he felt he could wait no longer.

Niais rubbed her eyes sleepily and yawned. Then she looked toward the av with a puzzled frown. Finally she shrugged her shoulders and sighed, clearly wondering about the incomprehensibility of males who told her "no" one sday and woke her up in the middle of the night the next to summon her. Nevertheless, she made no protest. She was languidly gathering up some garments when Cyn snapped off the av. He almost expected Mortchose to tell him to turn it back on, but there was no such order. Cyn wondered whether the killer was totally indifferent to that kind of sexual stimulation or was normal enough to fear that seeing Niais dressing might be a distraction. He had thought of leaving the av on for that purpose, but judged the idea useless. Mortchose knew his business far too well to give more than a glance or two at the screen, and that wouldn't be time enough for Cyn to get off his couch, turn around, and leap halfway across the room.

He sat quietly, waiting for orders, both because that would make him seem docile and because it was wasting time, but the inactivity was hard to endure. Doing something, anything, tended to mask his fears. Staring at the blank screen simply filled his head with images of what would happen to Niais if he displeased his captor—what might happen to her anyway. A few leaden smin passed. Mortchose shifted from one foot to the other. Cyn swallowed. Did he think that Niais was taking too long?

"Why don't you take that helmet off?" Cyn said quickly.

"Why?"

Cyn's hands twitched nervously. "Because you'd be more comfortable, and that would make you less jumpy. The last thing I want right now is for you to be annoyed by anything."

Tinny laughter greeted Cyn's reply. "You must be right about the ship putting me off balance because you're really too stupid to get away with anything. You think I don't know you can't see my eyes behind this faceplate? Mutt, just you believe that I'm looking at you—hard—every ssec."

"I didn't—" Cyn began, then shook his head as if defeated.

A tiny, very tiny flicker of brightness was added to the dim hope he nursed. He had succeeded in distracting Mortchose so that the time would seem shorter. As far as taking off the helmet, if the killer had agreed it would have made him vulnerable to any light weapon Aimie might be carrying; if Cyn's remark made him more determined to keep it on, there were still hopes on which to feed. Mortchose might become drunk and careless because he had not adjusted the oxygen output of the recycler correctly or, even better, the catalyst would be exhausted and he would be poisoned by the carbon dioxide in his own breath.

Cyn had started to think about a second intervention when the handle of the companionway door moved. The door did not open because Cyn had dogged it shut from the control room side, expecting he would prevent just the kind of surprise he had received. The blaster never moved, but Mortchose gestured with his free hand.

"When I tell you to get up, you can let the fem in. If that lame-brain Wakkin is with her, shut the door in his face. If you don't, I'll take off this bitch's feet. If I have to, I'll fry everyone. I'm not going to survive anyway if you get this ship away from me again, so I have nothing to loose." He giggled, a thin, high sound, shocking as it came from the helmet speaker. "Now. Go to the door."

Cyn stood up, not too quickly, and went directly to the door, waiting like a robot to be told to open it, to shut it. Again his implicit obedience was as much to waste time as to pander to Mortchose's need to feel powerful. That giggle had made his heart jump, but if the killer was getting an oxygen high, he had better appear to be totally docile. Nonetheless he had to take the chance of saying, "I'm sorry, Niais. Just do—"

"Shut up and dog that door again," Mortchose ordered. "You, doll, get over to the desk and sit down in the seat that faces the door. That's right. Now slide it in as far as it will go and lock it in place."

"How?" Niais asked.

"Push down the black lever at the right side," Cyn said.

A flicker of fear had crossed Niais's face when she first saw the blaster in the suited figure's hand, but that had been replaced immediately by an expression of submission. Cyn knew she would be no help. Her short life had probably taught her that submission was the best way to avoid pain and punishment. Since Cyn didn't believe that Niais could think quickly enough to take advantage of any slight opportunity to disarm Mortchose, he wanted her to obey quickly without irritating the killer.

When she had reached down and locked the lever, Mortchose added, "Now, slowly, reach as far forward as you can over the desk and drop everything within reach to the floor. Do it very, very slowly. If you try to throw anything, I'll burn you. I'll burn off your hair and ears. Then I'll cut off your nose, and your eyelids, and your lips—"

Mortchose's voice stopped suddenly, as if he had heard himself begin to linger dreamily over the last few words. For an instant, Cyn closed his eyes, wincing away from the horror of violence that might follow Niais's comprehension of what awaited her. But neither hysterical nor agonized shrieks preceded the soft thuds of articles being dropped from the desk; Niais was following her instructions. Incredibly, her face showed nothing beyond a faint disapproval.

In the midst of his terror, Cyn had to swallow a hysterical laugh. He felt he suddenly understood how Niais's mind worked. Apparently it was true that she had no imagination. The threats had no reality to her because the "sin" was one she would never commit. Niais knew it was unmannerly—not nice—to throw things at people. She would never be guilty of such a solecism; therefore, the punishment threatened would never be inflicted. Cyn offered thanks and an urgent prayer to the Powers that Be that the child would not learn differently.

When the desk was clear as far as Niais could reach, Mortchose said, "Now pilot, go lock the lift door, and go back to your seat."

Cyn did as he was told without expression. He had not expected Mortchose to forget his own method of entry. Besides, it was nearly impossible for anyone except Mortchose's partner to know what was happening in the control room. After he was seated, he heard Mortchose begin to move. Then he heard the second chair slide back and creak as the suited killer sat down.

"Let's get started, mutt," he ordered, "and don't make any mistakes."

Cyn fired the real space engines, directing the puter to echo his instructions on the screen. He could only hope that Mortchose would understand enough about the displays to believe that he was trying to find the planet and get there but not enough to realize that the Pot could do the same thing itself, much faster. Numbers flashed, marking acceleration and the power used to compensate and keep the ship at 0.7 gravity. Soon the rs showed a tiny shift in the position of the red sun.

Time passed. Twice passengers had called on the av: once Wakkin, asking where Niais was, and once Hachisman, wanting to know when they would arrive at Mantra. Each time, after a hesitation, Mortchose had directed Cyn to answer, his voice angry as if he were being constrained to keep the others content.

Once Niais had asked to use the desk autochef and been told to shut her mouth. Now she slept, her head pillowed on her arms on the desk. Aimie, who had twitched restlessly from time to time, now lay perfectly still. Cyn sat watching the screens, sucking his tongue in an effort to bring some saliva to his dry mouth to allay his thirst. His stomach growled with hunger.

At last, exhausted by tension and anxiety, Cyn himself dozed until an alarm he had set peeped. He jerked, heard an oath, and froze. "The planet," he said. The screen now showed the huge, bloody sun as no more than a rosy glow in the corner. The dark planet was clearly visible. "How close do you want me to come?"

"Put the ship into orbit for an easy shuttle landing."

To Cyn's intense disappointment Mortchose's voice seemed as clear and alert as when he had first spoken. He had hoped . . . Better not think about it, he told himself, or he might transmit the idea. There was still time. For another thirty smin Cyn tried to think of something he could do to thwart Mortchose. Finally he flicked on the com unit. A faint background static was the only sound it recorded. He knew there would be nothing, but it was an excuse to turn around.

"I have to ask a question," he said.

"Ask."

No good. The voice was still sharp. Any attempt to move would doubtless bring disaster. "I don't get any homing signal," he pointed out. "Where do we go from here?"

"Homing signal?" Mortchose laughed. "What kind of idiot would use a homing signal for a hideout, you stupid mutt?"

The scorn was so rich that Cyn clenched his teeth, even though the question had only been an excuse to turn his body toward his captor. If Mortchose saw the bunching muscles in Cyn's jaw, he was too content to bother insulting him further.

"Take an equatorial orbit," he ordered, "and let it decay until you spot a chain of volcanoes. There will be three in a row and one off at an angle of thirty degrees. Lock orbit on that volcano."

Cyn had to turn back to the console, but he hoped he had at least established turning around as a safe motion. "Cutting speed to a decaying orbit," he said obediently. "Keep your eye on the screen. When you see what you want, I'll lock in."

"You keep your eye on the screen," Mortchose sneered. "I'll keep my eye on you."

"You know I can't do a thing from this position," Cyn protested. "I don't want to miss the target and get blamed for it."

His gorge rose at the whine in his voice, but if whining would save Aimie or Niais, he would whine or crawl on his belly and lick the killer's boots if it came to that. He knew they were not at the planet Mortchose wanted to reach, but he did not dare try to explain that to the killer again. He could only hope if Mortchose himself could not find the landmark volcanoes, he would accept the fact that they had come to the wrong sun—and not burn either fem in his rage.

Cyn let the orbit decay quickly. The planet was not large and its gravity was no threat to the Pot's powerful engines. He had so little expectation of seeing any volcanoes—planets of a red sun were usually far too old for volcanic activity—that he was hardly watching the screen. But suddenly, they were there, three tiny sparks of orange on the dark maroon background. He was so surprised that only the automatic reactions of ingrained training brought his hands to life on the console.

The rs spotted and measured; the puter calculated; the Pot matched speed to the planet's period of revolution. Cyn stared at the screen feeling stunned. Of all the billions of suns in the galaxy, was it possible that coincidence had brought them to the one sun Mortchose wanted?

CHAPTER 13

"We're locked in orbit on your target," Cyn said flatly.

Nothing showed in his voice, even though he was now sure that no miracle of coincidence had taken place. It was enough of a coincidence that this planet should have four volcanoes positioned roughly as Mortchose described—but the three were not really in a straight line on closer inspection, and the last was certainly offset closer to 50 degrees than 30.

What had convinced Cyn, however, was not the imperfect correspondence of position; that might have been a result of carelessness in the description given to Mortchose. Three volcanoes and then one offset, all large and active enough to detect from space, would be sufficiently unusual not to need great particularity in other details. Nonetheless, Cyn was certain, in the first place, that no rational beings—not even idiots who involved themselves in Imperial politics—would set up a hideout on a planet with the type of indigenous life this one had. Secondly, some rough mental calculations—possible because the ship had followed a straight trajectory—proved that no matter which direction they had moved after being "lost," the Pot must have carried them much further than the 5.27-degree skew could have offset Mortchose's destination.

Cyn made no attempt to convince Mortchose he was in the wrong place, however. It was far too late for that. Once those volcanoes appeared, if anything did not match what the killer believed, he would only be convinced that Cyn had tampered with the ship or the instruments—and Niais or Aimie would suffer. He could only go on taking orders and keep hoping Mortchose would make at least one mistake.

"Now," Mortchose said, his voice higher than usual but still hard and clear, "turn on the life support for all entrances to the lift. While that works, you're going to make a little recording. You're going to tell everyone that life support has been turned off and they better get down to the shuttle. You're going to explain that the control room is locked off and that they've got fifteen smin before you blast off in the shuttle. Anyone not in it by then gets left behind in a dead ship. You're going to set the recording to play ten smin after you shut off the life support and we leave here. You're going to set it so we can hear it in the shuttle. If anyone is in the shuttle before us or the recording starts early, you know what will happen."

While Mortchose was giving orders, Cyn sat frozen, staring at the console. The killer was still getting enough air to keep him alert, and the thread of hope Cyn had that Mortchose would make a mistake getting down to the planet was gone. Mortchose was using Cyn's own technique for getting the passengers into the shuttle—with refinements. He would never have to watch a whole group. They would have to file through the lock one by one, climb down the ladder, and into their seats. There would be little chance of distraction and less chance of rushing Mortchose, especially with his partner with the passengers.

The recording was made. There was air and heat in the lift chamber, enough to last while Mortchose got them through it into the shuttle. Gritting his teeth, Cyn set about shutting down all life-support in the Pot. He worked as slowly as he dared without wakening Mortchose's suspicion, but he knew he was only delaying the inevitable. Finally, he had to report he was finished.

"Right on time," Mortchose said, and giggled.

Cyn tensed, but the next words, addressed to Aimie, doused the flash of expectation. No doubt there was a humorous aspect to the situation from Mortchose's point of view.

"Now that you've worked yourself free, smart bitch"—the killer's voice carried the sneer that must have been on his face—"You can get up. Don't worry. I can see you. Just keep your back to me and edge around until you face the lift door." He giggled again. "Thought you were getting away with something, didn't you? Well, all you accomplished was that I don't have to let anyone near enough to you to take the first blast if you act up."

Afraid to move even so much as turning his head, Cyn held his breath when, from the corner of his eye, he saw Aimie stiffen. He was terrified that she might still deny she had loosened her bonds, but she must have heard the yearning in the words "first blast." She must have known, too, that her weapons were not capable of penetrating a heavy-duty suit. She shucked off the loose line and stood up slowly, following Mortchose's orders exactly. Next Cyn was told to get off his couch and sidle around, facing the wall. Whether or not Mortchose was getting light-headed, he still knew his business. Neither was allowed to get close enough to touch the lift door until Mortchose was on his feet directly behind them.

By then Cyn did not hope that either he or Aimie would be able to overpower Mortchose on the way to the shuttle. With all of them crammed into the lift, the only significant movement that could be made was the killer's finger pressure on the firing stud of the blaster. Outside the lift, Cyn stood nearest the shuttle lock, Aimie and Niais side-by-side in front of the blaster. Docilely, Cyn opened the lock and passed through into the cargo section. Aimie followed, her face as expressionless as an exquisite image, but she stepped just a bit to the side. Cyn's heartbeat quickened as he slowed his pace and looked back, as if uncertain of what to do next. Niais came just ahead of the killer, puzzlement and concern just beginning to show in her limpid eyes.

The notion that he and Aimie together might be able to throw Mortchose off balance and wrest the blaster from him in the more open area of the cargo section lasted only until the killer stepped into the shuttle after his captives. With a brutal shove, he sent Niais flying forward to collide with Cyn. Before he had regained his balance, Mortchose had struck Aimie on the temple with the barrel of the blaster and had the weapon again aimed at Niais, who was still clinging to Cyn.

"Didn't expect that did you, stupid?" The giggle that seemed to punctuate every statement Mortchose made scaled upward into an unpleasant titter, but the blaster was rock steady. "Let go of him, doll, and step back here near me— nice and slow. You, stupid, pick up the smart bitch, carry her through, and strap her into a next-to-the-last-row seat next to the hull. Unhook the strap from the next seat. Tie her hands and shove them under the seat strap."

Woodenly, Cyn obeyed. He could have taken the weapon from Aimie's suit while he bent over her, but he decided not. For one thing, he didn't dare take it when Aimie wasn't conscious, in case she got a chance to use it and didn't know it was gone; for another, he wasn't sure what it was, how it worked, or whether he would be able to figure it out in the ssec or two he would have.

When he straightened up, Mortchose said, "She'd better be secure. If the straps aren't tight enough when I come by,

I'll burn her hands so she can't use them."

Cyn swallowed and tightened the seat strap another notch. Mortchose giggled.

"Stupid, stupid, stupid," he said. "It doesn't get into your thick head that I know all the tricks." Another giggle. "Now go up to the pilot's seat and strap yourself in. Hands on the console where I can see them. With the others coming in, I'll be a little nervous. If you sneeze or breathe too hard, I'm likely to burn the doll before I think about what you've done."

The warning was sane enough—considering the insane situation—but the voice was getting higher and shakier, not slurred but hysterical. Cyn breathed carefully and felt sweat beading his face and sliming his palms. Something was wrong with Mortchose, maybe simple fatigue, maybe something the recycler could no longer clean from the air in the suit. Was it a race now between the killer losing consciousness or becoming irrational and burning them all for amusement? If he felt himself passing out, wouldn't Mortchose use the blaster indiscriminately anyway? He had said he wouldn't be allowed to survive another failure.

Cyn jumped and gasped as the announcement he had taped began to play back from the shuttle's speakers. Mortchose had placed himself in front of the door that was used for dirtside entrances and exits with Niais standing just off the ladder/aisle in the opening made by a tipped-up seat. She was barely out of the direct line from the lock to the ship. Faintness or irrationality seemed to have no effect on Mortchose's ability to arrange those he needed to control.

"Move one hand," Mortchose directed. "Activate the av to the corridor. When you hear them coming, you tell them to come through the lock one at a time, that the door will close as soon as someone appears in it—and you see that it does or someone will get burnt. When the first in is strapped down, open the lock again."

Soon the av picked up sounds in the corridor and Cyn made the statement Mortchose had demanded. Then he opened the lock from the control on the console. Fr. Rocam appeared in the opening. As soon as she stepped through, he thumbed the lock shut. She did not see Mortchose at first, turning toward Cyn in the pilot's station and asking in a voice that trembled just a trifle, "What's wrong?"

"Don't ask him." Mortchose tittered again. "He's a dummy. He only talks when I tell him." There was a rasp in the helmet speaker as if Mortchose had cleared his throat. Then he said, rough and angry, "Take a seat and strap yourself in. Keep your hands in your lap, in plain sight, and keep them still."

She was white with shock when she passed him, but Cyn did not turn. In his mirror he saw that she had not collapsed, as he feared, nor did she sink into the first seat but walked on toward Mortchose, seemingly fascinated, until he barked, "Sit" at her, and she sat promptly—just in front of Aimie. Despite his agony of spirit, Cyn almost grinned. Her clothing was all huddled on anyhow, but her peculiar hat was tied most properly flat on top of her head. The impulse died swiftly. Power only knew what would happen to her now, hat and all.

"Open the lock," Mortchose ordered.

Wakkin was the next in. He had said no more than "What—" when Mortchose ordered him to sit and strap in. Cyn saw the infinitesimal change of expression, the barely perceptible stiffening that preceded action—but the killer saw them just as quickly.

"I'll burn the blonde doll first." Mortchose's voice gloated.

"Who—"

"Just take it out slowly, real slowly, hold it at arm's length by the muzzle, and drop it down the ladder. I've got the blaster on spray, so I'll get the doll and you too if you try to be funny or if it hits me."

A moment's frozen silence was broken first by Niais's soft whimper and then by a thud/clatter as Wakkin, moving carefully, did as he was told and his weapon went down to lie near Mortchose's feet.

Demoson either had no weapon or was too clever to betray it by displaying the hint of threat that Wakkin had shown. Otherwise, his reactions were much like Wakkin's, first surprise and anxiety and then horror.

Hachisman, the last, came through the lock already talking. "This is disgusting," he raged. "I'm going to complain—" In looking toward the pilot's station as the others had done, his eyes fell on the screen that duplicated the ship's navigator. "You incompetent!" he howled. "That isn't the right planet." His voice caught on a sob as his head swiveled away from Cyn, who sat as if frozen. "That—" he choked. "That isn't Mantra."

"It's the right planet for me," Mortchose snarled, all hint of titter gone from his voice. "Sit down and strap in—just like the others."

In the mirror Cyn saw the blaster waver from Niais to Hachisman, but that was no advantage. There was still no opportunity for Cyn to undo his straps and drop down on the killer. He, Niais, and Hachisman could all be fried before he finished the betraying wriggle that would shuck his harness.

"Undock and take us down. Land on the flat plain north of the offset volcano."

Cyn signaled the shuttle housing to open and began the undocking procedures automatically. That part of his mind not numb with despair was wondering if his inability to land where he was told would bring the moment of truth. If the volcano was part of a mountain chain, there would be no plain. A creak brought his eyes up to the mirror. Mortchose had eased himself down into the seat nearest the door. Cyn swallowed. Was the killer growing weaker as his air failed? But he could not see through the faceplate at all. He could only make the descent as slowly as possible and hope.

During the uneventful drop to the planet, Cyn watched the killer in the mirror and a new problem forced its way through the roiling fear and hope in his mind. Mortchose had not favored any of the passengers. Each had been treated with the same threat and suspicion. But one must be his partner. One must have revived him. No one could unfreeze himself, no matter what his training or conditioning. If Mortchose did collapse, would the partner try to take over? And which one was it?

Demoson had been the calmest; in fact, he had been the most self-possessed all along. But did that mean anything? Cyn studied his face in the mirror for a moment, but it showed only the same anxiety as all the others. He shifted his eyes to Mortchose again. The aim of the blaster was as steady as ever, and he glanced at Hachisman, who seemed almost more angry than fearful. But he had been born angry, Cyn suspected.

"Why is it taking so long?" Mortchose barked.

"It's dark down there," Cyn answered. "I took a circuit to look for the best landing."

"Don't take another. I told you once, stupid. I'll warm the doll good if you don't bring us down."

"Don't!" Hachisman cried.

"Shut your mouth. It's none of your business. She isn't even a person. She came in the cage. I'll cook her if you try to tell me what to do. Land this boat, pilot. North of the volcano, on the lava plain."

Mortchose's voice was high and shaking. Cyn knew he had to bring the shuttle down, and there was a plain. Rather than north, it was southeast of the orange glow of the volcano, but he didn't think Mortchose was in any condition to notice that. He fired maneuvering blasts, bringing the tail down.

Despite the pervading gloom, he had little difficulty landing on the relatively flat, ancient lava flow. During his free trading years, he had made night landings on worse terrain, usually to conceal outworld identity from primitives. Here the danger was less absolute darkness, which mandated reliance on the shuttle's sensors, than the erroneous belief that you could see. The light from the tired, swollen sun, a dull maroon glow, was perceptible to the eyes but actually provided little visibility. No novice, Cyn was not deceived and ignored the screens. The braking blasts cut; the landing braces shot out, heavy hydraulics adjusting to any unevenness.

"What now?" Cyn asked when the shuttle was stable.

"Spell out 'safe' in basic blinker code with your lights," Mortchose replied.

Cyn choked back a protest that the lights, which gave off heat as well, would bring the creatures of the planet upon them. He blinked out the message, repeated as ordered, and then, under instruction, set the shuttle's "eyes" to scan the surrounding area. Meanwhile Mortchose had ordered the passengers to put their hands on top of their heads and had maneuvered himself beside the door where he could control the movement of the others. To Cyn's infinite relief—either because he was getting muddled or because he felt free to kill the pilot now that they were grounded—Mortchose was taking fewer precautions. He had left Niais in the seat where he had originally placed her, and told Cyn to activate the screens provided for those passengers who liked to watch.

"But don't get any ideas," he said, tittering again. "You can't tell whether I'm looking at you or the screen. We don't need you anymore, and I'd like an excuse to fry you."

Cyn did as he was told, but hope was coming alive again. He had no intention of dying sooner than he had to, but now he was free to take chances he would never have taken while Niais was threatened. Unobtrusively—for there were small movements of the helmet that indicated which way Mortchose was looking—Cyn squirmed out of his harness and in another interval, activated the shuttle's emergency environmental analysis. At least the atmosphere was breathable and would not be immediately fatal, although it contained unpleasant constituents. It was bitterly cold, but they could probably survive for some time even without suits. The problem was the beasties. If only—

Mortchose's tinny laugh interrupted Cyn's hopeful thought that the creatures would be few and far between. "You did real good," he said. "You landed closer than I thought. They're coming for us already."

"No!" The single whispered protest forced itself from Cyn's throat as his hand flew out to fix transmission to the eye now displaying on the screen.

Certainly something was coming for them—a huge, black hemispherical something. Cyn strained his eyes against the deceptive light, but he could make out no more than the sense of movement and the blackness that seemed to absorb what little light the sun shed without any reflection. It was impossible to judge distance, but the thing was moving with disconcerting swiftness.

Cyn stared with growing horror, realizing that the necessities of existence on this dying world could have evolved no other form. The hemispherical shape exposed as little surface as possible to the cold while providing adequate surface for rapid locomotion and protected sensory organs. The huge size was conducive to conservation of heat. Icy drops beaded Cyn's forehead. It didn't look like a monster, he thought despairingly. In that lightless light, Power help them all, it looked very much like a large, armored transport.

A terrified half-sobbing laugh escaped Cyn. Until this moment he had counted on the fact that the beasts would be clearly monstrous and that Mortchose would be enough distracted by that for Cyn to jump down on him and, if necessary, push him out of the shuttle. Even if he weren't distracted, the monsters would have proved they were on the wrong planet. Mortchose would never have lasted the trip back in the suit. But now Cyn knew he would never have a chance.

Mortchose had backed up alongside the exit door where he could not be knocked off his feet. That maniac would force them out one by one, and the beast would swallow them, one by one. Cyn closed his eyes briefly to shut out the horror, realizing that Mortchose, sadistic idiot that he was, would never notice. He wouldn't care about any screams, if anyone got a chance to scream. He would assume the prisoners were being roughly handled as they were taken aboard the "vehicle."

Cyn managed to drag his eyes away from the screen, but a single glance showed him that Mortchose was again watching the passengers. He tried to think of some way to jump Mortchose so that he would avoid being killed instantly or being so badly hurt that he couldn't operate the shuttle. But his eyes were drawn back to the horror approaching them, and all he could think of was the gruesome joke of being swallowed one by one.

Mortchose, who had been interested in the screen only long enough to be sure that the "vehicle" was heading directly toward the shuttle, was now issuing detailed instructions on what they were to do when their transportation arrived. He hardly glanced at Cyn, secure in the idea that he was now free to kill the pilot. That would make the passengers docile or, if it didn't, it wouldn't matter because the men in the transport would back him up.

There was a funny sound, and the shuttle quivered. Cyn gasped in horror and pushed back his seat. As he turned, he could see the passengers. All were tense and frightened. Aimie was conscious again and alert, although her brows were drawn together in a frown of pain. Beside her, Rocam looked pathetically disheveled. The strings of her ridiculous hat, usually so neatly and carefully tied, were hanging loose, and the veil that usually secured the bird ornament had fallen back on her shoulders. Cyn started to slide out of his seat. The poor old lady, starting out with such happy excitement. She would never get to her niece's wedding.

At Cyn's movement, Mortchose's helmeted head swung slightly toward him, and laughter came from the speaker. The killer did not even deign to tell him to sit still, merely reached with his free hand to the manual lever controlling the shuttle lock and pulled it down. Cyn's eyes flew back to his screen.

"Close it!" he yelled. "Space and Power! Look at the screen. Look what's out there."

For answer, Mortchose swung the blaster. His intention was obvious and Cyn, already half out of the chair, tried to drop sideways between it and the console, knowing that the movement could not save him and that the brief agony of his own death would be better than what was coming to the others.

As he slid down, Fr. Rocam's hat launched itself into the

200

air and flew! Wide black wings spread, flapped, struck Mortchose's helmet, and flapped again, obscuring the face-plate as the creature curved away. The killer screamed thinly, reversed the swing of the blaster toward this new threat. Cyn squirmed to a crouch, prepared to launch himself down, but a chorus of gasps and shrieks froze him. A long grey trunk, thick as a big man's thigh and shiny with slime, snaked into the open lock, wrapped around Mortchose, and withdrew—carrying the screaming and struggling killer with it. Cyn completed his spring, but to close the lock rather than to rescue the killer. Gasping with fear, he slammed the control home, just as another of the repellent appendages slid forward.

It hit the shuttle with enough force to make the metal clang, and they could hear it questing blindly and fretfully, seeking the warm opening that had vanished. Shaking and panting, Cyn leapt up the ladder and into his seat, his hands flying over the controls. The shuttle lurched and fell back. More yells and whimpers of fear came from the passengers. Cyn almost screamed himself as he cancelled the order to lift. The whatever-it-was must have a grip on the shuttle so it couldn't rise. Cyn knew he had to make it let go, but the shuttle had no weapons, and firing a blaster at that thing, even if he had one and dared open a lock, would have the effect of poking a ram doosey with a straw.

A blow hit the shuttle that made it rock on its landing gear. Loose! Cyn's mind screamed. We've got to get loose! Terror sped the catalog of the shuttle's capabilities through Cyn's head, and suddenly his hands began to fly over the console again. The lights in the shuttle dimmed and went out, the whisper of the air circulation equipment died. "What are you doing?" a male voice called, but Cyn was too busy to explain or to offer comfort.

He drew breath through his teeth, his eyes jerking from the

screen to the gauge that indicated the charge of stored power. Another blow hit the ship. Cyn's eyes flew back to the screen. More tentacles or trunks were snaking toward them, and the creature was raising itself slightly as if to throw its entire bulk at the shuttle. The landing gear would never support that weight. Cyn forced his eyes away from the horror and back to the gauge, grinding his teeth with impatience.

The shuttle rocked more dangerously, but the noise the passengers had been making had died away to heavy breathing and Fr. Rocam's voice, very low, calming and praising her pet. Cyn raised his eyes to the screen again and wished he hadn't.

The trunks had a firm hold; the monstrous body was lifting farther, not to push the shuttle over, as Cyn had originally thought, but to clap against it a horrendous maw. For one unforgettable moment, Cyn stared into the bright red mouth? stomach? as it widened and widened. Then he flipped his switch.

A bright blue light enveloped the hull and ran down the landing gear. The tentacles snapped back; the maw contracted. Cyn slammed his lift lever to full thrust. The shuttle leapt from the ground, faltered. Cyn opened the switch. The blue glow of the hull died. The lift resumed with renewed confidence. A moment later lights and air fans came on again. At what he considered a safe distance, Cyn cut his speed to a more rational level and leaned back in his seat.

"Just like the good old times on Lystris," he sighed.

CHAPTER 14

As soon as the shuttle was settled into a trajectory that Cyn had calculated would intersect with the Piss Pot's orbit, he swung his seat around to face his passengers.

"If anyone else," he said wearily, "has a desire to make a stop that is not currently on our schedule, I would like to make a suggestion. Let me get to the carrollpause at Mantra before you begin operations. All things considered, we were lucky this time. Power knows where we'll end up the next time someone fools with the navigation. I'm a good pilot and a fair navigator, but if we jump outside the galaxy, even I won't be able to find my way back."

A babble of protest all insisting on purity of motive and total innocence drew a cynical smile and shrug. The following babble of praise made Cyn laugh. He came out of his seat and drifted down the ladder to free Aimie.

"You'd better throw your credits at Fr. Rocam," he remarked, holding up a hand to silence the praise and bowing toward her. "Her marvelous hat trick is what saved us all."

A faint flush rose in the old lady's face. "Cotchkelah is not a trick." Her voice trembled a trifle and her expression showed a mingled anxiety and indignation. "He is a real bird, and a very clever one, even if he was born without legs. You won't—you won't make me cage him and leave him in that cargo section, will you? He would be so lonely. He's never been away from me, nor caged. I—"

"As far as I'm concerned," Cyn assured her with heartfelt sincerity, "that bird can eat from my plate, sleep in my bed, or do any other damn thing it wants on my ship. You name it, the bird can have it!" He eyed the creature, now in her lap and again so immobile that it looked more like a queer hat ornament than ever. "Just tell me, freefem, how you keep it so still?"

"I don't," Rocam replied with a tentative smile. "Cotchkelah can't move much if he isn't in the air. He's heavy, you see, and he has no legs, so he can't launch himself. He can move a little by swinging his body, but if I tie him down with a veil—" She looked around anxiously and added, "He doesn't mind, indeed he doesn't," as if someone had accused her of cruelty. "And of course, at home he flies much more." Her cheeks got pinker again. "I must confess that I let him out in the recreation room last night. I knew I shouldn't, but the cabin is so small and it's been several sdays since he had a good flight."

Aimie's full throated laugh brought an answering grin from Cyn. There was the mysterious black flicker that hadn't touched the ground she had seen on the av. But Cyn wasn't going to be diverted. Mortchose had had a confederate, who was clever enough to conceal his or her identity even when the killer seemed to be in control. If the bird was a bird, that was just fine, but it might be a contrivance of some kind.

"But he doesn't even move his head, Fr. Rocam," Cyn said.

"He doesn't move it constantly, the way most birds do. I guess I did train him to do that, although I didn't mean to." The old lady laughed lightly. "I'm not as quick as I was when I was young, and I couldn't feed him when he bobbed his head. I kept missing his mouth. I had to hold his head still to feed him. He learned very quickly. I was really proud of him—so clever, so very clever to learn a thing like that, which is completely opposed to his inborn instincts."

"How did you get him?" Aimie asked, her eyes flashing once toward Cyn, who nodded at her and drifted back up the ladder to his seat.

"Cotchkelah was thrown out of his nest soon after he hatched because he acted differently from the other nestlings. Birds do that, and he couldn't have acted normally, being born without legs. I saw he was deformed when I found him, and I knew I shouldn't try to save him, but—" She made a wry, helpless gesture. "My children were gone; my husband was gone—and I knew the nest he came from. I knew the species was long lived. I—wanted something to care for."

"That's very natural," Aimie said.

She reached a tentative hand toward the bird, and Cyn knew she had thought of the same problem he had and was trying to test whether the creature was alive. It seemed to be. The head turned swiftly so that one beady eye could watch, but it was a single, quick movement without the usual head-cocking and neck-twisting motions in which most birds engaged. Now Rocam should warn Aimie off, but she didn't.

"You can touch him," she said eagerly. "He likes to be stroked. That isn't natural either, but I knew he would never be turned loose, so I—I imprinted him with people. After all, he had to live his life only with people, and he didn't need to be wary or afraid. His environment would always be safe and controlled. Why shouldn't he have what stimulation he could?"

Aimie had been stroking the bird gently while Fr. Rocam talked, and soon Cotchkelah stretched his neck to run his beak caressingly along her hand. The old lady smiled and scratched the top of her pet's head.

"He's so friendly." Suddenly Rocam's voice quavered and caught. "I pointed to where he should go, and he trusted me and flew." Tears started down the softly wrinkled cheeks. "I knew my poor Cotchkelah would be burned to death, but I had to do something! I couldn't let you be killed, pilot. I had to give you a chance. And then that—that thing—"

Awkwardly, unused to displaying sympathy, Aimie patted the thin shoulder.

"It was the will of Almighty God," Hachisman said suddenly. "Mortchose was a dangerous, insane killer."

Cyn stared at the stern, dark face, the intense eyes. God? Perhaps some Power or Powers directed the universes, but one Almighty God? Cyn knew there were civilizations that embraced that belief, and all too frequently punished or even murdered all who did not embrace it with them. Cyn didn't mind the belief—although how an old homo sap in a white gown and long beard was supposed to be the Almighty God of the White Worms, he couldn't guess—but he did object to the insanity that too often went with devoted monotheism, and Hachisman looked like a prime example. But what could belief in one Almighty God have to do with stealing mail ships?

"Oh, you mustn't feel sorry, Fr. Rocam." Niais's pure voice filled the slightly uneasy silence that followed Hachisman's pronouncement before it became really uncomfortable. "Mortchose was not a nice person at all. Inside he wasn't nice. Right from the beginning he wanted to hurt me. Me! I had never done the smallest thing to annoy him. And I liked him, despite what he wanted to do. I like everyone. He must have been quite mad, so he's better dead—isn't that right?"

Wakkin unbuckled his seat harness and moved to the seat beside Niais. Cyn watched the maneuver, noting that it was almost as smooth and practiced as his own would be. Fr. Wakkin had done a lot of traveling.

"Insane—perhaps," Demoson remarked, "but not suicidal by intention. He was far too careful in controlling us to have desired to die. He had some purpose, all right. But what the hell did he want on that planet? And what was that thing?"

Cyn's eyes flicked to Aimie and caught her almost imperceptible nod. He didn't believe that Mortchose's clever partner would give anything away, but he thought the other passengers should be warned and that they deserved an explanation of the frightening things that had happened.

"As to the beastie," Cyn said, "I have no idea and neither does anyone else, I guess. Can you imagine getting close enough to investigate it? The planet is prohibited because the creatures are so dangerous. All that's known, or at least all I found in the Overstars manual, is that they find their prey by heat-seeking."

"Then you do know the planet," Hachisman said accusingly.

"Yes," Cyn admitted dryly, "but I had no intention of stopping to call. Neither did Mortchose, but he wouldn't believe me when I told him we hadn't arrived at the destination he wanted."

"He wanted?" Demoson repeated. "But why did he want to divert the ship? Did he tell you?"

"He did not. He didn't tell me a damned thing, except what to do and what he would do to Fr. Aimie and Fr. Niais if I didn't follow orders." Cyn sighed. "All I know is that two other ships disappeared in this quadrant, and both of them were making stops at Empire Star on Mantra. It's very interesting to me that everyone here is in a great hurry to get to Mantra."

"Not me," Niais said. "I'm going to Ingong."

"Unfortunately," Aimie remarked, "we have to get to Mantra first."

"What are you carrying that's so damn precious?" Hachisman asked.

"Nothing—except far more passengers than an OM ship usually carries."

"Nonsense," Demoson said. "It's far more likely that you're carrying papers of value. You don't open the mail and read it, I suppose."

"No, and I considered that, but an important document can't be the reason. Mortchose did give away one interesting bit of information. He said he couldn't afford to kill anyone aboard because his employer or employers didn't yet know which one they needed—he didn't say for what the person was needed."

"You still haven't told us how you got to that planet of horrors," Hachisman complained.

"Fr. Aimie told you that Mortchose had tried to take over the ship and we had caught him at it. He had put in a journey button, but either it was damaged or he didn't understand how to set it. In any case, it landed us in a galactic hole outside of Empire space—too far to pick up an Empire beacon. I spent a bit more than a sday trying to find a known solar system—and the one I found had unfortunate similarities to the place Mortchose was looking for. He insisted on landing."

"But a journey by button doesn't take two sdays," Wakkin protested. "Most travel time is spent getting to and from the carrollpause."

"I don't think Mortchose realized how much time had passed. There's no brig on this ship. We stuck him in the freezer."

"Who revived him?" Demoson asked.

"You tell me," Cyn said. "I'd be a lot happier if I knew—and someone else would be in the freezer."

"You mean someone here was helping Mortchose?" Wakkin's eyes jerked away from Niais's face, and his voice rose almost to a squeak. "Someone might still try to steal this ship or abduct the rest of us or whatever?"

"Unless one of you revived Mortchose by accident," Cyn remarked with gentle sarcasm. "And also managed—by mistake—to cancel the automatic alarm that sounds if the freezer is turned off. I've heard of lots of strange abilities, but aside from a methane ice wriggler, I've never heard of anyone who could get out of a freezer to turn on the **REVIVE** process for himself."

A constrained silence followed. Cyn watched with interest as five pairs of eyes moved from face to face, flinching away when any two pairs met, and finally coming to rest, rather ostentatiously, on some neutral object. Niais had been looking at him all along, puzzled and faintly anxious; Wakkin, Demoson, and Hachisman looked studiously at the seat backs in front of them; Aimie smiled at Cyn, gently rubbing the temple where Mortchose had struck her; Rocam looked at him too, her eyes bright with interest.

"Do you think, pilot," she asked, "that the various attacks on this ship might have to do with the current disagreements between the Emperor and Empress?"

"I haven't the faintest idea," Cyn replied, "but I do know that a mountain of credit is involved. Think of it: a spaceship with a mammoth tractor beam; suborned Planetary Police; the attempt on my life on Xiphe—right under the nose of the Patrol; a professional killer and a partner. How much would that cost? Who would have that kind of money and that kind of influence?"

"IntraGalCorp," Demoson said.

Cyn smiled. "It would do my heart good to think I had done them out of that much credit, but give me a reason why they'd spend it for either a mail ship or a person? What person who would travel a mail ship? Anyone important in IntraGalCorp has his or her or its own racer. And why only ships going to Empire Star? IntraGalCorp has only diplomatic offices there—a bunch of flunkies to tell the Planetary Council what they want done."

Demoson looked rather offended but Aimie gave him no chance to answer Cyn. "And why only within the last few swiks?" she put in before he could speak.

"The Planetary Council will be going on recess," Rocam said.

"Holy God," Hachisman exclaimed, casting his eyes up. "What has that body of do-nothings got to do with anything? What can it possibly matter whether they're in session or not?"

"I have no idea," Rocam admitted. "It just came to my mind because the pilot mentioned them and my niece—she's my great-niece, really—is getting married the sday after the recess begins. Her husband-to-be is an aide to one of the representatives and they plan to return to his home planet on the diplomatic ship so she can meet his parents. It saves them the fare, you see."

"Speaking of fare," Hachisman growled, "I think we ought to be reimbursed, pilot. We will never reach Mantra on schedule."

Cyn uttered a bark of laughter. "The funny thing is, unless someone pulls something new and different, we will. I had just about finished calculating the jumps from this Power-forsaken system to Mantra when Mortchose surprised me, and we are actually closer to Mantra than Xiphe and in an emptier quadrant. I hope to be able to make up most of the time we lost, and I don't think we'll be diverted by outside forces again because I'm going to be screaming for Patrol as I enter the system. Power knows, what with making an unscheduled stop in a forbidden system and having a passenger eaten by a monster, I have enough to report."

"You mean I'm not going to be a sday late for the GMA?" Demoson asked.

"I wouldn't bother sending any more messages about arrival time," Cyn said. "You'll still be nearly a sday late because of the stus we've lost getting to this planet. We'll get back to where we can jump into the void much faster, since I was deliberately going as slowly as I could without Mortchose noticing, but there is still a problem aboard."

"We should get a refund," Hachisman insisted angrily.

Cyn shook his head firmly. "The delays were caused by passenger interference in normal operation, so you couldn't get your credit refunded anyway. I've reported the reasons for delay both to Overstars and to Patrol and have a creditable witness in Fr. Aimie, who is Overstars Security."

"You are a very loyal employee, Pilot Cyn," Rocam said, smiling at him. "Do you think the Empress's stand about letting the federated planets make their own destiny is better than the Emperor's wishes to mold them into a more consistent pattern?"

"Me?" Cyn exclaimed. "I've got no opinion. Officially I'm a servant of the Empress—Overstars Mail, if you don't know it already, is in the Empress's bailiwick—but my job is only to get this ship to its scheduled stops. I carry mail, cargo, and people regardless of the political opinions wrapped up in them if any—and the way I feel now, I wouldn't cry too much if a plague hit both sides."

"Not in this ship," Niais said sweetly but firmly. "No plague until after you get me to Ingong. You promised."

Everyone laughed and the tension, which had hung in the air after Cyn had exploded his quiet little bombshell about Mortchose's revival no matter who was speaking or about what subject, diminished. Cyn swung around toward his console and soon picked up the Pot on his screen. Not long afterward, he was matching orbits and docking. When the shipputer responded without a hitch to his shuttle console, he had to swallow back a sharp ache in his throat. He had heard nothing when he was forced to stand face to the wall waiting for Mortchose's order to leave, but he had feared—oh, how he had feared—that the killer had done something that would maim his ship.

They had to wait some time for the life-support system to be restored and stabilized, and the passengers got up and moved around the shuttle. Cyn didn't protest, even when Wakkin went and picked up his weapon, which was caught in the corner near the door, having for some reason not been swept out with Mortchose. Even so, Cyn took no precautions when he gave permission to leave the shuttle. No passenger would dare attack him with all the others suspicious, warned, and ready. Then, too, he hoped that the lesson they had had on the dying planet would quell the enthusiasm of Mortchose's partner for navigational experiments.

Still, Cyn was not so foolhardy as to rest any confidence on his hopes. As soon as he got the Pot underway, he began to monitor. By then, the passengers were all in the rec room, wolfing down the mediocre meals provided by the autochef with the ravenous appetites and deep appreciation of those who had not expected to eat again. An unspoken truce had been declared; no mention of political matters was made, but Cyn felt they looked less at each other than people usually did when talking.

Not that the conversation was desultory. Cyn was amused

by the enthusiasm with which the adventure was discussed. Now that they were safe, it took on a kind of glamour. Doubtless in their descriptions to friends once they reached their destinations, they would all play quite different roles from the terrified passengers of reality—all except one, Cyn thought, his amusement fading. But his own relief was still too intense for him to feel any real anxiety yet, and he was soon grinning broadly, imagining all of them dining out for years on the tale of their journey.

Relief notwithstanding, after the meal was over and the talked-out and now-weary passengers separated, Cyn asked Aimie to come up and sit guard over the control room and navigator while he did a survey of the cargo areas. He spent several stus examining every packet and shelf, the robos, the walls, ceiling, and floors to be sure that Mortchose had left no little surprise for them. He found nothing, but he was beginning to worry again and wondered, as he returned to the control room through the lift, avoiding the passenger level, whether he could demand to examine the passengers' luggage.

He had a bad moment as the lift doors opened, when he saw the control room was empty. He came in with his stunner at its highest level, but as soon as he had palm-locked the door, Aimie called his name and stepped out of concealment.

"It's been delightfully quiet," she reported. "Fr. Rocam called up to ask if she could fly Cotchkelah in the rec room. Everyone else was in his cabin, except Niais, so I said it was all right. The damn thing does seem to be a bird. If it's wired for something else—"

"It can't do much harm in the rec room," Cyn said, grinning. "If it blew up the autochef, I'd be grateful. The new models must be an improvement."

Aimie laughed. "I know the service better than you. If

they've designed something new—which I doubt—it'll be worse. The Pot's made two transitions." Cyn nodded; he'd felt them, and Aimie continued, "Oh yes, Niais." She laughed again. "She's in your quarters. I tried. I swear I tried, but without shooting her dead, I just couldn't think of a way to stop her. She said you'd promised to 'deal with' her."

"Power blast that fem! She's got a new catch phrase. I told her if she used 'play games' in that sense again, I'd strangle her. For some obscure reason—at least obscure to normal minds—she's convinced I can't say words with sexual connotations."

Aimie smiled slowly. "Can you?"

Cyn's lips twitched. "I don't know. It's not usually necessary to say anything." He hesitated, and then added, "Let me go and get rid of her."

"By all means," Aimie murmured. "If you can."

But when Cyn looked into his bedroom, Niais was fast asleep on his bed—quite naked as usual. He sighed and closed the door softly; then, after a brief hesitation, jammed the handle again. As he turned back toward Aimie, who was still smiling—or smiling again—he muttered, "Blast them all. This stupid Emperor/Empress tangle has spoiled what might have been the best trip of my life."

Aimie widened her eyes. "You can't say that. If Imperial politics hadn't saved you, I would have been investigating you and laying bare all your secrets."

"By all means," Cyn said, closing the distance between them. "And I don't think you should let politics interfere with your primary duty any longer. I'm ready to lay bare anything you want to investigate."

He slid an arm around her, and she yielded readily. When their lips parted, she murmured, "I'm beginning to think Niais may be right. You've got an inhibition against using words to state a sexual purpose clearly."

Without speaking, he drew her toward the second couch, skillfully getting it to recline fully without releasing her. Aimie examined his face, the eyes languorously half shut, the lips a bit fuller than usual as he undid the catches of her jumpsuit and then the fasteners on his coveralls.

"On the other hand," she sighed, as her suit slid over her shoulders, "you seem to be quite correct about not needing to say much. You sure get your point across."

CHAPTER 15

When the navigator chimed, Cyn swallowed, cleared his throat gently, and turned his eyes toward the console. What he saw was perfectly satisfactory, and he looked back at Aimie. Now that they were on a known course, with no need to mark or compare jump times, the navigation was fully automatic. The chime and brief pause simply gave the pilot a chance to change his mind.

"Wow!" Cyn exclaimed softly.

"Flatterer," Aimie said.

Cyn shook his head and sighed. "No. I'm grateful that the navigator waited until I was ready to look."

"I wonder what would have happened if it hadn't waited."

He passed his tongue over his slightly swollen lips. "I don't know," he replied quite seriously. "And let me tell you that's an enormous compliment—in case you didn't realize it. To anyone else I'd have said, quite glibly, that I wouldn't have paid any attention. That would have been a lie. A Free Trader responds to his instruments. This time—I'm not sure."

"After three sdays in the nymph's Garden?" Aimie asked with her brows lifted.

"That's quite different," Cyn said, frowning in his effort to clarify his thoughts and express them. "Being with a nymph is like falling off a mountain—very exciting, but not an experience I'd want to repeat. Being with you—" his startlingly pale eyes raked her and his tongue came out to caress his lips again "—I could develop quite a taste for you, and you aren't the kind to go stale."

"Well, thank—" Aimie had begun, when there was a metallic rattle and a loud thump.

Both were off the recliner, crouched with weapons in hand, facing opposite directions, when Niais's voice came. "The door is stuck again. Do please let me out."

Weapons drooped in suddenly relaxed hands. Cyn cast a jaundiced glance at the door and raised a questioning brow at Aimie. After the briefest hesitation, she nodded her head at him and reached for her clothing. He waited just a moment to make sure she wouldn't change her mind, then called out. "All right. Just a smin. I'm coming."

"You didn't have to jam the door," Niais said in gentle reproof. "I'm not so rude as to interrupt. But now you're finished, I thought I would like some company."

A startled glance passed between Cyn and Aimie. They had not been completely silent while making love, but the sounds they did make were soft, not the kind that would carry across the control room and through a closed door.

"How did you know we were . . . ah . . . finished?" Cyn asked, wondering if his mind was so utterly decayed that he had inadvertently left the connection between the operating console and his bed panel open. If he had, of course Niais could have heard them. But, if he had, something was really wrong with him far beyond fatigue. Locking the bed panel into the disconnected position should be as automatic as heartbeat and breathing. It should not be something one could forget.

"I always know," Niais responded innocently. "It's like perfect time sense or perfect pitch. Well, I could never be—"

She stopped abruptly, looked frightened, and then smiled blindingly. "That's why I came up the other two times. You wanted to—wanted—" A look of total bewilderment came into Niais's face. "Well, I don't know what words to use. You always get angry when I say 'play games' or 'deal with' or—"

"It's all right," Cyn said hurriedly. "There's no need to say any more. Your meaning is quite clear."

His first reaction was relief that he had not forgotten to disconnect his panel; his second was the now almost habitual desire to strangle Niais. But immediately overriding the mixed embarrassment, amusement, and irritation, an idea was forming in Cyn's brain.

"Blast it!" he said to Aimie. "Stop giggling and think. Can we use her as a solar wind to show the direction of danger?"

"Danger?"

"I don't know. Look, both times when Niais came up here before, I was asleep—had been asleep long enough to relax deeply. I don't say I never think about—" Cyn paused, laughed, and went on, "about playing games when I'm awake, but it's pretty far in the back of my mind when I'm doing navigational calculations or wondering what lunatic is going to attack me next, so she does have empathy—"

"On one level," Aimie remarked, grinning. But she sobered immediately and turned to Niais. "Love," she said gently, "you've been in every male's bed except Mortchose. Why?"

"Because he didn't want—want to—"

"Say 'make love,' pet," Aimie suggested. "Our pure and noble mail-carrier will just have to have his ears sullied. Mortchose didn't want to make love at all?"

"Not at all," Niais assured her earnestly, her alabaster brow wrinkled. "There was nothing in him. It was all empty, black and empty."

Cyn nodded, remembering the naked lust in Mortchose's face that even he had recognized was not sexual lust. "What about the others?" he asked. "Is there any difference you feel from one to another."

"Yes, of course." Niais smiled with delight at giving satisfaction. "Fr. Rocam wasn't interested at all. Fr. Aimie wasn't interested in me. You only wanted—just wanted, not me, but that's the same—those two times. Fr. Demoson and Hachisman each wanted me once and I went right away because I knew it wouldn't last. Most of the time there's something more important and they don't want to be bothered. Fr. Wakkin—

Aimie laughed. "We know about Fr. Wakkin. Even the pilot and I can sense what he wants. One doesn't need empathy."

But Cyn still had his mind on using Niais to point out which of the passengers had been Mortchose's partner. Rocam seemed the most likely. Her loosing Cotchkelah at Mortchose did not exonerate her. She could have known they had arrived at the wrong planet and that they would all die if she didn't save the pilot. And Rocam did seem to see everything in political terms. But it was so hard to believe.

"Demoson and Hachisman felt the same? No difference from the way Wakkin felt? Are you sure you didn't concentrate on Wakkin because he was younger, more attractive, because you liked him better?"

For a moment Niais stared, perfectly dumbfounded. Then she exclaimed, "How could I like any one better? I like everybody. I like everybody exactly the same. I can't like one more and one less." Then she frowned anxiously. "Younger? More attractive?" Her voice grew tremulous. "Maybe I don't see the same as you?"

Cyn wondered again how Niais had failed to win residence

in the Garden. He was certain that Myrrha would have answered him in the same way—except for the last, frightened question. "Don't worry about it, love," he said quickly. "I'm sure your eyes see the same. You just don't think the way we do."

"Oh, think!" Niais laughed.

Almost Cyn heard the peal of bells. He sighed. She had failed because she was too stupid, he feared. And his idea had not paid off. Rocam might well have no strong sexual impulses at her age; preoccupation was not the only suppressant of libido. Demoson and Hachisman had made no secret of having urgent and preoccupying business, and both were men of experience, so it was not really surprising that they were not obsessed with Niais. And the fact that Wakkin was, did not exclude him from being Mortchose's partner. A criminal, even a killer, was not necessarily preoccupied with his purpose; he could be prepared to do his job when the occasion arose without rejecting what Niais offered.

Aimie had been smiling, her eyes registering amused disbelief either at Niais's statement or at the idea anyone could so lightly dismiss thinking. Then she stretched and yawned. "I think I'll take a turn in your bed, Cyn. When you need to sleep, wake me. And maybe you'd better keep Niais up here. I told Rocam to lock herself in after Cotchkelah flew and she agreed, but you'd have to nail Niais's head to the bunk to keep her out of someone else's. Having her loose would make it too easy to grab her as a hostage."

Cyn nodded agreement, and a short time was spent pleasantly enough in choosing and eating an evening meal. All too soon, Cyn was regretting the need to keep Niais with him. Conversation with her was nearly impossible, nor was it possible simply to retire to his couch and watch the Pot operate. Niais got restless. He compromised, at last, on a simple card game.

At first Cyn credited his constant winning to Niais's stupidity and made attempts to explain her mistakes. She did not repeat the mistakes and her play improved for a few games; however Cyn soon started to win too steadily again. It didn't take him long to discover the reason, because her cheating was very clumsy.

That Niais should cheat did not surprise Cyn; Niais seemed to have a system of morals, but they were skewed to her own logic. Nor did it surprise him that she should cheat herself to give him the games. Any commercial partner of pleasure pandered automatically to the ego of his/her/its companion. What surprised Cyn was the rapidity and accuracy with which she had absorbed his instructions about the game.

Certainly she was not stupid about learning, nor about correcting mistakes, honest or intended. She had seen that Cyn was bent on teaching her, so she shifted to cheating to gain her ends. That wasn't stupid either. Some men enjoyed childish partners they could instruct, but Cyn didn't and she had been quick to read that aspect of his character. Did her empathy go farther than she understood—or admitted?

He stared at the cards, wondering. Niais kept insisting she had to go to Ingong. If that were true, she could have no connection with events on Mantra; if it weren't true, it could be one more cover in a surprisingly tight cover story. She wasn't even on the list of passengers. Her youth, her overt idiocy—neither meant anything. Depending on where she really came from, she might be many syrs older than Cyn was and idiocy could always be assumed. Mortchose had threatened her, but he hadn't even touched her.

"What's in the package you carry so carefully, Niais?" Cyn asked.

"I can't tell you that," she responded readily.

"Why not?"

"Because I don't know. It's a present for someone on Ingong."

"Aren't you curious?" Cyn insisted. "Haven't you looked?"

"I'm not a curious person," Niais reminded him, then shrugged. "It doesn't matter. I can't look. I can't get it open."

"Don't be silly. It's just wrapped in cloth."

He got up and came around the desk. Niais did not resist when he lifted the package from her lap, but he almost dropped it because of its surprising weight. He looked at Niais's slender arms with an awed respect, and realized that part of the weight was Niais's arm, which had risen with the package. Then he saw that she didn't cling to the package for support, as a child clings to some toy or cloth for security. The package was attached to a broad bracelet on her left wrist. But Cyn clearly remembered Niais holding the package with her right hand, her arms spread widely apart, while he was fighting Mortchose. And she had been shifting it from her left hand to her right just before the blaster exploded on Xiphe.

"Niais," Cyn said softly, "you can loosen the package, can't you?"

"Yes," she agreed without the smallest hint of reluctance, "but it's very dangerous, very, very dangerous." Suddenly she shuddered. "I know I mustn't touch it, that it cuts flesh, but—but it went right through that male's blaster when I tried to pull it away from him, and it blew up and hurt him." Tears glittered in her lower lids. "I didn't know."

"What went right through his blaster?"

For answer, Niais touched one of the protrusions on her bracelet and her arm dropped. At first Cyn saw nothing, then some movement made a sparkle of light run along the invisible line. Cyn blinked wonderingly. He had heard of monofilaments but had never seen—or not seen—one before. It was a single enormous molecule. Laser might cut through it, but almost no other force could break the bonds between the atoms; it required a chemical reaction—a very specific chemical reaction. His eyes fell to the package and he could see it was part of the thread. What in all of space could be in the parcel when the worth of the covering could buy a man ten sdays in the Garden?

Cyn shook his head and returned the parcel to her lap, the thread reeling in with the slightest relaxation of tension. What in space was the bracelet made of to resist that thread, which had sheered through the metal of a blaster? The question was purely rhetorical, but it reminded Cyn that Niais had saved his life and, incidentally, prevented the pilot on Xiphe from taking his place. He relaxed and went back to his seat.

"Honey," he said, "I don't like to win all the time. I like a good fight better than winning. Play the best you can, Niais, or let's quit."

The direct approach was always best with her. Given a clear directive, Niais could home in on a goal. Her limpid eyes grew brighter; her warm red lips pursed in concentration. Niais played that hand as if her life depended on the outcome. Cyn lost. He concentrated harder himself, and lost again. In smins he found he was enjoying the game. A few smins more and he was playing as if his own life depended on it.

Peripherally Cyn detected a flash of color. His head snapped up, eyes fixed on his console. He stared intently, checking each light, but every one was its normal green and none that should be dark were lit. Still uneasy, he rose and peered more closely, particularly at the navigation displays and Carroll system function. Nothing. He started back toward the desk, then stopped short. Niais had been in bed with him when the homing caller had been placed in the shuttle. Try as he might, Cyn could not decide whether she had distracted him deliberately—after all, he had been asleep when she came and might well have missed a minor warning like a light flashing on when the shuttle lock was opened. And she had saved him on Xiphe. Nonetheless he turned back toward his console.

"You've stopped playing?" Niais asked.

Her voice held no disappointment, no reproach. She seemed only to be asking confirmation of the obvious, but Cyn felt vaguely guilty. He had known she was enjoying herself, enjoying a respite from straining constantly to please— was that why she was so insatiable sexually? Because it was the only way she knew to please without doubt? He hesitated, remembered that the homer had been set while she was in his bed, and said, "Yes. I have something I must do now." Hesitated again, then smiled and added, "But I have time to teach you a card game you can play against yourself. Would you like to do that while I'm busy?"

Niais agreed. Cyn showed her a simple solitaire. When he returned to the console, she was dealing out, her head bent in concentration. There had been no further sign of unusual activity, but Cyn asked the puter to trace back electric signals from the console lights. In ssecs he had notice of a brief change from green to red in the av. Aimie had mentioned that the av might be malfunctioning . . . No, that had been Cotchkelah flying, hadn't it?

Even while the thought ran through his head, he was requesting a trace of av function. The puter reported all OFF switches in the passenger level were bad. That was fine; Cyn had done that himself. Then a brief hiccup in the av in

Hachisman's cabin showed. Cyn immediately called up an image of that cabin; a visual of the small darkened area appeared without a hitch. Everything in the cabin looked perfectly normal, including the humped form in the bunk. Cyn strained, but he could not make out the hair or face; the blanket seemed bunched high on Hachisman's shoulders.

Cyn returned to the search for electric disturbances in the av. Another blip in Hachisman's cabin. That wasn't much of a surprise. If the av in that cabin was malfunctioning, it might do so more than once. Cyn called the image of Hachisman's cabin again. The view on the screen was identical. The body in the bunk hadn't moved. Not much time had passed since his last look and people did sleep very still sometimes. But . . . Cyn glanced at the chrono. Four stus. Well, that would have to do.

"Aimie," he called from the doorway to his quarters. "There was a hiccup in Hachisman's av. He seems to be asleep, but I think I'll go down and make sure of it."

She woke alert, and said, "Two smins," heading for the fresher as she spoke. Nor did she take much longer to emerge and ask Cyn what he wanted her to do.

"Like before. Don't let anyone in. Let me know if any odd lights come on . . . Actually, I should be back in no time. I'm just going down to peek into Hachisman's cabin."

He removed the all-unseal from its drawer as he answered, opening it with the right sequence of thumb and fingerprints and prodding the "Check passenger cabin" dipswitch as the reason.

Cyn knew his way through the rec room in the relative dark, progressed silently to Hachisman's door, unlocked it, opened it a slit, and stood listening. Nothing. But this time "nothing" was wrong. Either Hachisman was alive and not breathing, thus not homo and worthy of further investigation;

dead and not breathing, also worthy of further investigation; or not in the cabin at all. Cyn pushed the door aside, entered and shut it—in case his reasoning, or ears, was faulty and Hachisman began to shout complaints about being wakened.

The hump under the bunched blankets was not a body. Just as Cyn's hand had ascertained that fact, Aimie's voice came over the av. "Rocam's missing. Not in her cabin. Not anywhere else I can see on the passenger level."

Cyn muttered an obscenity. "Where are the others?"

"Demoson and Wakkin are together in Demoson's cabin. Demoson's at that everlasting puter and Wakkin's reading. I don't—" Her voice checked sharply, and when it resumed, the pitch was high with tension. "Cyn, we're out of Carroll's void and the navigator's beeping."

"On my way."

He was up the companionway and at the console before he let out the breath he had caught. He keyed a query. The puter reported that they had made the eighth transition completely, had passed out of strong carrollpause influence on the ninth, entered the void—and had been thrown out of it by a very large gravitic influence. Cyn checked everything he could think of and several systems that had no possible influence on Carroll operation. His results were either negative or reported that there was a gigantic gravity well very near the Pot. Cyn turned on the visual screens and scanned, shaking his head, knowing what he was doing was ridiculous.

Nothing showed. Well, there couldn't be anything there. The proximity indicators, which operated outward from the hull, were silent, but even if they had been malfunctioning Cyn knew no physical anomaly was causing the problem. Had the ship been that close to any object of such gigantic gravity, they would be falling into that object with increasing velocity. But the Pot wasn't accelerating. It was moving with no change in the small velocity established when it emerged from the void.

The trouble wasn't outside the ship, so it must be inside. Cyn began to trace each system and very soon found that a contradiction appeared in the report from the shuttle systems. The "whole system" was showing itself as OFF on the puter scan, but a strong draw of power was also indicated.

Cyn didn't bother with further analysis. He sat cursing himself for being stupid and wasting time. Mortchose's partner was the one who had electronic bafflers; whoever had convinced the freezer alarm not to go off when Mortchose had been revived would likely have little trouble feeding false information into the shuttle sensors and faking an OFF signal. Rocam was gone and Hachisman was gone. Gone where?

"Not out into space, stupid," Cyn muttered to himself. "Where else could they have gone but the shuttle?"

"The shuttle?" Aimie repeated.

"Rocam or Hachisman or both are in the shuttle sending a false gravity signal. The Carroll system thinks the shuttle is a black hole."

"What are you going to do?" she asked.

"I'm not sure what I'm going to do," he said, "except to get into that shuttle and turn off whatever is on." His lips were thinned and his pale eyes unnaturally bright. "This can't hurt us and it can't be another attempt to take the ship. No organization, no matter how big, could know where we are. A trick like this can only delay us, and it can't even delay us very long because we're inside the Empire now and I can yell for help. That means one or two sdays must be important."

Cyn got up as he spoke and got out his space armor. He put a fresh recycler into the breather and began to make adjustments to the suit radio, setting the suit-to-ship channel to sound over the av system just as if he were at his console and the suit-to-suit channel to transmit to a particular headset.

"Yelling for help could notify whoever's friends."

"Not if I give a false ident," he said, handing her the headset. "I know several other mail ship designations. I'd have to be an idiot not to think of that. So would whoever."

"What's this for?" Aimie lifted the headset.

Cyn told her and then began to get into the space armor. "I don't know why, but I have the feeling Rocam was trying to tell me something when she talked about the Planetary Council recess. A warning? A plea for help? I don't know, but I'm sure either she or Hachisman doesn't want us to reach Empire Star before the recess." He latched the suit closed and donned the helmet, leaving off the gloves and keeping the faceplate open. He started to turn toward the lift but stopped and snarled, "I've had it! I swear we'll get to Mantra on time even if I have to get out and push the Pot there myself."

Aimie started to laugh, but stopped when Niais said plaintively, "Are we lost again?"

"No," Cyn told her. "I know just where we are, and we'll be on our way as soon as I get that pain-in-the-ass out of the shuttle and into the freezer. Be a good fem, Niais, go back into my quarters and stay there. You can take the cards if you like." He watched her go and jammed the door once more, telling Aimie briefly about the danger of the monofilament line, but ending, "I think she's just what she says, but there's no sense taking any more chances."

"No," Aimie said thoughtfully, "not for the next two—or is it three—sdays, anyway. I think I know why whoever doesn't want us to arrive before the recess. Remember what I was saying to you about a challenge to the Emperor? The challenge has to be made before the Planetary Council."

"So what?" Cyn was checking the supplies and tools hooked on the suit belt and in its pockets and pouches.

"So if any harm comes to the challenger after the formal challenge is made and before the Council has made its determination, the challenged Imperial is automatically deposed—whether or not the Imperial is involved in harming the challenger. A new Emperor or Empress, whichever was challenged, must be chosen and enthroned."

Cyn looked up from his examination of the charge in the small metal-cutting laser. "Are you sure?"

"Of course I'm sure. It's happened three times. The first time was how a nonhumanoid species came to the throne. There was no fem heir and Queen Mother Nnuzissun challenged the then-Empress, who had the Queen Mother killed—not very discreetly. One of the first big scandals in Imperial history. It's taught over and over in political science classes."

"So once the challenge is made, the challenger is protected." Cyn shook his head and removed the laser's backup magazine from his belt to make sure it, too, was fully charged. "It's still crazy. The Council's been in session a good part of the syr and the trouble between the Emperor and Empress has existed for a long time, long before he was enthroned, I've heard. Why let him be crowned? Why leave a challenge to the last sday?"

"I don't know why the Empress 'let him be crowned,' " Aimie said. "Maybe she couldn't stop it, but why the challenge was left to the last few sdays—we were supposed to arrive two sdays before the recess—that's easy. The challenger has to be another son of the Empress, so the Council couldn't possibly deny his challenge without 'proper examination.' I can't see the Council delaying the recess. In fact, the representatives would be more eager to go home to discuss the situation. So, the challenger would have the whole period of the recess to make his case to the Councilors and their governments—and in perfect safety."

Cyn had started toward the lift as she explained but he stopped with his palm almost against the lock, turning his whole body, since the helmet wouldn't turn, to look back at her. "No wonder the Emperor's party is so desperate to stop us. No, wait. The ship with the tractor could have vaporized us. The Planetary Police could have blown us away too. Why spend a fortune and operate such complicated schemes?"

"Because there were, or are, decoys. Remember the two ships that disappeared? The Emperor's people have to be sure they have the real challenger—maybe they'll try to fix his mind so that he'll deny intent to challenge before the Planetary Council. Above all, they can't afford to vaporize him. Don't you see that with the Empress's backing any number of false challengers could be presented? No, they need the male himself."

Cyn hesitated, then said, "There's only Wakkin and Demoson left. Which? And is it the real thing we've got aboard?" And then, before she could answer, he added, "No. I don't want to know. It's none of my business. Blast them all! I just want to deliver the mail on time."

He lifted his hand toward the palm-lock again, but this time Aimie said, "Wait. There's one thing we've overlooked. I've never seen Wakkin and Demoson in a cabin together before. Is one the prisoner of the other? And which one?"

She turned the av on as she spoke; Demoson was still working on his puter and Wakkin was leaning back against the wall, the reader on his lap between lax hands. No weapon was in evidence.

"Leave it as it is," Cyn said. "I've got to get us started before anything else."

CHAPTER 16

Cyn darkened the interior of the lift before he opened the door into the passenger level. The rec room was dark and quiet. Stunner in hand, he stepped out then into the medic compartment, right next door. There he picked up two canisters of anesthetic gas with valves and tubes. He was about to step back into the lift, when an odd sound coming from the passage to the shuttle lock caught his attention. He froze, listening. A very faint, but totally inhuman squawk, then another. Cotchkelah!

Trying hard to walk softly—no easy feat in space armor—Cyn entered the passage. The panel protecting the manual device for opening the outer door of the lock was open but the lock itself was closed. Closer, Cyn could hear the frantic squawking better. He hesitated for a moment. Lock doors were not made to spring open, and the slow slide would be a warning to anyone in the lock and give whoever a good chance to level a weapon.

Nerves, Cyn reproved himself. The armor would protect him against anything but a laser long enough to use his own stunner, and the chances were that the person in the lock—if there was a person in the lock—was not dangerous. The one who wanted to stop the Pot from getting to Mantra was in the shuttle. Nonetheless, Cyn's fingers itched to move the setting on the stunner to full as his free hand pulled the lever to open.

As the door slid, the light came on automatically. Cyn's eyes were first drawn to the bird, flapping awkwardly on the floor, screaming its rage and frustration. A thin, weary whisper, "Hush, Cotchkelah, hush," drew Cyn in immediately.

"I've found Rocam," he said into the suit-to-suit speaker.

The old lady, white as paper, was trying to lift herself from a crumpled position against the shuttle door. Her eyes widened momentarily in terror when Cyn's armored form loomed over her, but her expression altered to one of relief when she made out his features.

"Are you hurt?" Cyn asked.

"No, not at all," she sighed. "So foolish. I'm sorry pilot. I have been very foolish." Her lips quivered toward a smile and mischief filled her eyes. "One forgets one's age. When I saw Fr. Hachisman leaving the passenger area so—so surreptitiously, I—I followed."

"Are you sure you're all right?" Cyn repeated, repressing a strong urge to take the woman, who was old enough to be his grandmother, over his knee and paddle her.

Clumsily he knelt beside her and helped her to sit up. This was a passenger list to end all passenger lists, he thought. Taking into consideration the political situation, the agent of the Emperor or his supporters and a decoy or—Power help him—the real challenger were almost reasonable, but how had he offended the Powers that Be in such a way that they would visit on him in addition a nymphomaniac idiot and an old lady in a funny hat with a taste for adventure?

"Oh, yes. I'll be better in a moment." Fr. Rocam lifted a shaking hand and touched it to her temple. "Would you please catch Cotchkelah? He will break his wings. Oh, dear, I have been foolish. I should have warned you at once, instead of allowing my curiosity to . . . But he's such a troubled

232

person, and not at all violent. But—I didn't wait long enough, you see. I thought he would be busy in the shuttle and not notice when I opened the door."

"There's a light on the console to warn the pilot if the lock opens," Cyn said.

He captured the bird and handed it to her, then lifted her to her feet. She wavered but managed to walk the step or two through the outer door. Cotchkelah folded his wings and fell silent as she stroked him.

"I didn't know," she whispered, gazing apologetically up at Cyn, who was still supporting her. "But it should have been obvious. How stupid of me. Well, of course, he turned around and saw me through the opening. He said, 'You!' as if I had betrayed him. We had talked, you see, and I was sympathetic to some of his ideas. I suppose he stunned me. I don't remember."

"He'll have this lock dogged," Cyn muttered to himself, half his mind on what to do with the old lady.

"I'm so sorry." Then she seemed to take in Cyn's armor and her brow creased in a frown equally compounded of headache and puzzlement. "What has he done?"

"He's blocked the Carroll's void system," Cyn said absently, wondering if he should take her up and leave her with Aimie. "He's got something in the shuttle that's telling it we're at a carrollpause."

"How long have I been here?"

"Not long, less than thirty smins anyway."

"Then the charge he fired at me must have been very light. I don't know much about weapons, but I know that much."

"Didn't want to scramble your brains, I suppose. Probably his people want information."

Fr. Rocam's eyes dropped to the armament attached to Cyn's suit belt. "What are you going to do?" she asked faintly.

"Do? I'm going to get that misbegotten son of a slithian slave trader and a wraxian whore out of that shuttle, even if I have to extract him through the air-tight seals atom by atom."

The old lady's breath caught. The light, half-jesting words and tone didn't match the hard, pale eyes. "Pilot," she said hastily, "this man is not another Mortchose, even if his purpose is the same. I'm sure he didn't change the setting on his stunner when he fired at me. That means the weapon was set at that low charge. He didn't want to hurt anyone."

"Are you suggesting that I let him accomplish his purpose?"

"No! Oh, no. If what I guess is true, we must get to Mantra on time. I only want to say that this man is not a killer by intention. Be as gentle as you can."

Cyn laughed. "I don't want to have to explain two dead passengers, even with Security personnel aboard to support my story."

But Fr. Rocam's insistence that Hachisman was not basically violent had reminded Cyn that she had earlier said they had talked and that gave him an idea. He looked down at the frail old woman, who was standing on her own again, opened his mouth, and then shut it firmly, shocked at what he had been about to do. She laid the hand that was not supporting Cotchkelah on his armored arm. It had so little substance that he wondered how she carried even a bird's small weight. Cyn could not feel the hand but he saw it move and looked higher, into her face. Her eyes were young, alive with interest and expectation.

"You were going to ask me to help," she said eagerly. "Don't hesitate, please. I'm not afraid and—and I have so little to lose, much less than you, pilot."

Cyn couldn't doubt her sincerity. She needed to be useful and had so little opportunity—only Cotchkelah. And there shouldn't be much danger.

"All right," he said. "There's a speaker mechanism next to the lock. If you're willing, I'd like you to keep his attention and keep his ears busy. Now don't you be foolish again and make me feel I've murdered you. If you hear him at the door, you run. Yell for Fr. Aimie and lock yourself in your cabin."

She nodded and started back to the inner door. Cyn held her back. "Don't make him mad and don't frighten him. I don't know what weapons he's got in there. A laser can fire right through the lock, maybe even through the hull of the shuttle. I don't know how much energy there'd be left in the beam, but it could well be enough to make a nasty hole in you—and it wouldn't do my shuttle any good either."

Rocam uttered a smothered giggle. Cyn frowned at her.

"I'm going to leave this door open so you can run. He'll see that on the telltales. If he asks about it, tell him you went out and came back."

"What are you going to do?" she asked in a hushed voice.

Cyn looked at her squarely. "It's better that no one but me knows. If he asks, tell him anything you think he'll believe. It won't matter."

"Of course." Rocam shook her head. "How silly I am. If he heard us while we were still near the inner lock, he might try to catch me and make me tell him what I know. What I don't know, I can't tell."

With all too vivid memories of Mortchose's idea of the way to extract information, Cyn nearly changed his mind, but the old lady gave him no chance. Smiling, with her eyes twinkling, she had already trotted to the lock door and pushed the speaker button.

"Fr. Hachisman," she said, "I don't know what you're doing in there, but I'm sure it's wrong and may be dangerous. I realize I startled you, and I'm sorry, but you're very fortunate I wasn't hurt when you stunned me. I'm an old fem. Now come out of there and we'll forget the whole thing."

Cyn clamped his jaws together hard to repress a most inopportune temptation to laugh. The tone was that which an indulgent but disapproving grandmother would use to a naughty child. It would be almost impossible to resist, he imagined.

"Go away! A sweet old lady like you—the Empress is a monster to use you to prevent progress."

Cyn went back to the lift. The voice came through his helmet earphones on the ship-to-suit com line. In the control room, Aimie would be hearing the same thing. Hachisman's near hysteria was clear. Cyn hesitated before he pushed the **DOWN** button. If Hachisman burst through the lock and hurt Rocam, Cyn would never forgive himself. However the old lady replied at once.

"I assure you I have no connection with the Empress at all, not even through my husband. Ecology is in the Emperor's domain." Her voice was patient and indulgent. "I only know that when someone sneaks around in the dark as you did, his activities are not healthy, and I'm very much afraid if you don't come out that someone will get hurt. Come out, do."

"If I come out, billions of beings will continue to be hurt, to live in slavery, and be warped and tortured. Is that what you want? Is that what you believe in?"

Cyn felt considerably relieved. If Hachisman was willing to talk politics, the chances were slim that he would attack Rocam. And 'grandma' was already having an effect; her concern seemed to be making him less hysterical.

The lift stopped. Cyn fastened his faceplate and pulled on his gloves, nulled the buzzer that was designed to warn lift passengers the area beyond the doors had no life support, opened the door manually, jammed it open, and stepped out of the lift on the cargo level. He had left the lift lock dark, cold, and without air because he did not know how much Hachisman could get from the shuttle instruments. Certain adjustments would advise on the condition of the cargo/lift lock. He walked as softly as he could toward the lock door, unhooking the metal-cutting laser from his belt.

"Fr. Hachisman," Rocam was saying, her voice soft with sympathy, "I am an old fem. I have lived a long life and traveled with my husband on ecological projects to many planets. It seems that intelligent beings will always torture each other. This makes me very sad. I don't know why it is so. I hope that some time the reason will be discovered and the sickness cured. Until that time, there is nothing I can do—and I have tried, many times—or that you can do either to change this."

"You're talking about personal relationships," Hachisman said. "I'm talking about laws. The Empire is a sick monster. Many of its limbs are diseased and rotting because the Council is corrupt. Medicine must be administered, and only one strong man can administer it."

"My dear young male," Rocam sighed, "it is difficult and dangerous to try to administer strong medicine to an unwilling patient. If the patient should dismiss his doctor, the condition would surely grow worse—even become fatal."

Cyn lay down on the floor and felt along the door until he found the edge. Inside the shuttle he knew there was a projection where a shelf for small boxed cargo protruded. He had no idea whether Hachisman had turned the lights on throughout the shuttle. If he had, probably the glow of the metal heated by the laser would not show, but if he had left the cargo hold dark, it would. Cyn hoped the projection would hide any light given off by the melting metal.

There was another danger: that the life-support sensors in the shuttle console would record the escape of air into the airless lift lock; however, Cyn was making only a very small hole. He didn't think the air pressure would change significantly in the few smins before he pushed a narrow piece of tubing in and started feeding in the anesthetic gas.

"You are presupposing a sane patient," Hachisman replied, his voice scaling upward with passion, but the passion was old, unrelated to events in the ship. "When the patient is mentally incompetent, he cannot dismiss his doctor."

Jaw set with distaste, Cyn put the barrel of the laser against the corner of the door. He hated to damage his ship; it hurt, almost as if he were planning to burn a hole in himself. The only reason he could do it at all was to save his Pot from what he believed would be a worse violation. He drew a deep breath, vowing to take the damage out of Hachisman's hide, and switched the laser on.

"Unfortunately sanity and insanity are not matters of fact but matters of judgment," Rocam said reasonably. "What you might consider insane—"

"To hell with metaphors," Hachisman interrupted. "The slave planets are a blot on the Empire. Slavery is a sin against God! Slavery must be wiped out!"

Yellow, red, white and at last a white rim surrounding a black center. Cyn watched the plastel change, cursing the fact that the helmet prevented him from properly lining his eye up with the hole the laser was making. The angle prevented him from looking through the black hole in the center to see when he had cut through. Then he told himself not to be a fool. He would know.

"Slavery is a disgusting and heinous practice," Fr. Rocam agreed soothingly, "but—"

"There can be no buts!" Hachisman screamed. "You were born free," he panted, "but I—I was born a slave."

Cyn's finger slipped from the on button. The white rim of

plastel started to sag and dull toward red. It was one thing to frustrate a person who wanted to enrich and aggrandize himself by gaining influence with a corrupt or foolish Emperor; it was quite another to turn over to the tender mercies of the Empress and Council a being who had suffered far too much already.

"But you are free now," Rocam pointed out, her thin, old voice steady, "and without any help from a dictatorial authority that could easily be a worse monster than—"

"I am free because **GOD** put out **HIS** hand and lifted me out of the degradation of my state. **HE** consecrated me to the duty of saving the universe. Any government, any single being, who permits slavery to exist anywhere is **DAMNED**."

The shrill fanaticism of the voice restored Cyn to his normal first-things-first pragmatism. He remembered Rocam saying, "You will enslave us all to make some free." What Hachisman wanted was no solution—and probably wouldn't happen anyway. If he could find a way to let the man go after they arrived at Mantra, Cyn thought, aching with empathic pain, he would do it—but one male's grief and horror would not weigh much in the balance of hundreds of burning or decaying worlds. And that would be the result, Cyn was sure, of trying to use force to establish uniformity. He pressed the on button again.

"I am as eager as you to wipe out involuntary slavery," Rocam said, "but to destroy the Empire would not accomplish that purpose. If the Empire collapses, the slave planets would have no external controls on them. They might spread their practices to new planets, or high civilizations might degenerate as trade became disrupted and fall into slavery."

"I'm not trying to destroy the Empire," Hachisman snarled, "I'm trying to build the Empire into something good and **HOLY**."

"But force is never holy," Rocam protested, "and it would surely rupture the thin lines that hold the Empire together. You must know that it was only possible to form the federation that we call Empire because each member planet was promised total autonomy. The Empire governs only trade and relationships between planets. If the right of any member—"

"Slavery is not a right!" Hachisman raged.

"Neither, to my way of thinking, is murder," the gentle old voice persisted, "but the Empire does not dictate to its members what the punishment for murder should be or even whether murder is a crime at all. Each culture must decide for itself the rules by which it wishes to live."

The pencil of color that was not light had eaten away the sagging lip of the hole and begun to bore inward again. Cyn gritted his teeth with impatience, but there was nothing he could do to hurry the process; the material of which the shuttle was made was tough. Nonetheless, he thought it would not be very long before the hole was drilled. He braced the laser on the floor and found that it was possible to hold it with one hand. With the other, he drew out a coil of thin metal tubing with a short length of elastomer at one end.

"I do not say your god did not help you to freedom," Rocam continued, "but you helped yourself also. You desired to be free. In your culture lie the seeds of freedom."

"All slaves desire to be free."

"Oh, no." The denial was gentle but very positive. "I have been to two planets where the masters could not free themselves from their slaves. Slavery was no longer economical, but the slaves would not accept responsibility for their own lives. My husband was sent to study the culture and find a way to convince them they could live in freedom."

"I don't believe you! The Empire supports slavery."

A sudden change in the beam of the laser made Cyn lift his finger. This time when the beam of energy was cut off, the lips of the hole did not sag. Cyn could not hear the whistle of escaping air, but the dim ready light from the lift was enough to illuminate the moisture carried with it, which froze instantly into glittering microcrystals. Hurriedly he laid down the laser so he could manipulate the tubing into the hole. The push of emerging air tended to repel the tube and Cyn's gloves were clumsy. Still, it did not take long. Cyn pinched the elastomer end of the tubing to cut off the flow of air out of the shuttle and drew a deep breath. So far, so good.

"If you want the bald truth," Rocam replied, "the Empire didn't care a minum's worth about either masters or slaves. By charter, the Empire cannot interfere in any planet's internal affairs but must help a member planet that requests help. The most limited and inexpensive help the Empire could provide was to send my husband to 'study the situation.' That he actually solved the problem for one culture was a miracle—"

Cyn pulled at one of the gas cylinders on his belt, trying to detach it, but he dared not let go of the elastomer he had pinched shut. The cylinder, just too fat for his hand to close around, was awkward to maneuver one-handed. He managed to unhook it, but as he brought it around the end came in contact with the shuttle door. Cyn froze. He had heard nothing, of course; one cannot hear where there is no medium to carry the sound, but there was air in the shuttle. Hachisman might have heard.

However, his angry voice interrupted Rocam. "The Empire should care!" he cried.

The breath Cyn was holding started to ease out, but his relief had come too soon. In the next moment, Hachisman added querulously, "You're talking to me like this for a reason."

"Certainly," Rocam responded promptly. "I'm trying to get you to see reason, to convince you that what you're doing will not accomplish your very worthy purpose."

"You don't care whether my purpose is worthy or not."

Something was wrong. Even through the filtering of the com line Cyn could detect that Hachisman's voice was different. Cyn couldn't put a name to that difference except perhaps a note of abstraction, as if Hachisman was thinking of something else while he spoke. Sick between the need for haste and the contrary need not to make another sound, Cyn struggled to fit the elastomer over the tube from the valve of the gas cylinder. He had to let it spring open to do that, and again the betraying sparkle of freezing water vapor gave evidence of the hiss of escaping air. Cyn could not hear it, but Hachisman might.

He heard Rocam talking and another statement from Hachisman, but that seemed very short, almost indifferent, and his voice blurred several times as if it were turned away from the com. Cyn's jaw ached from the force with which he had his teeth set, and then the elastomer slid into position and he was able to turn the valve. He was careful, fighting the temptation to open it all the way; the hiss of ingoing gas would be as betraying as that of outgoing air. He had decided to content himself with a half turn until Hachisman suddenly shouted, "What are you doing? I hear you! Get away from that door."

Cyn turned the valve on full and dropped the cylinder, groping for the stunner on his belt as he scrambled to his feet.

"I'm sorry, I fell against the door," Rocam called. "I just got dizzy for a smin. Oh, I can't leave you alone in there. Please come out, Fr. Hachisman. If—if you don't come out,

I'll—I'll have to tell the pilot where you are."

Half furious, half grateful, Cyn didn't know whether he wanted to kiss or kill Rocam. That redoubtable old fem was trying a final, very dangerous gambit in her effort to hold Hachisman's attention. Cyn bent to grope for the laser he had left on the floor, cursing himself, praying that Hachisman wouldn't decide to keep the "secret" of where he was by dashing out to silence Rocam for good.

Her gambit paid off, however; instead of opening the lock and trying to seize her, Hachisman snarled, "You think I'm stupid, don't you? You think I don't know the pilot can hear every word we say over the com and that by now he's probably right next to you trying to get the door open? You think I didn't guess that you were talking to me to hide the noises he was making? Well, getting the door open won't do him any good. I don't want to hurt anyone, but I will if I have to. I won't use a stunner on him. I've got a blaster and—and I'll use it. Pilot, listen, if you won't be reasonable I'll use it. I will!"

"Whether or not the pilot is here, I meant every word I said," Rocam cried. "You cannot achieve your purpose this way. I'm sure if you will come out, the pilot could be convinced to forget everything connecting you to Mortchose."

Cyn had found the midpoint of the far edge of the lock door and was playing the laser on the area he believed held the latch. He tried the manual lever, but it would not move to the open position. He needed to cut farther.

"In God's name, pilot," Hachisman yelled, "leave me alone for two sdays. I'll turn off my device then and we can go on to Mantra. I'll even let you take me prisoner. Just go away. Leave me alone."

"Is there something we can do, pilot? Wakkin and I are here with Fr. Rocam."

That was Demoson's deep voice. Cyn rolled his eyes. That was all he needed. His finger pressed harder on the laser trigger as if that would make it burn faster.

On the ship-to-suit channel, Aimie said. "I cut off the com to Demoson's cabin, but one of them must have opened the door and heard Rocam."

"You!" Hachisman shrieked simultaneously. "You devil!"

Cyn swallowed an oath, not daring to make a sound. The gas didn't seem to be working. Either there wasn't enough or it was diffusing very slowly and hadn't yet reached Hachisman at the top of the shuttle. He turned off the laser, hooked it to his belt, and knelt down to replace the first gas cylinder with the second. In his haste, he forgot the first cylinder and when he rose, he hit it with his heel and it rolled. Cyn neither felt nor heard it, but it must have hit the shuttle lock because Hachisman's sudden howl of rage overrode all other sounds.

"What are you doing at the cargo lock?" he screamed. "You can't get in. I'll burn you if you open it. You deserve to die for making so much trouble. God wants you to die. If you hadn't interfered every time, we'd all be safe and I would have accomplished God's will without doing harm."

Inside his helmet, Cyn drew back his lips in a snarl. If this was one of god's messengers, Hachisman's god could take a spacewalk without armor.

Hachisman was still yelling, "Don't you dare open that. All the air will go out. That would be deliberate murder!"

When I do it, Cyn thought, it's deliberate murder, but when you plan to fry me with a blaster, that's god's work. But he knew there was no chance that Hachisman would be harmed by the open lock. The cargo hold was sealed off, and the amount of air that would rush into the lock itself was small. Then he realized that the last few words had been fainter and slower. If Hachisman had come down to face the cargo lock door, maybe the gas had gotten him.

"Don't be a fool, Hachisman," Cyn said. "You've done nothing really serious until now. You'll get off with a fine and a reprimand for interfering with Overstars traffic. Killing me would be something else entirely. No one else knows how to run the ship. You could all die."

There was no answer and Cyn's spirits soared. He yanked on the lever—and it gave, falling to the open position. The door did not slide aside, however. Cyn thought he must have burned through the wiring as well as the latch that held it. That was no problem. Shifting the laser to his left hand, he pulled a thin pry bar from his belt and worked it into the opening the laser had made. A single forceful push, levered against the frame, drove the door back into its slot.

"Murderer!" Hachisman screamed. "You won't succeed! I've fooled you! I've proved you deserve to die."

Blinded by the light within the shuttle—he had forgotten he had been working in near dark—Cyn hesitated.

"Out!" Hachisman shouted. "Out or I'll burn you down."

Cyn's breath caught. He had been misled by the hysteria in the man's voice. Hachisman might be a fanatic, but he wasn't a fool. Some time during his conversation with Rocam, when his voice changed that time, he had put on an emergency life-support suit. No wonder the gas had no effect.

"Out!" Hachisman screamed again.

Simultaneously he fired the blaster—but either he was no killer or had never handled such a weapon before. The bolt went wide, searing the wall beside the door. In reflex, Cyn pressed the stud on the laser. Although his aim was better, even left-handed, he did Hachisman no more harm than Hachisman had done him. The laser was a short range tool, and its focus was not long enough to reach its target.

245

Hachisman, however, was startled by Cyn's obviously lethal intent. He backed away, firing wildly again. The edge of the blast washed one of Cyn's arms with heat, and Cyn spat obscenity but the shock restored his rationality. Instead of returning fire uselessly, Cyn lunged forward. He still held the laser leveled, but he had no intention of using it. For one thing, he suspected Hachisman was almost as terrified of burning Cyn as he was of being burnt. More important, Hachisman had backed up the ladder toward the front of the shuttle and the boat's instrumentation was behind him. If he got close enough to catch Hachisman in the laser's beam, he would also be close enough to damage the shuttle's instruments if he missed his target.

"Stop! Stop! I'll kill you if I have to! I will!"

Cyn laughed and surged toward the ladder. It was too late for killing on either side, he thought—and then he gasped with pain as heat washed his armor. The cooling elements whined in protest at the sudden burden, but they could not compensate. Searing heat transmitted from the armor to Cyn's midsection. He cried out and threw the pry bar, saw Hachisman raise his left arm to ward it off. Using the back of a seat, Cyn drove himself upward, then shouted again in shock as blaster fire washed over his faceplate. Blinded anew, he fought back a desire to trigger the laser and sweep it in wild arcs until he cut his opponent down. To stop himself, he flung the weapon up at Hachisman. He heard the male yell and a hiss and crackle as a seat burned and pushed himself up again, blind, sobbing with pain, flailing his armored arms.

And he connected! Hachisman's shriek of pain and terror, nearly deafening in Cyn's earphones, was music nonetheless, the impact as satisfying as an orgasm. He swung his other arm with all his strength and twisted, knowing he would lose his footing on the stair/ladder. But his arms were tight around

Hachisman, and they fell together and landed on the cargo section floor with the shrieking fanatic underneath.

Cyn struck down at where he thought Hachisman's helmet must be. The agony in his chest and belly had abated enough for him to think, but unfortunately he could not see and the blow missed. Hachisman struggled weakly, but he was no fighter and in any case there was little he could do, pinned under Cyn's armored weight. Cyn struck again. His eyes were finally recovering from the blast that had temporarily blinded him, and his second blow connected but had little effect. He raised his fist again.

"Don't kill me! Don't break my helmet! Don't!"

Cyn knew Hachisman would not die, but he made no answer. The few moments of fear the male survived would be all the revenge Cyn would get personally. His fist came down. Once. Twice. On the third blow the faceplate cracked. Hachisman's screams and pleas deafened him as his fist descended once more. But this time the fingers opened, clawed at the cracked plastic, pried it apart. The shrieks were muting into whimpers. Cyn peered down through his fogged faceplate cursing with frustration. He couldn't see Hachisman well enough to detect whether he was shamming.

Cyn's obscenities grew more intense and colorful as he came to realize he had not won; he had only achieved a stalemate. He couldn't tell whether Hachisman had clung to his blaster, and as long as he wasn't sure the fanatic was really unconscious, he didn't dare get up and let him move his arms. And Cyn couldn't open his helmet to see or he'd be in the same state as Hachisman if he weren't shamming. And with all the people listening to him, he couldn't even ask one to come in and help him. There was no way in because he had jammed the lift in the cargo section and the passenger lock was dogged shut. He had painted himself into a corner and he couldn't yell for freefall and float out.

An insistent voice in his earphones, tight with anxiety and excitement finally drew Cyn's attention but he felt strange, vague and light-headed. He needed to concentrate to understand what Aimie was saying.

". . . if you can't talk, use tap code. If you can't speak, use tap code. Tap what's needed. Reply in any way. If you—"

"I can talk," Cyn said, his voice slurring. "Sorry. Things here were a little exciting for a few smins."

There was a dead silence on the ship-to-suit com.

"Aimie!" Cyn shouted, feeling as if a lifeline were slipping from his hands. The fear cleared his head momentarily. "Don't faint now," he yelled. "Tomorrow, when we have time, we can both faint together."

A shaken laugh came across. "I'm not going to faint, but— I heard blaster fire. I knew you were alive because I heard you cursing, but I thought you were badly hurt. Demoson and Wakkin are trying to open—"

"No!" Cyn exclaimed. "I've got the shuttle flooded with anesthetic gas. That's the trouble. The blaster got my faceplate and I can't see, but I can't open the damn helmet either."

"Would the emergency suit helmets fit the armor?" Aimie asked.

"Yes, of course." Cyn shifted, grunted with discomfort as the skin of his midsection pulled tight instead of stretching in its normal way. Simultaneously something soft shifted under him and he gasped, remembering why he was where he was. "I can't get up," he mumbled. "I'm sitting on Hachisman, and I can't see whether he still has his blaster or whether he's faking being asleep."

"From the sound of your voice, I'd say he wasn't faking," Aimie replied, speaking louder. "I think you've got cracks in your faceplate and the gas is starting to get to you. Breathe as little as you can. Now listen, find his shoulder; feel down along his arm to his hand; if he's holding anything, take it away."

Feeling stupider and stupider, Cyn managed to follow her directions. There was nothing in Hachisman's hand, and he was contemplating lying down atop the male and resting, until Aimie prodded him into getting up and changing his damaged helmet for that of one of the emergency suits.

"Hold your breath," she shouted. "Do you hear me? Cyn, answer me. Hold your breath when you take off your helmet and flush the new one. Flush it! Do you hear me."

"I hear."

He really didn't want to be bothered, but the voice nagged at him so insistently that he struggled to his feet and to the cabinet where the life-support suits were kept.

"Hold your breath," he mumbled. "Flush the helmet." As he spoke the words also rang in his ears.

CHAPTER 17

Cyn found himself sitting on the cargo section shuttle floor staring down at Hachisman's limp body. Somewhere near his feet there was a steady squawking. He blinked and shook his head, which was beginning to feel its normal weight rather than as if it were about to float away. The tinny noise was coming from the com of the discarded helmet lying beside him. Cyn smiled, turned off the squawk, and flicked on the com in the new helmet.

"Hold it," he shouted across the din Aimie was making. "I'm here and wide awake."

He then proceeded to outline what he was going to do: bind Hachisman, put a respirator on him, and put him out in the lift lock. Clear the atmosphere of shuttle, lock and lift.

"Then I'll try to remove the device that's generating the false carrollpause," he said, biting back an exclamation as he tried to flip Hachisman onto his face and his midsection warned him he was tearing something.

"You sound as if you could use some help," Aimie said.

"Not yet," Cyn told her. "You've got to stay in the control room; Rocam's just not strong enough; and frankly I don't want another able-bodied male in here, no matter what his sympathies. Sometime between when you commented on Wakkin and Demoson being together and now, I began to wonder if one could be bodyguard to the other."

He had succeeded in flipping Hachisman over, then un-hitched a coil of line from his belt and begun to bind his wrists and ankles together as he spoke.

"No," Aimie said. "I thought of that too. They were apart too much. Anyway, Wakkin can't be the bodyguard. Who-ever heard of a bodyguard spending half his time sleeping with a rather mysterious fem? And Demoson can't be the bodyguard because no bodyguard would permit his subject to bed a suspicious character like Niais."

"Right you are," Cyn agreed, pulling the line up from Hachisman's ankles and running a double loop around his neck. As long as the fanatic lay still, he would be relatively comfortable; when he started to struggle, he would strangle himself—but the rope could not tighten around the suit enough to choke him, only enough to force him to lie still or gasp for air. "So," he went on, eyeing his work critically, "I'll lay minums against stellars that one of them is a pilot."

"And you don't know which and you don't want either one near any controls."

"Uh huh," Cyn grunted breathlessly as he dragged Hachisman's body out through the lock. "Busy a smin," he gasped.

Every movement hurt more and more and Cyn could feel a broad damp area on the coveralls under his suit. He won-dered why he had been unaware of the pain and damp earlier, and then realized it must have been the effect of the anes-thetic gas. He could only go on with what he was doing, hoping he hadn't ripped his burned flesh badly enough to bleed, because until he rid the shuttle of its current contami-nated atmosphere and refilled it, there was no way he could get out to the medic without contaminating the entire air supply of the Pot.

He glanced at the lift doors; if he closed them he could clear the lock at the same time he cleared the shuttle. Cyn sighed. It was much safer to leave them jammed open and repeat the air-clearing procedure. The few smins to evacuate and restore the small area of the lock and lift could not affect his condition. But if he closed those doors and freed the lift, one or another of his passengers—a group like none other in the history of Overstars, he was sure—would be down to "help" him before he turned around.

Groaning he levered the shuttle door closed, climbed to the pilot's station, and sank into the seat. There was a strange device lying on the console, a wire trailing into an open panel. Cyn looked, twisting this way and that, but he could see no other lead and no branching in the lead that emerged from the box. Then he sat and stared. It was a very small device, not much longer and wider than his thumbnail and not as thick as his finger. Too small, he thought, to carry much of a destructive charge, so it probably would not explode. Life support was always separate from all other systems too, so the device might not be able to detect the operations of that system. Cyn shrugged and initiated the evacuation process.

"I'm bleeding the shuttle to vacuum," he reported to Aimie. "You'll see telltales on the console go red. Don't let it throw you. They'll be green again soon."

When the anesthetic had been purged from all contaminated areas, Cyn levered himself painfully to his feet. He was frightened by his exhaustion and continued pain. He glanced at Hachisman's device, but knew he was in no condition to deal with it. He was in no condition to argue with anyone about what to do either; he had to get to the medic. Cyn pulled his stunner, and undogged and opened the shuttle door. Demoson and Wakkin both waiting at the lock, backed away as he came through. One spoke, but Cyn could not hear clearly through the helmet and he ignored it, talking into the suit-to-ship com as if he had not noticed.

"Go away. Go to a cabin and close the door."

The stunner moved suggestively. Both protested, he thought, but he made no attempt to try to untangle the dim and garbled words. He followed into the rec room, placing his feet carefully and bracing each knee because he felt his legs might buckle. When both were inside, he jammed the door handle. Then, he staggered to the med compartment.

Inside, he laid the stunner in easy reach and stripped off his gloves. Raising his hands to remove the helmet called forth lancing pain from his abused body, but he persisted, sobbing with effort, only pausing once to tell Aimie, who was calling frantic questions, to stay at her post, that he was with the medic and would tell her more later. Ridding himself of armor and the charred coveralls took what seemed his last shred of strength, and he fell back on the table, triggering the automedic as he lay down.

"You look terrible."

Cyn's eyes shot open. His groping hand knocked his stunner to the floor. Niais bent, picked it up, and handed it to him. She was frowning very slightly.

"You promised to take me to Ingong," she said. "I don't think you should get into any more fights. You seem to get more banged up each time. If you go on like this, you won't be able to keep your promise—and that's not nice."

Cyn closed his eyes, opened his mouth, then reversed.

"You promised," Niais said, her voice faintly tremulous.

"Overstars will get you to Ingong," Cyn said, closing his eyes again. "No matter what happens to me. You have a contract with Overstars. They will assume responsibility for notifying anyone expecting you, if you will be more than two sdays late."

"But you promised."

Cyn opened his eyes; Niais's were full of tears. "Stim," he said to the medic, and after a brief hesitation he felt the icy sting of an injection. A moment later, he felt like pushing away the mechanism the medic had extruded over his midsection, dragging Hachisman into the shuttle, and forcing him to remove his device, wrenching the truth from Demoson and Wakkin, and engaging in some new and fascinating sexual acrobatics with Aimie—all at once.

Fortunately, the stimulator did not turn off his brain when it turned on his muscles. He lay quietly until the medic withdrew. A drawer in its side popped open, exposing two printed cards and three plas-wrapped packages of pills. Cyn took them from the drawer and automatically slid his hand down his side. There was, of course, no pocket. He looked at the charred wreck that had been his coveralls and sighed. This trip had been unusually hard on coveralls.

"Honey," he said to Niais, "remember when I gave you a pair of coveralls to wear?"

"Of course I remember."

"Bring them out here to me."

Niais looked at him, then sighed. "You look better without them, even with that funny thing around your middle."

"I'm used to wearing clothes. And on your way, just take out the screw I used to jam the door of Demoson's cabin."

When she was gone, he went to the av and asked Aimie to come down and bring his boots. The coveralls, Demoson, Wakkin, and Aimie arrived at about the same time. As Cyn stepped into his clothing, he asked Aimie to look into Rocam's cabin. The old lady was asleep, but she woke when the door was opened and trotted out, Cotchkelah held carefully in one arm.

Cyn looked from Wakkin to Demoson. "Which of you is the pilot?" he asked.

After a brief hesitation Demoson nodded at Wakkin. "He is."

Cyn explained what was holding his ship in real space. "Do you know anything about such a device?" he asked.

Wakkin said, "I'd have to look at it, but from what you say I doubt it's booby trapped." He went back into the cabin and brought out a piece of hard-sided luggage that was clearly heavy. "You don't trust us," he said to Cyn, "and I don't blame you, but I've got some instruments in here that will read all kinds of system interference. I'll try to explain how to use them if you like, but it'd be quicker if you'd let me try."

"You could have got the ship to Xiphe—or directly to Mantra," Cyn said. "Why in the hollows of space didn't you take over right after we had that trouble at Healtha?"

"First, you got the drop on us so neatly, I never had a chance. I'm a pilot and engineer, not a burglar or bodyguard. Second, I checked the puter plot of your course and I couldn't have got to Xiphe any better or faster than you—"

Cyn knew that to be true, since the skew he had put into the navigator would have fouled any program Wakkin produced.

"My employer—" Wakkin nodded at Demoson "—didn't want to get to Mantra early anyway. Of course, neither of us expected the little side trip to wherever that was we went." He shrugged. "I guess none of that proves we want to get to Mantra rather than making another side trip."

Demoson sighed and reached into the neck of his tunic to pull out a duralloy card much like Aimie's. "I have this," he said. "If you've got a reader—"

"No," Cyn said. "No one's going to put a card like that into my ship's puter."

"I've got a reader," Aimie said, reaching into the ever-present shoulder bag.

It was a little thing about five cims square with a lens at one side, and slots for infocubes, buttons, and cards. Aimie smiled and shrugged. "Some suspects don't keep hard copy records and I don't have time to use their readers. Put the card in, press the button on the top, and point it at any light surface."

Demoson slid the card into the slot and handed Cyn the reader. When he pressed the button, the Imperial logo, followed by "**EMERGENCY OVERRIDE**," appeared on the surface of the rec table. What followed was an order to any Imperial service or official to assist, protect, etc. etc. the **IMPERIAL SON**, Demokarias, and to bring him, with all speed, to Empire Star.

Aimie and Rocam curtsied. "Don't!" Demokarias exclaimed, and added in a frustrated tone, "Oh, damn!"

Cyn stared for a moment at the ordinary-looking man, ran a hand through his hair, popped the card, which Demokarias took, and said, "Right. Since your orders and my own intention coincide perfectly and Wakkin says he is your man—" Demokarias nodded confirmation "—the three of us can go free the ship and freeze down Hachisman. I don't think Aimie, Niais, and Fr. Rocam are part of any conspiracy to stop you from getting to Empire Star." He blinked, recalling their various efforts to be helpful, then continued in a resigned tone, "But I will accept your decision as to whether to take them with us, leave them here, lock them up . . ."

Demokarias shook his head. "Oh, no, pilot. You've managed with rare ability so far. I'm not picking up your load; I've got a big enough one of my own." He grinned suddenly. "If you need muscle or information about the garment industry, I'll provide it. But it's your business to get me to Empire Star as soon as possible."

"I can use some muscle," Cyn said, touching the pseudo skin that covered his burns. "Mine is wearing out." He looked at the three fems. "Will you stay here?" he asked, resigned to the fact that short of stunning them and tying them up there was no way to control these three.

Niais shrugged. "You're all too busy now to want me."

Rocam smiled. "I think I've had quite enough excitement for this sday—but you will permit the pilot to tell us what happened, won't you, Imperial Demokarias?"

"You misunderstand my power completely if you think I could start or stop Pilot Cyn from telling you anything." Demokarias shook his head. "But I will promise not to try to persuade him to keep any secrets. I'd like to hear what happened myself."

Aimie met Cyn's eyes and nodded. He turned and led the way into the shuttle. Wakkin, as Cyn himself had done before, examined the tiny device with considerable care, opened his bag, and began to select instruments.

"I'd like to speak to Hachisman," Demokarias said. "I've heard it said that stasis can fix ideas or memory. If I could, I'd like to suggest a few new ideas to him."

"Why?" Cyn asked.

"Hachisman has intelligence and purpose. Just now that purpose is misdirected—not in its aim, but in its method. I would be very sorry to see him frozen with the notion that he was a failure because he was not vicious enough or that all free men are callous and indifferent to the sufferings of those who are enslaved."

This was an entirely different person from the half jovial, half sharpie businessmale Demoson. Cyn liked him better, but felt he was being impractical. "I guess you can talk to him while Wakkin works on that doohickey since I'm in no condition to help carry him to the freezer. But frankly I doubt that rational argument will have any effect on a person who thinks he has a direct com line to an only and all-powerful god. I can't say I care much for his particular god either."

"Ah," Demokarias said, his eyes bright with mischief, "But maybe that's pure prejudice. I heard Hachisman telling you that his god wanted you to die. I can see where you might prefer a different deity under the circumstances." Then the amusement died out of his voice, and his expression came closer to that of Demoson, calculating and cynical. "The Empire's tools are many and various. Madness does not by any means preclude valuable service."

Now Cyn wasn't so certain he preferred Demokarias to Demoson, but he led the Imperial to the cargo lock and told him to pry it open. As they came through, Hachisman began to scream and struggle.

"Please, Fr. Hachisman," Demokarias urged, "this can do you no good. More important, it can do your people no good. I want to assure you that the arrival of the Challenger before the Planetary Council ends will not be detrimental to your people. None of the Imperials regards slavery with indifference."

"Words," Hachisman panted. "Words are cheap. So it's Wakkin that old bitch was protecting. But you're almost as bad. You wouldn't chance a loss of profit to free a whole planet. That 'free' pilot standing behind you won't endure a black mark on his record for a few sdays lateness to lift slavery from a world. You'll all watch the Challenger hamstring the Emperor so he can't fulfill his promise to free the slave planets."

"You are mistaken, Fr. Hachisman. Rocam is only a lively

and intelligent old fem going to her great-niece's wedding and Wakkin is a pilot and engineer. I am the Imperial Demokarias and I swear that I am as eager as my brother to free every slave on every world. We differ only in method, not—"

Hachisman began to struggle so violently at Demokarias's confession that Cyn felt obliged to caution the Imperial not to let the frantic man strangle himself while trying to ease his mind.

"You must listen to me," Demokarias insisted. "It is you and the like of you that must free your own worlds. I do not wish to be Emperor. I refused the throne in the past, but I cannot watch my brother destroy the Empire which offers the one hope for advancement of all people—the interchange of ideas."

"Ideas cannot set people free!" Hachisman howled. "The Emperor promised us armies."

"Did he also promise the armies would leave your world once it is free? Or will you exchange one master for another? A slave planet must free itself. Are there more masters or more slaves?"

"What can an unarmed rabble do?" Hachisman spat.

"What will a rabble be after it is freed? Still a rabble."

Hachisman twisted and squirmed in an effort to reach Demokarias and Cyn suddenly leapt forward and dragged the Imperial away into the shuttle.

"People have been known to detonate," Cyn said when Demokarias looked at him in surprise. "Your brother might not want you dead because you'd be as inconvenient to him that way as alive, but a madman might stop caring about the Emperor's convenience if he were pushed too far."

"Are there a couple of blankets in the shuttle?" Demokarias asked, and when Cyn nodded, he said, "I'll just throw them over him. He won't blow himself up if he can't take me with him, and I know they'd never have put a high enough blast level into him to destroy anything but himself." He got the blankets from the cubby Cyn indicated, then looked at the pilot, brows raised. "You are a very clever fellow, pilot, to realize that my brother doesn't want me destroyed or even lost in space."

"Fr. Aimie told me the rules of challenge," Cyn said. "Don't credit me with more than I've got."

Demokarias only gave him a hard, flat stare and passed into the lock where he dropped the blankets over Hachisman, who began to sob. "Male," he said, "don't be such a fool. Listen to me. You can free your people. You, yourself. I said a rabble free was still a rabble, but a rabble armed and led by one of its own may be far more."

Hachisman caught his breath and stared with an arrested expression at Demokarias. Then his eyes narrowed and he sneered, "You'd like that, wouldn't you? You'd know all the free spirits then, and they could be gathered up and eliminated any time you felt you wanted to call in a credit from the masters."

Demokarias laughed. "Why should you think me fool enough to underestimate you? No rebel in his right senses tells anyone more than s/he needs to know. Whoever you dealt with would know only you. And you'd know one or two others—no more. So if you were caught you could tell very little. Do you think that in all the ages no revolts have ever succeeded, and that those successful changes were not studied and analyzed? You say your god freed you, and I will not argue with your belief except so far as to suggest that some more material presence helped. Are you very sure you know who was behind that presence? My mother—"

He broke off as the ship quivered in the way characteristic

of entering Carroll's void. Hachisman screamed. Wakkin dropped down the shuttle ladder and grinned.

"On our way," he said, shouting over Hachisman's shrieks and holding out the device that had been lying on Cyn's console. "Cute little thing. Doesn't do any harm except drawing a lot of power, but this class of vessel has plenty of that. You should check your fuel tanks at Mantra. You might want to top them up."

Cyn had snatched up the small rectangle as soon as Wakkin's hand opened. "Does it need any special care and feeding?" he bellowed.

"No." Wakkin's voice rang far too loud, and he lowered it to add, "And it's dead until it can draw power."

"Thanks," Cyn said, but the word was drowned as Hachisman began to scream curses and swear that god would punish them all. Cyn winced, wound the power cord around the device, and slipped it into his breast pocket. "Would you and the Imperial Demokarias please pick up that siren and bring it to the freezer so we can shut it off?"

Hachisman twisted and turned, jerked his legs and bound arms so violently that the two had difficulty keeping the blankets around him while moving him even the few mets to the lift.

"I'll go up with him," Wakkin said. "No sense our all getting bruised if he decides to fly apart."

Cyn's mouth opened, but Demokarias put a hand on his arm. "No need for heroics. I don't think Wakkin's in any real danger but we need one pilot on this ship whatever happens."

Nothing happened. Hachisman had even stopped yelling by the time Cyn and Demoson climbed up the shuttle and joined the rest of the party. Wakkin had braved Hachisman's possibly explosive condition and dumped him on a gurney in the med compartment. Before Cyn could pull off the blankets and slide the gurney under the medic, Demokarias came forward again.

"Take this thought with you, Fr. Hachisman. No matter who wins the Challenge, you cannot lose. I will add my promise to the present Emperor's. I will have you revived and trained and will find a way to supply arms, if you wish to go back to your people and lead them to freedom."

As he spoke, Cyn pressed an anesthetic hypo he had taken from a cabinet against Hachisman's neck. In ssecs, the male's eyes closed. The other two lifted him to the medic table.

"Human, male," Cyn stated to the robot. "Identify and remove any foreign objects."

The machine slid sensing units around the still body. "None," it stated.

Everyone breathed a sigh of relief. Explosive devices could be triggered by many inputs, including a drop of body temperature or any attempt at removal.

"Strip him and freeze him," Cyn ordered, and walked out of the medic compartment. At the bottom of the companionway, he turned to face the others. "I swear, if any of you comes near me without my permission or there are any more irregularities in my ship's behavior, I'm going to freeze you all—including the Imperial Demokarias." Then he went up the stairs.

By the time the Pot came out of its last transition, most of Cyn's bitterness had disappeared. He had been left strictly alone, though he had not locked the door. Now he set the Pot to the highest acceleration, tuned the rs screens to their greatest range, and sent a general call over the av for the passengers to come up to the control room. The av showed a near stampede, except for Niais, who stared at the others from Wakkin's cabin door—he had shot by her at considerable speed—with blank amazement before she followed at a more leisurely pace.

Cyn had swung his couch to face into the room. "We are not in any present danger," he said as they poured in—"unless one of you has prepared another little surprise for me?"

Hasty head shakings and denials and some laughter greeted his remark. Cyn sighed and continued, "At least, there's no ship on the rs screens now, and we're on our way at top speed toward Mantra. Mostly my question is for Imperial Demokarias, but I want you all to hear what we say. We've all been endangered equally and, I think, all deserve to comment. Imperial, do you want me to ask for Patrol surveillance, or is that likely to get us unwanted company?"

"I have a special code that I think won't be recognized by anyone except certain Patrol vessels." Demokarias grinned at Cyn. "The message is in clear and is addressed to the GMA. It's all about garment styles. If you're willing to use it, you can be rid of me in a few stus, I believe."

"You've got a coded message that will bring a safe Patrol vessel to carry you," Cyn said, wanting to be clear. Demokarias nodded. With his teeth showing, Cyn asked very softly, "Why the hell didn't you take a Patrol ship from wherever you were? Why did you get on my ship and drag us with you into danger?"

Demokarias stared at him levelly. "Because I am an Imperial. My concerns are wider than a few individuals—no matter how worthy. Because I didn't want an undeclared war between Patrol and Navy, as Patrol tried to get me to Empire Star and Navy tried to block us. Because I didn't want to offend the whole Navy—which, after all, will be my arm of enforcement if my challenge is successful—by seeming to distrust them. Because—"

"Right," Cyn interrupted. "My apologies. Nonetheless,

with all due respect, Imperial, nothing could give me greater pleasure than being rid of you."

Demokarias chuckled. "No offense taken. In fact, I feel you are utterly wasted as a mail-carrier. How would you like a birth as pilot of a royal yacht?"

"Oh, no!" Cyn exclaimed. "It was bad enough being a target earthed. I'll be fried on Mwg before I set myself up as a shooting gallery in space, too."

The Imperial laughed heartily. "It's very rare that a crisis occurs that makes an Imperial a target. And think of the delights of Empire Star. I've heard about your weakness for soft lights and fancy fems."

"The same ones in the same places? No, I thank you, Imperial. It would be too much like living dirtside." Cyn's eyes flicked toward Aimie. "Imperial yachts don't travel far enough often enough."

Demokarias nodded. "Very well, Pilot Cyn. But you've served me very well. Is there some reward you would like?"

"I didn't serve you," Cyn said. "I just did my job. However, if you win the challenge and want to dish out favors, give a thought to letting the Free Traders in on some of the gravy that IntraGalCorp licks up."

"No," Demokarias said. "Sorry. Free Traders are far too valuable doing what they do. The purpose of the Empire is the spread of ideas, and the Free Traders are the only route for new thoughts to reach outside the Empire. What I will do is tell my mother, the Empress, of your efforts in my behalf and of your heritage and ask her to spread through the Patrol a little more sympathy for Free Traders—"

Impulsively, Cyn got off his couch and held out his hand. "Deal," he said.

The Imperial took his hand. "Deal," he echoed, then smiled. "I know what it means, too. I really did work in fashion sales for many syrs." Then he laughed aloud. "But on the personal side, pilot, I'll see all your debts paid to Lystris in Imperial credit, and maybe enough into Overstars Credit Central for you to go back to the Garden."

"I'll find another good use for the credit, if you don't mind," Cyn said. "The Garden is once for the body and forever for the spirit. I don't need to go back."

"You are unusual in more ways than one," Demokarias remarked, and took a plas sheet out of his pocket. "Here is the message."

"Anyone else?" Cyn asked. "The rest of you might consider asking for a lift from Patrol too. If Hachisman's friends don't get the message, they won't know the Imperial is gone. It's possible there'll be more fun and games. I won't mind being deserted, I assure you," but as he spoke, his eyes flicked to Aimie again. He rather hoped that she would stay.

"You promised to take me to Ingong," Niais said. "Why should I leave?"

"I didn't dare ask before," Demokarias remarked. "It would have been out of character for Demoson, but why are you going to Ingong, Niais?"

"I have to go there," Niais replied.

Cyn groaned. He had heard this exchange before.

"Why do you have to go there?" Demokarias persisted.

"I have to be delivered in a cage."

"You have to be delivered to Ingong in a cage?"

"Yes!" Niais crowed with joy, as if she had finally hammered a most abstruse concept into the mind of a dull student. "And Cyn has promised that he will deliver me."

Demokarias's eyes were somewhat glazed but his lips moved as if he were going to ask another question. Cyn gave him full credit for courage and persistence. However, Wakkin put a hand on his arm. "Please, Imperial. I have asked several times in several different ways. I have offered her various inducements to reconsider. I have not had any notable success."

"But why to Ingong?" Demokarias asked the group in general. "The dragons are good people, but they aren't much interested in the doings of other species—except for scientific and philosophical concepts. I doubt if there are ten or twenty other homo sap on the planet. And why in a cage?"

"We aren't going to get any answers out of Niais," Aimie said. "But Overstars Security is now aware of the problem. We will get answers and, Imperial—" she smiled at him "—I will see that those answers are transmitted to you if you still want to know."

"I think I do," Demokarias said. "If something unusual is happening on Ingong, I think I do want to know."

Fr. Rocam extended a hand to Cyn, who took it. "I wish to thank you, pilot, for the best time I've had in many syrs. I have enjoyed myself. However, if I am delayed any longer I will miss my niece's wedding, and considering that she paid for this very expensive voyage, I feel obliged to be there. If you think the Patrol will make room for me, Imperial Demokarias, I would like to transfer."

Cyn laughed and thanked her again for her help and Cotchkelah's; Demokarias assured her that she—and the bird—would be welcome on any ship in which he traveled. There was some idle chatter as Cyn put Demokarias's message through the com, and then everyone began to drift down to the passenger level to pack or do whatever else they deemed necessary before leaving the Pot. It was only when the no-see-no-hear went on in Aimie's cabin that Cyn realized she hadn't said whether she would go or stay. The no-see-no-hear seemed evidence that she planned to leave and still had some secrets she preferred to keep from him.

Cyn frowned, oddly dissatisfied.

He should have been overjoyed at the prospect of being alone again. Of course, Niais would be aboard, but that didn't count. She was a good bed companion, but talking to her would only lead him into a home for the bewildered. It had been pleasant to have Aimie to talk to—not the terrible pressure of all the family on Lystris, but one person with a bright mind and an interest in profit and loss—and he had barely started to tell her about the intricacies of Trade.

CHAPTER 18

Before the sday was over, the Pot was hailed by a Patrol cruiser. Cyn did not acknowledge the hail—the Pot was still far enough away to run and escape—until Demokarias approved of the identification of the vessel. Much as he found he liked the Imperial, it was a relief to see him and Wakkin transferred to the Patrol personnel carrier. With equal relief, Cyn handed over to the Patrol captain, who had come for it himself, the journey button Mortchose had put into his navigator. But the relief brought no real pleasure and Cyn had to bite his tongue not to snap at anyone who spoke to him.

He roused himself to stroke Cotchkelah, to thank Fr. Rocam again, and make a note of her address so that he could keep in touch with her. He saw to the removal of Hachisman's stasis box. While he was occupied, Aimie slipped past him through the emergency lock into the Patrol's personnel boat. Then she was gone, without a word, without even a look—simply gone.

Cyn returned to his quarters and palm-locked the door. It was significant of his mood that although she was now alone in the passenger section, Niais made no attempt to reach him or talk to him. He felt guilty about shutting her out so completely, but he could not bring himself to bed her or try to amuse her. In compensation, and also to occupy his mind, he began to look for information on the great dragons of Ingong.

268

He found more than he expected, and he was not interrupted by any emergency during his search.

Cyn was not certain why the pursuit had ended so suddenly. He wondered idly whether there had been some undetectable homer in Hachisman himself. Or possibly the Pot's speed had frustrated any final attempt to stop them. Or was there some Empire rule he didn't know about not interfering with a challenger who actually came into Mantra's own system? Aimie could have told him. Was that why she had left, because she knew he would be in no danger? She had just been doing her job, then? Even in that interlude on the pilot's couch?

When the navigator indicated the Pot was in orbit around Mantra, Cyn squealed a report of the various delays and Mortchose's death to the OM office. He was not really surprised when he was not given clearance to bring his shuttle in immediately. Empire Star was probably the busiest port in the galaxy, and even though Overstars had its own landing field, the volume of traffic just before the Planetary Council went into recess might be more than all the fields could handle. He did mention that he was already late and did not want to be further penalized, but made no smart reply when the clerk snapped that his arrival time was already recorded.

He was furious, however, when the delay of permission to land lasted a full sday and a half. By the time it came and he was able to gather up the forms the clerk on Xiphe had filled out, the signed statements of the other passengers, and the sealed report by Aimie about Mortchose, and set his robots to clear all mail and cargo from the hold, Cyn felt he had had all he could stand of Empire bureaucracy and was seriously considering returning to Lystris. Niais cowered when he ordered her into the shuttle and did not say a single word on the trip down.

In the Overstars office, Cyn presented his records to be receipted, the report of Mortchose's death and the statements about him, and then shoved the forms concerning the "beast" in the cage into the clerk's hand. The clerk opened his mouth, looked at Cyn, then looked hurriedly down at the forms, and saw Cyn's ident number. He looked up once, clearly startled, and began to key his puter, hemmed, hawed, and nodded.

"This contract is to be confirmed, just as it is, but you'll have to—"

"What?" Cyn roared, yanking Niais forward and almost shaking her at the clerk. "This is a young fem, not a beast!"

The clerk shrank somewhat, but shoved the forms back at Cyn. "Don't shout at me. I don't make the decisions. You have to go to the Postmaster's office for special confirmation orders."

Cyn shut his mouth hard. The clerk was perfectly right; he didn't make the decisions. But, he wondered, can I really take Niais to Ingong? Put that child in a cage and drop her without knowing what would be done to her?

"You promised to take me to Ingong in my cage," Niais said, as if she had read and understood the conflict under his rage.

The tone of her voice, the too-well-known litany, reminded Cyn of what Niais was and what he had so recently read about the great dragons of Ingong. He began to wonder if he was worrying about the wrong problem. It would be a moot point, he thought, towing Niais behind him towards the office of the Postmaster whether Niais or the civilization of Ingong would suffer more. Any system built on logic and reason might well crumble under the impact of Niais's personality.

Even so, Cyn was bristling as he flung open the door—only to stop short, rage aborted. Aimie's elaborate shoulder bag lay on a chair in the antechamber. And this time, unlike all other occasions when Cyn had needed the Postmaster's attention, he was not kept waiting. The secretary told Niais firmly to take a seat and, having confirmed Cyn's identity, waved him through. On the other side of the door, the pouch's owner wriggled her fingers at him surreptitiously from the side of her chair while maintaining a perfectly frozen official expression. Cyn's face was now also correctly expressionless, but joy warred with wariness in his eyes.

"Fr. Pilot Cyn," the Postmaster—a roly-poly black and white creature native to Mantra, species arthes—said in pompous, formal tones, "first I wish to commend you for the devotion you have displayed in protecting the property and persons entrusted to the care of Overstars Mail."

"Thank you," Cyn responded.

"It is my second, far less pleasant duty, to reprimand you for the unorthodox methods you used."

"I am afraid I didn't have time to consult the Manual of Procedure, nor am I certain it would have covered precisely the situations I encountered," Cyn said, matching the pomposity.

From the corner of his eye he could see Aimie's lips twitch and fought a brief battle of his own to keep from laughing as he considered what the Manual of Procedure might have recommended for dealing with the creature that had eaten Mortchose.

"That may be true," the Postmaster agreed woodenly.

There was no humor in his voice, but his eyes were averted. Cyn suddenly had the feeling that he had walked into some elaborate trap. The arthes of Mantra were known to have a lively sense of the ridiculous. Any one individual of any species might, of course, be humorless, but surely so stiff a clod would have commented unfavorably on Cyn's irreverent remark about the Manual of Procedure.

"Nonetheless," the Postmaster continued, "a mail-carrier's position is not one in which imagination and initiative are desirable."

"Oh?"

"Ah, yes. Initiative and imagination, you see, can lead to all sorts of undesirable consequences." The arthes was now gazing with a rapt expression at the ceiling. "The long, empty stus of travel leave too much time for an imaginative man to think . . . ah . . . of ways to relieve the tedium or . . . ah, um . . . to make a voyage . . . er . . . profitable."

That was a very nasty suggestion. Maybe this wasn't a joke after all. "I've done nothing against Overstars rules," Cyn said, his voice tight.

"Nothing against the letter of the rules, no," the Postmaster said, "but definitely circumventing the spirit—"

"If you want my resignation," Cyn snarled, "I am quite ready to—"

"No! Not at all!" the Postmaster exclaimed, bringing his eyes briefly to bear on Cyn's. Then he looked carefully out of the window. "There is room in Overstars for all types," he continued sententiously. "Indeed, the service has great need of enterprising males like yourself—in another branch."

So it had been a trap! Cyn's eyes flicked to Aimie, but she was innocently examining a holograph of the Postmaster's rotund wife and his nearly spherical children.

"I must remind you, sir," Cyn said stiffly, "that I cannot work dirtside for more than a few sdays at a time. I was born a Free Trader, and I must live in space."

"Of course, of course," the Postmaster agreed.

He cast one curious glance at Cyn. In fact, Cyn knew he did not understand at all. Probably he felt that all spacers were quite mad, but the concept was familiar to him in theory.

"It would be totally uneconomical," he continued, "to pay you a pilot's wage and not use your skills. In fact, you will retain your ship and continue to deliver mail—but occasionally we will request that you make a special run."

"Security!" Cyn exclaimed. "Are you asking me to transfer to Security?"

"Um . . . it is not exactly a matter of asking. I am afraid . . . er, yes . . . afraid that you are being . . . ah . . . drafted. Yes, owing to exigencies in the service, you are being drafted into Security."

"Now wait," Cyn said. "Now just wait a smin—"

"Are you going to deliver Niais to Ingong?" Aimie interrupted. Her eyes met his steadily, unaffected by his glare.

Cyn closed his mouth. She had certainly put her finger on a very sore spot on his conscience. He looked back at the Postmaster—who, he decided had the appearance of someone who had eaten something and could not decide whether it had agreed with him.

"As I was saying," the arthes continued. "In view of the unsavory traffic in fems, which Fr. Aimie has brought to Overstars attention, it seemed most expeditious to use you since you were already involved. You certainly seem to have shown a predilection for operations that are not . . . ah . . . covered by the Manual of Procedure."

That time the bright shoe-button eyes looked most innocently right at Cyn. Cyn choked.

"However," the Postmaster went on, "it seems that the fem—"

"She's not an adult fem," Cyn protested. "She's hardly more than a child."

"Unfortunately we have no proof of that," the Postmaster

reminded him. "Some species retain the appearance of child-ishness almost until their deaths. Of course, if Fr. Niais is as young as she appears, that fact increases the problem and our responsibility to stop the abuse—if it is an abuse. All we know now is that she says she is not a child and, actually, insists on being delivered to Ingong."

"But in a cage?"

The arthes shrugged, an odd gesture that made his paunch rise almost to his chin and then bounce several times. "Now Overstars has rules against involuntary transmission of sen-tient beings, but there is no rule against delivering a free pas-senger in a cage—if that is what the passenger desires. There is not, in this case, even an argument about cheating on the fare. The cost of shipping live cargo in so large a cage is actu-ally higher than the passenger fare would be."

"But—"

"The cage has this advantage," the Postmaster continued, ignoring Cyn's second abortive attempt to protest. "It makes the transaction very suspicious so that Security has more than enough reason to investigate. I gather that the young fem cannot, or will not, explain why she is being sent to Ingong?"

Cyn passed a hand over his face, as if to wipe away the memory of his conversations with Niais on that subject. "That is correct," he said mildly.

The arthes nodded. "Very well. We cannot, as I have pointed out, refuse to deliver her as contracted, but we also cannot lay ourselves open to prosecution for participating in interstellar slave traffic, which is proscribed by the Empire. You are therefore transferred to Security and seconded to Fr. Aimie to investigate this matter."

Trapped. Cyn had seen it coming, but he had no choice except to resign and he liked working for Overstars, even if— He cut off the thought he suspected would follow the "even if" and signed and thumbprinted the transfer papers without further comment. That done, he rose, cast a challenging look at the arthes, who met his glance without flinching—or laughing—and stamped out into the antechamber.

"Come on," he growled, seizing Niais and pulling her along with him. "We're on our way to Ingong."

By the time he had picked up the mail and cargo for Ingong and returned to the shuttle, Cyn knew he must be feeling better. Niais was cuddling against him and asking innocently whether he was still wearing the funny wrapping around his middle. He began to laugh when he thrust her into a seat and told her firmly to stay there and was still laughing when Aimie arrived on a baggage robo. Considering what he had said to Imperial Demokarias when he refused his offer of a pilot's job, he understood quite well why Aimie had used such underhanded methods. He understood, too, why he had thrown away his life savings and gone into debt for three sdays of pleasure. He had been bored to death, and unwilling to admit it to himself.

"Fiend," he said, giving Aimie a hand off the baggage robo, having no intention of admitting to her what he had lied about to himself.

"I'm an angel," she replied, her brows lifting. "Look how well I've arranged everything. I got myself promoted to field work, which I realize I like better than analyzing numbers. You've got the job you protest every five smins that you love, plus danger pay, which you never got before. You know that if you'd gone ahead and nosed out the trouble on Ingong yourself, they probably would have fired you instead of giving you a medal. And we," her eyelids lowered and her lips curved suggestively, "we have a chance to get to know each other better."

She had an unanswerable argument, so Cyn punished her

with a long kiss, which reconciled him to his fate. There was movement around him—the baggage robot entering and leaving the cargo hatch, people passing in the distance—but it was all normal. When he entered the cargo section to make his usual checks, a flicker of shadow caught his eye. He jerked upright, his hand going for his stunner, and then he laughed when Aimie, in the entrance between the passenger and cargo sections, asked what was wrong.

"Your shadow," he replied. "I'm still jumping when anything I can't see clearly moves."

"Just nerves," she agreed.

They arrived at the Pot without incident and all went up to the control section together. Cyn felt it would be too unkind to leave Niais alone below—and wasn't sure she would stay there—but he was already envisioning difficulties. He might be proud of his virility, but he was not fool enough to think he could keep up with two fems like Aimie and Niais. He was thinking, rather ruefully, of locking himself in, away from both as he fed the navigator the new journey button for Ingong he had collected at Mantra.

In the background he heard the beginning of another of those "Why are you going to Ingong" conversations, and he grinned maliciously and lay back comfortably in his recliner. Let Aimie have a go at it. She was pretty good, but he would lay his odds on Niais in this competition. After about fifteen smins he heard Aimie's voice begin to rise. He sat up with a grin and swung around—just in time to see the lift door open and the snout of a weapon poke through.

"Cancel that journey button, pilot."

The shadow in the cargo section. "Oh, no," Cyn sighed. He knew the voice and felt no alarm. "Come in," he said cheerfully and without making a move toward his console.

"Oh, look who's here," Niais exclaimed with bright pleasure. "But what are you doing with that stunner?"

"I'm going to save you from being abandoned on Ingong!" Wakkin replied grimly.

"I thought you were Imperial Demokarias's pilot," Cyn said.

Wakkin shrugged. "His Challenge was recorded and acknowledged the morning of recess so he'll be stuck in Empire Star under heavy guard for swiks. I got leave as soon as I learned that Overstars wouldn't cancel Niais's shipping orders. Imperial—"

"But I have to go to Ingong," Niais protested.

"No you don't," Wakkin said hotly. "I've told you again and again that I'd protect you. You don't have to go anywhere you don't want to go."

"That's silly." Niais sighed. "I do have to go to Ingong."

"Why do you have to go?" Wakkin cried desperately.

"Yes, why?" Cyn and Aimie echoed.

Niais drew herself up. "Because it is necessary for me to arrive there in a cage."

The three looked at each other. The stunner wavered in Wakkin's hand. Cyn laughed aloud.

"Join the crowd," Cyn said to the younger pilot. "I've been on that merry-go-round all trip—that is, whenever I wasn't being threatened, coerced, or laid out as an appetizer. Overstars doesn't like this traffic in fems, if it is a traffic, any more than you do. But this one—" he nodded at Niais "—isn't going to help us stop it. Maybe she doesn't know the answer. Maybe she's just frightened, though she doesn't look scared to me. The thing is, she claims to be free and adult and that delivery in a cage is her own desire. By law and by contract, if she's a free sapient being, adult, and willing, we have to deliver her."

"Yes, and in my cage, don't forget," Niais put in brightly.

An expression of defeat appeared on Wakkin's face; he shrugged and holstered the stunner. "I guess I knew it wouldn't work," he said. "But Imperial Demokarias said that maybe she was too frightened by Mortchose and Hachisman to believe that we could help her, and that if I appeared threatening she might be more likely to accept me as a protector. And I just couldn't bear to think of her being left alone in that cage without any way to reach help."

"She won't be out of range of help," Cyn said. "Fr. Aimie and I are assigned to investigate the problem. We haven't yet decided just what tack to take, but we have four sdays before we orbit Ingong to think about it. You're welcome to join us, since Imperial Demokarias has approved your attempt to help Niais."

"Yes," Aimie seconded heartily. "We are delighted to have you along. Why don't you take Niais down to the passenger level and—and see what you can find out."

As Wakkin and Niais enthusiastically complied with this suggestion, a horrified expression appeared on Aimie's face. She turned and stared accusingly at Cyn.

"It's contagious," she said. "Now you've got me using delicate phrases for the obvious."

Cyn cast a glance at his console. Assured that progress was normal and all screens recording only approved traffic, he slid his arm around Aimie's waist. "I never did," he protested. "I told you before. I don't think there's much reason to use any words at all." Then he transferred his hands to her shoulders and looked her straight in the face. "There'll never be much need for words between us. You knew I'd about had it being a mail carrier—and that I couldn't go back to Lystris, no matter how much I love her, either."

"At least I knew you were a square chip and mail-carrier was a round socket. I wanted a field job and I thought if I asked for a 'hero'—Imperial Demokarias was very emphatic on that subject to Overstars—for partner I'd get it. And I wanted you—"

"Thank the Powers that Wakkin came aboard. I was trying to think of a locking mechanism I could wear that would keep Niais away. With you here and her response to 'wanting'—"

"Speaking of wanting—" Aimie's expression had changed from languorous to curious. "What could the dragons of Ingong want with a humanoid fem?"

"I don't know," Cyn said, grinning, "but if it's nasty enough maybe we should let them have her before we investigate."

Aimie laughed aloud, but then grew serious. "That's the trouble. It won't be nasty at all, if it's the dragons themselves who want her. I'm afraid something may be going on that they know nothing about. I tell you, I smell a real stink."

"A real stink is something I don't like at all," Cyn protested. "I'm curious. I'd like to know why Niais had to be listed as a beast and delivered in a cage, but I've had about all the real trouble I want for a while."

Aimie chuckled softly as she patted his shoulder. "I know, lover," she replied soothingly. "If we're lucky, I can foresee spending syrs and syrs listening to you complain that you're a peaceful person who hates trouble as you wade into the nearest fight with fists, boots, blasters, or knives." Then her brow furrowed. "But I think, seriously—"

Cyn silenced her by the satisfactory expedient of covering her mouth with his as he turned her toward his sleeping quarters. He reached back with one long arm to channel alarms to the panel over his bed.

"Shush!" he said, finding it awkward to maintain the kiss while they walked. "I forbid a single serious thought until we have to save the Empire again."

About the Author

Roberta Gellis has a varied educational background—a master's degree in biochemistry and another in medieval literature and an equally varied working history 10 years as a research chemist, many years as a free-lance editor of scientific manuscripts, and nearly 40 years as a writer. She has been the recipient of many awards, including the Silver and Gold Medal Porgy for historical novels from *West Coast Review of Books*, the Golden Certificate and Golden Pen from *Affaire de Coeur*, The *Romantic Times* Awards for Best Novel in the Medieval Period (several times) as well as the Lifetime Achievement Award for Historical Fantasy, and The Romance Writers of America's Lifetime Achievement Award.